A Dragon's Night

By: N.P. Webb

Copyright ©2025 Line By Lion Publications
www.pixelandpen.studio
ISBN 9781948807395
Cover Design by Adam Prack
Editing by Dani J. Caile

For more information, email www.linebylionpublications.com

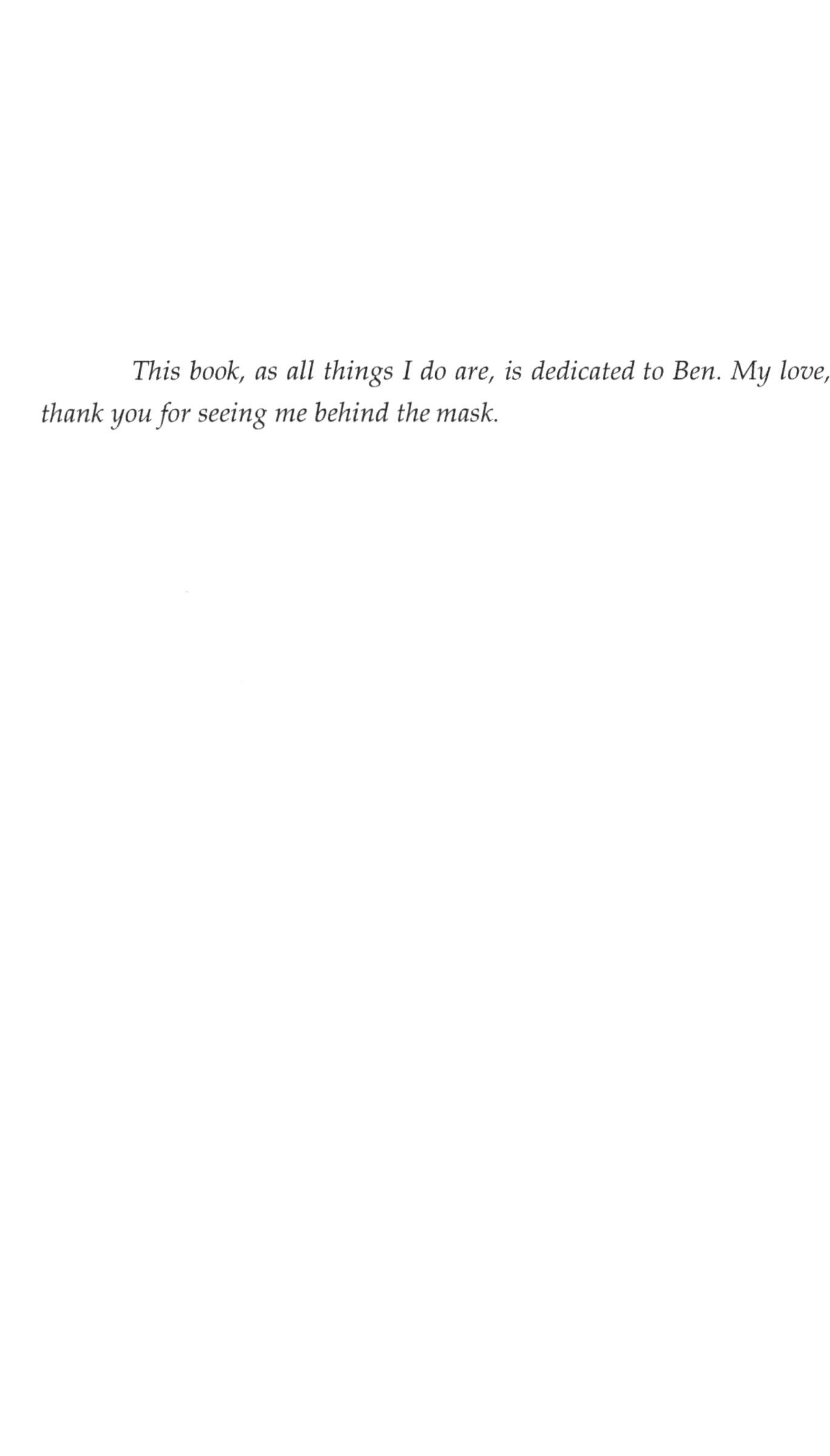

This book, as all things I do are, is dedicated to Ben. My love, thank you for seeing me behind the mask.

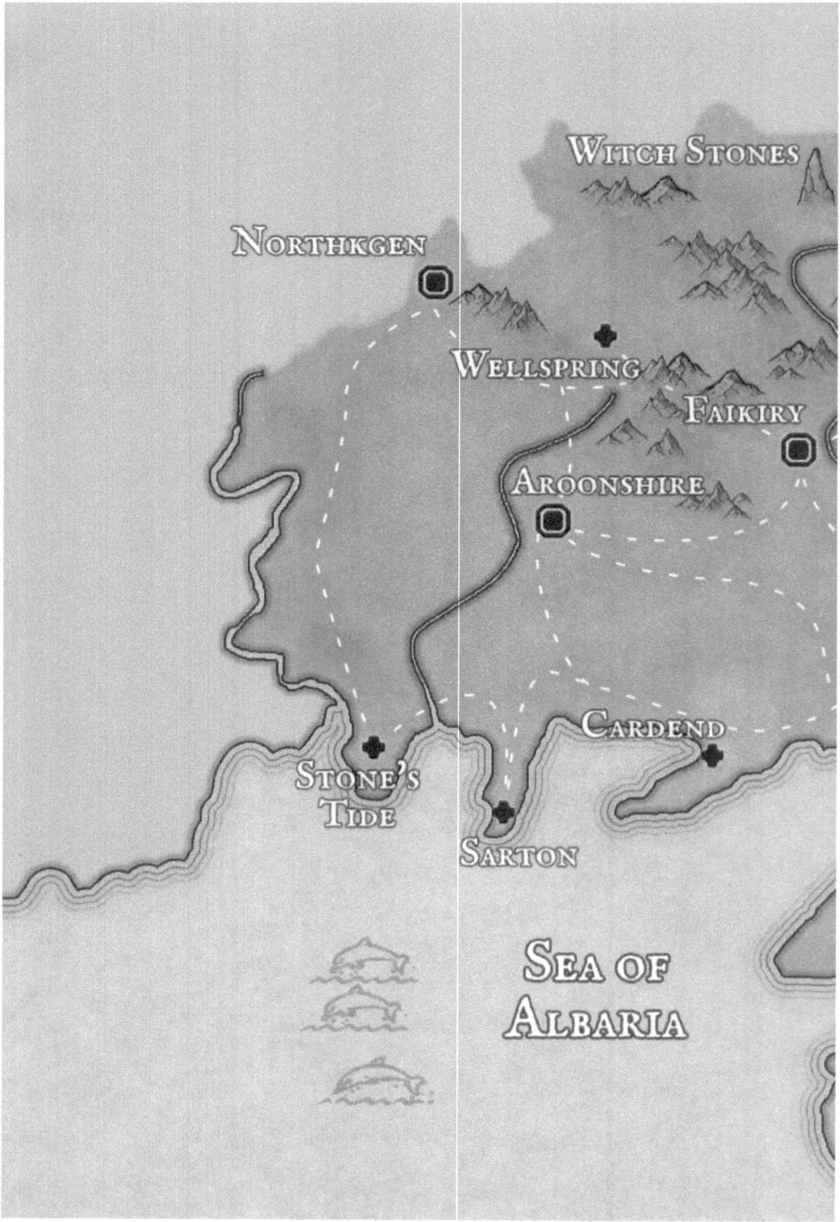

WITCH STONES
NORTHKGEN
WELLSPRING
FAIKIRY
AROONSHIRE
CARDEND
STONE'S TIDE
SARTON
SEA OF ALBARIA

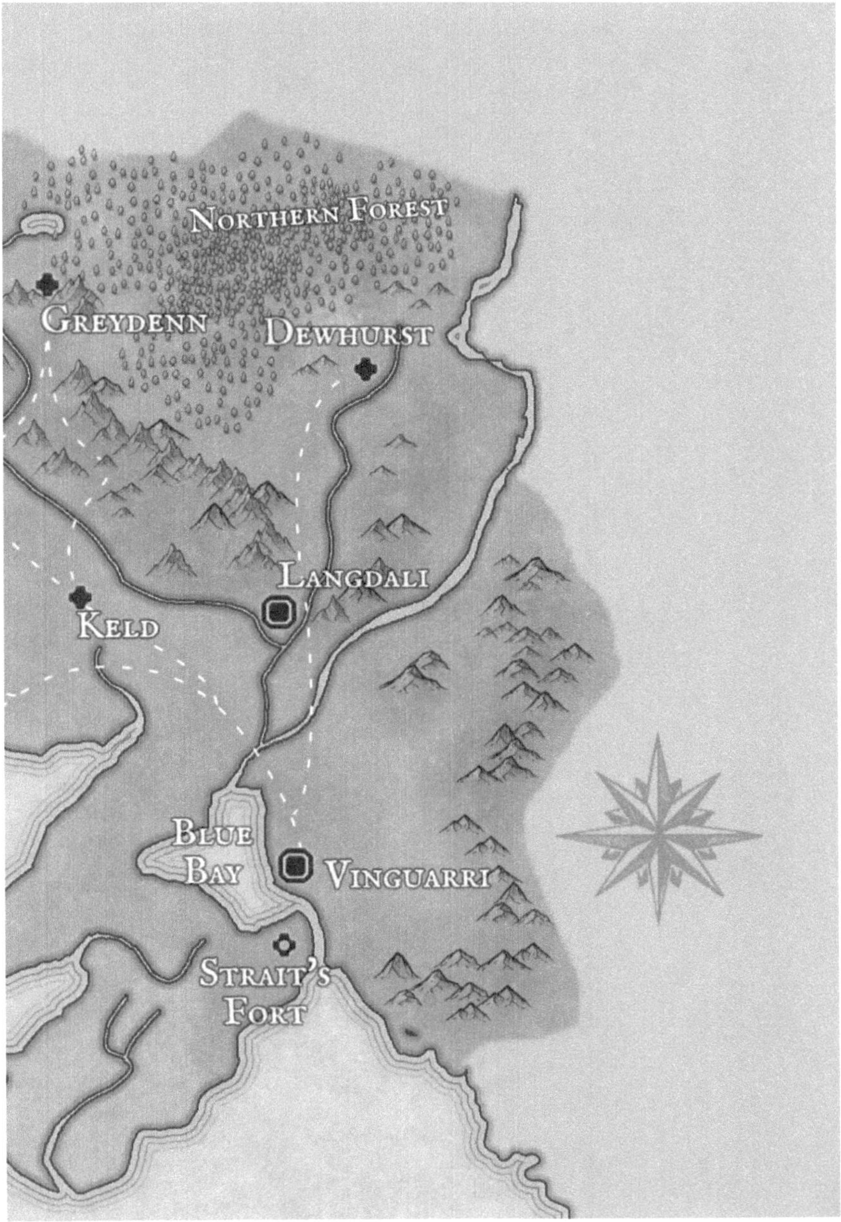

NORTHERN FOREST
GREYDENN
DEWHURST
LANGDALI
KELD
BLUE BAY
VINGUARRI
STRAIT'S FORT

Proclamation

King Elrick Arthur Galterius, long may he reign, issues a proclamation to commemorate his great coronation. Whoever can slay the dreaded Mirador Dragon and save his beloved sister, Princess Elora Adhelina Galterius, will be given the Princess's hand in marriage, Mirador Castle, as well as Lordship of Greydenn and all associated rank and honors. King Elrick wishes luck and good fortune to all who take up the sword in defense of the great country of Albaria."

Chapter One

THE wounded knight squirmed under my claws as he tried to free himself. A steady stream of blood flowed from his temple down his grime-covered face as he thrashed and clawed. After a moment, the man's eyes widened in horror as he realized his efforts were pointless against my scales. He heaved a great sigh and fell back, his armor clanging against the stone pathway. He cast his eyes towards the night sky one last time before returning his gaze to me. Now was my time to strike. I hoped that this would be the last battle, that he would take my bargain, but I knew neither were likely. This was my life now, to be hunted by these wretched creatures sent to 'rescue' the princess.

As if I had ever needed saving.

It had been three months since the King's proclamation—a full season since I had known true peace. What a shame, it was my favorite season, too; Spring. There was *nothing* in the world as delicious as the feeling of warm spring sun on my dragon form, illuminating my purple scales with an almost iridescent light.

"Young knight," I said with a voice like gravel. The harshness of this form's voice was always a shock to me. Until the bounty, speaking was never something I needed to do, nor considered. "You have fought valiantly, and for that, I am prepared to offer you a deal. Swear that you will leave now, and never return, or die." What the young man would choose was apparent to me from my vantage up above, but I hoped the lie about his prowess would goad his ego enough to make him reconsider. In truth, the battle was over before it even began–he was a weakling sent to slaughter by the new King and was about as irritating and threatening as a pebble caught in my scales. He was something to be quickly dispatched and never considered again. A mere speck of ink in my story.

"You devilish beast," the knight screamed. His nasally voice was a curse to my ears. "I will never rest until Princess Elora is safe! She is to be my wife and I will slay you!" A chortle rose from my throat before I could stop it. Such confidence for a man one muscle twitch away from nothingness. Just a tiny shift of my weight is all it would take to end this creature's useless existence.

"Last chance," I breathed. Smoke exhaled from my nose as I attempted to drive my point home.

The knight's eyes widened in terror as he clawed against my feet. "THIS CASTLE WILL BE MI–"

And there it was. It was never about dear Elora, only about the baubles that came along with her hand. I made good on my threat, reducing that prideful, greedy man to a wet, red stain on the castle's cobblestone path with just a minor shift of my weight before he could finish that cursed statement. The remnants of him clung to my body as I launched into the moonlit sky, my icy blue wings stretching under the starlight. I sent a silent prayer to whoever was listening, if anyone: *please let this one be the last.* I had long since tired of senseless killing.

*   *   *

A few miles into the forest from the castle built into the mountain lay my personal haven, a small mountain lake surrounded on three sides by rocky cliffs no human could traverse and a dense forest no human would dare venture through. It was here that I finally cleansed off the aftermath of the fight, the visceral remains of the knight flowed downstream quicker than the memory ever could.

I couldn't allow myself to mourn the man, the one sent to die by the king like the other eleven had been, nor dwell on the thought of his family. The King did not care about these men when he sent them to their death. Their families would go poor and their deaths unnoted if it wasn't for *my coin*.

Once the remains had been washed away and the bloody cloud dissipated, I shifted to my other form, my bones shrinking and shifting while my scales disappeared to reveal bare pale skin. Walking between forms wasn't painless, but the pain never daunted me. How could I dwell on the pain when I knew the ability to fly was just a moment away? No, from the first moment I tasted the sky and felt the rush of my wings, I knew this is something I could never give up, much to the chagrin of my parents. No threats they threw at me were as powerful as the call of the sky.

As my shift completed, I relished in the feeling of the cool water on my bare skin–the coolness eradicating the tension that had taken over my muscles these last few months. Nothing like a bounty on your head to make you tense, let alone one placed on you by your own twin brother. Elrick was a bastard who wanted me dead from the moment I could remember, but the proclamation on the day of his coronation was a shock even to me.

I pushed the thought of my brother from my head, the bounty, all of it, as I floated on my back, my dark hair forming a halo nearly reaching my fingertips. As the water soothed my frazzled mind, I set my eyes on the heavens above and took in the star-speckled sky above me. These stolen moments were when I felt the most free–the most like myself. A shooting star danced across the sky far above. As I sank into the clear water's icy clutches, I wished for a world where I was always this free.

*   *   *

DAWN'S light was creeping over the mountain when I finally flew into my cave. The small opening was nestled deep in the backside of the mountain, on the opposite side of Mirador Castle, where no one from Greydenn dared venture. I swore and I shifted back to my human form as quickly as possible. It felt like my body was burned away by molten metal as my bones shrank and muscles changed. I was late, and being late could spell the end of this decade long charade. I bolted to the stairwell at the back of the cave where a secret passage led to my chambers. It would be mere minutes before people started arriving at Mirador.

When I arrived ten years ago, the castle workers were told I was cursed to be guarded by a mighty dragon at night. For their own safety, everyone was banned from Mirador from sundown to sunrise. All the workers were moved to housing in Greydenn at the base of the mountain, and every morning at this time, a wagon full of castle attendants would be making the trek up the stone path.

Unlike those traveling up the side of the mountain in the rising sun, my passage was narrow and damp, carved directly into the white-stone mountain that Mirador was built into by the finest stonemasons my father could find. After a decade of walking them, I knew every chip and divet like the back of my hand.

I finally turned the last corner and slipped on the nightgown I stashed before pressing my ear against the hidden door. My pulse thrummed in my ear as I waited for a heartbeat. The room was completely devoid of sound as I pushed the door open. Light crept into the dank corridor as I peered out the crack. A sliver of my chamber came into view. I scanned what I could see of the room and nothing was out of place. The plush tapestries lining the wall glowed in the morning sun coming in from the numerous windows and the lush purple covers of my bed were mussed, just as I had left them the previous night before my fight. The passage door was hidden by a large painting of Mirador Castle and the village below that hung just to the right of the chamber entrance. My father had the passage chiseled into the stone before I arrived at the castle as a clever way to attempt and hide the fact that his daughter, cursed to be guarded by a night dragon, was actually the dragon herself. All of the architects and workers on the chamber lost their heads for their work, or so the rumor goes. The good King Rainard couldn't have word getting out and jeopardize his legacy. He was the one who negotiated the end to the war, after all.

I had always wondered when my father commissioned the passageway. When did he decide to send me away? Was he already preparing to be rid of me while I still toddled at his feet, hanging on to his every word? The unanswered question burned in my mind. He took that secret to his tomb and my only consolation was that I knew my nightly flights had him rolling in his grave.

"You're late, girl," said the wrinkled woman sitting in the corner of my chambers. I nearly jumped from my skin at the shock of hearing her voice. "And you smell like a beast." She wrinkled her nose. Her steel-colored hair was bound tightly at her nape.

"I'm surprised you can still smell at your age, Olgara." I walked over to the old woman and plopped a chaste kiss on her head, causing my old nanny to swat at me with disdain. Olgara was exempt from the castle ban. Even my parents knew that I was too young to be alone all hours of the night, dragon or not. They told others that the dragon would not harm Olgara since she was with me when I was supposedly cursed. I was eleven when I arrived, just a young girl sent away from the only home I had ever known by the people who were supposed to cherish me, or at least marry me off to a nice man. That was the duty of a princess–to marry well and strengthen diplomatic relations, or stop a war, as my parent's marriage had done. A princess is just a kingdom's most prized heifer sent to slaughter.

"I saw young Sir Lawcet met his end last night. Smashed to pulp and ground into the stone," Olgara said with a shake of her head. "Poor thing," she muttered.

My spine stiffened. "Oh yes, poor Sir Whatever, how dare he not be able to cut off my head in order to become master of his own castle." Olgara looked at me flatly as I continued.

"Shall I serve myself on a silver platter to the next suitor? Is that what you prefer?"

Olgara turned her attention back to the fabric on her lap. She looped her needle through the fabric as she attached beads in an intricate design. "I was talking about the poor soul who is going to be scrubbing entrails from the grout for the next three days, dearie." Olgara set down the sewing in her lap and looked up at me with a neutral expression. "We both know I like my job of taking care of you, who knows what young King Elrick would make me do to earn my keep if it wasn't babysitting his beastly sister." Olgara winked and I instantly relaxed. It was freeing to have someone see me for who I truly was, beast and all, and still have a fondness for me, a fondness I never received from my family after I first turned. Olgara did not love me, the closest thing I could assume that my old nanny loved was harassing young guards and a good soup. No, Olgara did not love her charge, could not, but it was the closest thing to it I could remember receiving.

"I ran you a bath. Go wash up before the chambermaids arrive–you have about a quarter of an hour," she said as she returned to the embroidery in her lap.

I stated my thanks to Olgara and rushed to the washroom connected to my chambers. When I opened the door, I was hit with a wave of lavender and herb-scented steam coming from my tub. It wasn't my favorite smell, but one Olgara always drew up for me on stressful mornings. On top of the water floated Olgara's trademark–a sachet of herbs. I climbed in and let the warm water soothe my tired muscles and relished in the warmth, so different than the coolness of the isolated lake I left only an hour ago. The warm water soothed me. Soaking in the warmth was not an option this morning, I thought as I began to preen in a way only a princess could–from washing my long, dark hair, then scrubbing my body and oiling my skin until I was pink and the smells of my other form were washed away. Once I was sure the traces of my secret were lost in the water, I exited from the bath and began combing out my long hair. My friends would be happy to do it for me when they arrived, but as I sat in front of the bathroom mirror, I relished in the alone time and my routine, and soon lost myself in my own reflection. My reflection was a game as I tried to pinpoint the shadows of my other form I swore were always visible on my face. Both my forms were stunning mixes of ferocious beauty with high cheekbones and green eyes that rivaled the purest emeralds, so green they seemed to glow. I could see my dragon form just under my skin, like cracks in a mirror allowing one to see what truly lies beneath. Our features were sharp, regally austere. To me, it was so apparent what I hid. How could no one around me see what so obviously was there? What would happen if they did? I did not know what was worse, never being known or being known and reviled. These questions were a mental prison I had built for myself on too many occasions. If I let my mind dwell here too long, I would be trapped forever.

I started to braid my hair back, further losing myself in my morning routine. In truth, though I craved freedom, I liked the routine. I liked flying back into my cave and sneaking up my stairs to only be chastised by Olgara. I liked scrubbing myself in the bath and then putting myself together for the day. I liked talking to my maids and going to the village. I liked taking care of others and helping the inhabitants of Greydenn in any way I could. I liked my lessons on history and music and science in the afternoon and I liked that everyone was kicked out of the castle before sunset. I liked sneaking away back down to my cave and taking on my other form whenever I could.

I liked all these things, but I *loved* flying. There was no freedom like soaring high in the sky where nothing could reach me. I had a confidence as a dragon that it was hard to feel as a woman, even as a princess. A confidence that has nothing to do with appearance, as I could so plainly see both forms written on my face. I sent a silent prayer to whatever god would listen that no one else was able to see the resemblance as clearly as I could. The names of our gods were lost to history long ago, but I hoped my plea would reach listening ears. The only god we still had any reverence for as a people was the goddess of death. Her name was long forgotten, but the Unseen still caused people to pale in fear. There is no power in life as formidable or assured as death. It never surprised me that she was the only one still remembered.

When my parents told me about my curse, I was but a joyous five-year-old who, a few moments before, had been excited to show them the amazing *thing* I could now do. I saw myself as magic, they saw me as a beast–a beast who had stolen their daughter. Cursed. How could such power and grace be a curse? I thought I could change their minds, prove to them that I could be the daughter they wanted, but it was to no avail. The role of the meek, powerless princess never fit as easily as my wings. I knew my parents had some love for me, they tried to find ways to break the curse, but they sent me away so quickly without even deigning to hear my side of things after. The prophecy spoken on our birth assured my parents that whatever Elrick did to me was justified.

A knock at my door pulled me back from my thoughts. I tried not to think of *that* day when I could–too many dark memories to pull up today. A weakness of will could not be tolerated when it came to that matter.

I quickly threw on a dressing gown and opened the door connecting my bathing chambers to my bedchamber to greet my two maids; Selena, a short and curvy woman with beautiful brown skin framed by a halo of dark curls and golden brown eyes, and Katherine, a willowy woman with straw-colored hair cut to her chin, freckles, and a devious grin usually planted on her face. Her metal grey eyes always glinted, like she was waiting for a moment to pass only she knew of. The two women had been with me since we were girls. Once we all three arrived at Mirador ten years ago, our relationship changed. At High Castle, the line between princess and maid had to be clear at all times, lest the adults get angry and take it out on the young servants. Once we arrived at Mirador though, a real friendship blossomed with our new freedom. We were girls together, and there is no bond as strong as that. The only secret I kept from them is the same one I kept from everyone here, except Olgara.

"Good morning, ladies!" I opened the door with a smile before taking in the somber expression of my friends.

Selena was the first to speak, her usual bubbliness gone from her voice, "Good morning, Elora. We come bearing bad news." Selena paused as she rubbed her hands together. "The Knight that arrived yesterday to slay the dragon, Sir Lawcet, he did not survive the night," Selena said with downcast eyes.

"Oh heavens, how did he die?" I asked, trying to feign shock as best I could.

"Judging by the stains currently being scrubbed from the bridge, rather smashedly," Katherine muttered.

"*Katherine*," Selena exclaimed. I couldn't help but giggle at her exasperation with Katherine's sharp tongue.

"What? How else am I supposed to cope with seeing a man become nothing more than a stain on a path," asked Katherine. She was always quick with her words and for as long as I had known her she had a remarkable ability to make light of the horrors around her with a biting tongue.

"Here I thought the only place people were smashed in Greydenn was at the pub," I paused as this caused the other two women to lose themselves in embarrassed giggles.

Selena let out a large sigh that made her seem twice her age. "At least the dragon issued him a quick death this time. The last one was not so lucky." Selena flinched at her own words, like she was surprised they fell from her tongue. She looked to Katherine with wide eyes.

Katherine grimaced, obviously recalling the memories of the last knight to try and slay me. I felt no remorse for the long death I dealt to that beast. He brought it on himself by what he attempted to do to Katherine. I could not let myself dwell on what might have happened had I not stumbled on them when I did. A burning rage built inside me as I thought about what damage he could have done. "What are servants for if not to use?" he asked me, oblivious to how much of a beast *I* could be when it came to those I love, regardless of form. His words were too common a sentiment among the nobles of Albaria. They did not see those around them as people, but as things to be used and destroyed at a whim.

No, I felt no remorse for grabbing the man in my claws, flying him high and dropping him on one of the metal gates. I felt no remorse that because of the way I so carefully dropped him, sharp metal impaled him through his torso and out his mouth, and it took him hours to die. He choked on a mix of metal and his own blood, and that felt too merciful of me. Any monster who attempts to force himself on someone deserves their fate. If that made me evil, I was fine with that. When I walked out on the grounds the next day and looked upon his skewered corpse, I did not feel shame, but an ease in knowing that the beast would *never* harm anyone again.

I wondered if my friends would think I was a monster if they knew the truth. Would they desert me like my family did? Just a beast in their story? This was my greatest fear, that I would lose my friends if they ever realized what I was capable of. And if something happened to them, I feared what kind of beast would be truly unlocked in me if an awful fate befell one of my friends. I knew deep down that I was capable of becoming a beast like the prophecy, worse even than others could anticipate, if those I loved were threatened. The worst part? I do not think I would feel shame if it came to that.

Katherine cleared her throat as she straightened her spine. Her shoulders shook lightly, like she was shaking the memory away of the knight. She turned to me, her pained grey eyes juxtaposed with the light smile that spread across her thin lips. "You will have a busy day today." She lightly mussed with the dressing gown before touching my hair. "Time to ready you for your duties," she said. We quickly dropped the morbid topic in order to ready me for the day. A night after a dragon sighting always meant a busy day. I would have to meet with Greydenn officials, check for damage, and make sure money was sent to the family of the fallen knight directly from my purse. It was the least I could do with the dowry that would never be used.

Selena and Katherine expertly laced me into a beautiful, gauzy grey gown with fluttering sleeves and delicate beaded flowers on the bodice–Olgara's handiwork obvious on the dress. As the waste was cinched, I thought that *this* was the part I didn't like. I did not like having to put on a restrictive gown, even though this was one of my more comfortable options. I did not like having to go to the small council and hear how evil the dragon was. I did not like feeling guilty for death, even if it was in self-defense. This guilt for the families of my foes is what led me to sending money and a personal leter to the family of the knights I removed from service. I did not like knowing my brother, the person I shared a womb with, had put a bounty on my head deliberately. I did not like having to lie to my friends. I did not like fearing that if they ever did find out my secret, I would lose them as friends. In so many ways, they were my last connection to humanity–my one tether to this form. If it wasn't for them, both the Princess and the Dragon would have long since disappeared into the night.

Chapter Two

EVERY moment felt like an endless eternity. The battle and flight of the night before was making me painfully aware of when my last meal was. By the time Katherine and Selena finished readying me for the day, I was famished. The palace cook arrived with all other workers after dawn, so breakfast was usually a quick affair and today was no different. The sight of the food before me–porridge with fruit and fresh honey, smoked meat, and tea with cream–caused my stomach to rumble. As the first bite of food hit my mouth, I had to muster all my years of training to maintain my composure and eat like the princess I was. No, shoveling food into my mouth would not be acceptable and would draw questions I never had the answer for. Beasts eat without manners and I knew I had to maintain the illusion I was *not* a beast.

After breakfast, came a debriefing on my walk to the village below with Selena to assess the damage from the fight the previous night, while Katherine stayed back to assist Olgara with whatever task she had decided on for the day. Days after dragon sightings were always the busiest. The walk down the path of the mountain took a good fifteen minutes, which gave

Selena plenty of time to inform me of the events from the night before in Greydenn. Selena informed me of everything that happened in Greydenn, from what different people saw during the dragon's battle all the way to who slept in whose bed the night before. For as long as I could remember, Selena had always had a special skill to know everything about everyone. She oftentimes knew more and in greater detail than even my fellow council members. If it happened after dark in Greydenn, Selena knew about it. She bounced with joy as she shared the gossip and I felt ever grateful to have someone like her by my side.

"Why do you have that look on your face?" Selena asked. Her dark skin glowed in the morning sun as her loose curls danced in the summer breeze.

"I'm just thinking how much more efficient the Greydenn Council would be if you also sat on it," I said with a smirk.

Selena blushed, "You flatter me, and I *would* be better than some of the members, but I just can't be bothered to do that much paperwork," she said with a sigh before throwing a coy smile up at me. I smiled back before turning back to the path.

The view from the mountain pathway never failed to take my breath away. In truth, Mirador Castle was not built on a mountain top, but on a small rocky plateau. At some point in the distant past, a lord decided he needed more space, more grandeur, so the architects turned to the only space left to expand. The back half of the castle was carved directly into the mountain. A stone bridge connected the grounds to the long winding path that was carved into the side of the mountain, just large enough for a cart to pass through. A spring bubbled up from the castle grounds and cascaded to the distant valley below in a beautiful waterfall. The valley under the mountain was rich and green, with beautiful blue-watered rivers running between the hills. Small farms dotted the rolling hills surrounding Greydenn, producing the main exports of the farming hamlet. The village was nothing more than a network of cobblestone streets and white-walled cottages with thatched roofs. The serenity of Greydenn was so different from what one would see in Vinguarii. When I first arrived, it felt like a completely foreign land altogether.

Sweat dampened my brow by the time we finally made it down the path. At the base of the mountain, we were greeted by Greydenn's small council, led by Mayor Gordby. Gordby was a short and stout man who tried desperately to hide the thinning of his grey hair, unsuccessfully, with just a comb and a prayer to the gods. Unfortunately for him, the long-forgotten gods did not grant their blessing.

He was also dressed in his best purple cloak, which meant he was in a good mood. Usually on days after a dragon attack, especially one that claimed the life of a visiting knight, Gordby would be nothing if not morose.

I quickly glanced at Selena, who was just as stunned as me at the choice of garb. She mouthed one word at me: *Purple*, with a quizzical look mirroring my own. Gordby clearly had something to discuss today.

Aside from Gordby, the council consisted of Commander Collins, who oversaw the guards, Angela Baccha, who spoke for farmers, and Louis Hevante, who spoke for Greydenn merchants. They were all good people and for the most part, had the best interest of Greydenn at heart. Quarrels were common among the council members, but love for Greydenn united us in unexpected ways. Working with them in the last decade brought joy to my heart–the type of joy that can only come from duty.

My role in Greydenn seemed ever evolving, and much more difficult to pinpoint than the others on the council. I was just grateful the people here no longer looked at me as they once did, when they only saw me as a scared and cursed little girl exiled to the furthest reach of her parents' kingdom, out of sight and mind. I wasn't sure when the shift happened, but gradually, the people here began to see me as someone who had value, someone to lean on, someone who could help. The place designed to be my prison had become the warmest home I had ever known.

I wasn't the town's ruler, not that I wanted to be. I didn't have lordship over the castle, but I did oversee things like tax collections, hold discussions with the town council, help settle disputes, and the day to day functions of Greydenn. I did not act as a liaison with the King, though, and wasn't ever expected to have contact with the Lords of other townships. Gordby, thankfully, saw to that.

Regardless of the complexities and long hours, I enjoyed my role wholeheartedly. Over the years, I had always tried my best to be of use to the town. Though I could feel guilt about the stress my night-time antics caused the town, I never did. I paid every person handsomely for any damage incurred. For a dragon-besieged town, the folks here were *happy*, and better off than the smallfolk in other places, but especially those in Vinguarii. If you looked out the windows of High Castle, you weren't greeted with smiling people and a beautiful veranda, but people who looked like they hadn't seen enough food in their entire lives. The smallfolk there struggled in ways that would seem foreign to those in Greydenn.

"How did Greydenn fair last night?" I asked the council before me, knowing the answer.

Gordby lowered his eyes as he wrung his plump hands. "We faired well, your Highness, but unfortunately the knight who arrived two days ago was not so lucky."

"Selena informed me of this on the way down. Mayor Gordby, will you please find the family of the late knight? I want to make sure they are compensated for their great loss." The lie fell effortlessly from my lips. No one should see the death of that man as a great loss.

"Of course. I should have that for you by the end of the week, Princess," Gordby replied with a nod.

"I hate to interrupt," said a smooth voice in the back coming from a tall, strong woman with olive skin and red hair, "but one family did lose some livestock in the attack last night. A sheep, I believe."

For once, my shocked face at the admittance of lost livestock coming from Angela was genuine. I *definitely* was not the culprit of this sheep's disappearance, unlike usual. Late night snacks of an occasional livestock or the wild animals of the region were common for me to partake in, but there was no time last night with the battle and my night swim. If I had partaken last night, I would not have had to count my breaths during breakfast so as to not inhale my food. The missing sheep could have been picked off by wolves, but anything that goes missing on a night when the dragon is spotted is always blamed on me, much to my chagrin. At times, I wondered if all the livestock and property damage blamed on me even existed.

Though, to be fair, it usually was me. Mutton had always been my favorite, and the char from my fire made the most delicious flavor. It rivaled even Chef's greatest creations.

"I will make sure the family is compensated for this. Who was it?" I asked.

"The Willoughbys," Angela said.

The Willoughby family, like everyone in Greydenn, was well known to me. They were not ones to be dishonest in the past, so it was more than likely that something did pick off a sheep. They were a young couple with several mouths to feed, and I knew the coffers I sent them would be well used.

The small council disbanded shortly after with Gordby running off excitedly saying he had 'important business to attend to' and to make plans to reconvene in the town square in two hours. With that, Selena and I also went our separate ways– I wished to go grab some things in town while she completed some tasks for Olgara. Olgara rarely made it down the mountain, even with the wagon service, but she somehow *always* had a list for one of us to gather for her. At times, she would even send Selena or Katherine to gather rare herbs under the light of the moon on dragon-free nights. For some reason, no one ever questioned *how* Olgara knew which nights the dragon would not be seen. Those nights she would send me to much needed sleep, assisting her in random tasks, or I would explore the castle grounds under the light of the moon. Even in my human form I rarely sat still for long.

I made my way down the cobblestone streets alone. The bakery was on the way to the Willoughby farm. Sweet treats seemed like the perfect gift to bring for the small children. Normally, I would send Selena or Katherine with my goods for them, but since the council would be meeting later, it seemed like the perfect opportunity to check in on the family myself. The beauty of Greydenn always left me awe-inspired. From my first step on these cobblestones, I felt at home. My exile to this town had been a gift, though it was meant to be a punishment. Greydenn was considered a backwards town, one of the furthest away from the capital city in all of Albaria.

I rounded the corner a few blocks from my destination, when unseen hands grabbed me by the arm and pulled me into the shadowy alley. Before I could make a sound, a rough hand was pressed over my mouth. Heat built in my throat as the dragon stirred under my skin. My eyes adjusted to the darkness quickly and the feeling of shock drifted into annoyance. A tall, strong man stood before me, all tan and swagger with dark hair drifting over his brown eyes. I scowled–he always loved the dramatics.

Even though it had been five years since he went to train as a guard, his hands still held the rich scent of saddle oil and horses. Once a stable boy, always a stable boy. I scowled at him as Dameon's face lit up with a devilish smile. "Hello, princess. Did you miss me?" he said with a voice like deep honey as he stared down at me. I was tall for a woman, but Dameon towered over even me.

He removed the hand from my face and stepped back, giving me space to adjust myself and further cement the scowl on my face. It had been less than six days since I last saw him. He looked surprisingly good for being in the woods the last few days, his tan skin was even more sunkissed and the extra dirt on his face seemed to accentuate his wide smile and boyish grin. He looked absolutely roguish.

"When would I have had the time to miss you, Dameon? You are nothing if not a perpetual thorn in my side," I said.

Dameon, ever the dramatic, gripped his side, mocking pain. "You wound me, Princess. Here I was dutifully fulfilling my oath to protect Greydenn and our *beloved* princess, and this is the thanks I get when I return home?" Dameon widened his eyes and puckered his lips as he dropped his shoulders. "Why do I continue putting myself in harm's way if not for the favor of our beloved princess." His voice dripped with honey, but I knew him well enough to detect the biting undertones.

"Don't worry Dameon, I'm sure the horses will be so excited to see you and the whores will be grateful for your coin," I said with a wink. In truth, I hadn't ever known him to frequent the upper levels of the tavern at the edge of town, but most young men visited at least once. It wasn't like Dameon had a sweetheart, though he definitely would have his pick of the ladies in town with his charm and looks.

"Oh I know my girls have missed me, I brought them peppermints," he said as he flashed a pouch full of the red and white treats with an innocent look on his face.

I raised my eyebrows quizzically. "Which ones, the whores or the horses?"

"Both," he said while popping a candy in his mouth before offering one to me. The smile on his face felt dangerously contagious.

I took the candy and as the sweetness hit my tongue, I couldn't help but smile. As much as I hated to admit it, I did miss Dameon. He brought laughter to my life in the darkest times. As a child, I would often sneak to the stables when I could and he would tell me fanciful stories. His habit of sneaking horses away at night to explore got him in hot water numerous times, especially when I would sneak away on dragonless nights with him. Through his nightly journeys, he became exceptionally skilled in traversing the local area. Once the awkwardness of youth was shaken from his body, Commander Collins plucked him from the stables and started training him as a guard.

"So," I said, speaking around the candy, "to what do I owe the pleasure of being pulled into a dark alley by someone who has so many treats to give out?" I say while batting my eyelashes in a way I knew will make him blush. He had always been all bark but no bite. Selena and Katherine always remarked that it was strange I never took him to my bed as I occasionally did others. There was no worry about a princess being pure when the princess would never marry, I always told myself. The knowledge of my trysts stayed only with my friends and me. But it always felt like a strange idea to me, like it wasn't right. I always secretly feared losing him if I was to do so.

Dameon's tan skin darkened in the blush I was after, but he quickly composed himself. He took a deep breath and as he exhaled, the boyish rogue I knew was replaced by the stern face of a guard. "I came to warn you, Lor. I saw a royal envoy on the road. It is a few hours out. I rode like hell to get here in time." Gone was any hint of amusement in his features.

"Oh, thank you for letting me know," my own smile faded from my face before I realized that my reaction wasn't the normal one for the princess. I should be ecstatic about the possibilities of being free from my dreaded beast. I tried my best to place a look of neutrality back on my face, but I knew

Dameon was fully aware of the effort it took by the way his own eyes saddened, for what reason I did not know.

"Why so much secrecy, Dameon? This should be something to celebrate–I might be free of the dragon soon," I said with a sigh. The smile I planted on my face hurt my cheeks. I sent a silent prayer to the gods that it looked genuine enough for Dameon to believe it.

Dameon hesitated. "I just…" he stopped. "I just don't like the look on your face when one comes by surprise." His face softened with his words into something I recognized but hated with my whole heart–pity.

I felt my face soften, "Thank you, it's just hard to always get my hopes up," I said as genuinely as I could pretend to be.

"Come by the stables sometime, some new foals just dropped and I am sure that they will brighten your mood." He patted my shoulder before he turned to walk away.

I did not want our reunion to end on such a melancholy note. "Is that how you depart from royalty, Soldier Grey," I asked in the most authoritative voice I could muster. The mask of superiority I had to wear at High Castle was never one I could bear.

Dameon stopped. I so rarely used his last name–the name that marked him as a bastard child. He turned. "My apologies, Princess Elora." He began to do his best mock version of a woman's curtsy as he mimed grabbing skirts and all. As he stood, he turned around and walked towards the street again, before calling over his shoulder, "Oh, and Lor, it's Captain Grey now." He threw me a devilish grin before quickening his step and rounding the corner.

I smiled genuinely at his declaration. He had been working so hard for years for this. The toll of the bell tower stopped me from following. If I still wished to visit the Willoughbys before the council reconvened, I would need to leave now.

I walked out of the darkened alley and into the light of the street and instinctively looked for Dameon, but he was long gone.

*   *   *

THE trip to the bakery and to Willoughby's farm was uneventful. The parents were just as gracious for the treats I brought the children as they were the coins for their loss. As I made my way into town again, the memory of the sticky hands and red-cheeked faces clung to me. The small ones made short work of their treats. Much to their parents' horror, the youngest babe crawled into my lap and left a sticky kiss on my cheek. That kiss seemed to remove the negative emotions that lingered from my conversation with Dameon, filling my cup in the best way possible. I felt ready now to hear whatever was thrown my way by the small council.

"I have a strange feeling about today. Something is off." Selena's melodic voice held a tone of worry in it. She had a habit of sneaking up on me. So much so that her sudden voice didn't even alarm me at all as we strolled towards the town center together.

"What could go wrong on a purple cloak day?" I said with a smile I hoped she believed. The look that drifted across her face as fast as a spring current made me fear that she saw the smile for what it was–hollow.

Selena looped her arm through mine and we walked the remaining few blocks to the town hall. The usually bare walls of the building were draped with fresh flowers and freshly cleaned purple banners displaying Albaria's crest; a mountain pierced by a great sword surrounded by a circlet of stars. The beauty was stunning and caused a twinge in my heart. The last time Greydenn had been decorated like this was for my arrival a decade ago.

My breath hitched in my throat. No, it couldn't be. He wouldn't come here now. He couldn't.

Selena squeezed my arm and pulled me to take a step. I wasn't even aware I had stopped walking. I took a deep breath and cemented a soft smile on my face with the same ferocity a soldier wears armor. Groups of people passed us on the street, people who would not understand *why* a royal envoy is a negative thing for me, regardless of the dragon. I had to be more careful.

"Beautiful flowers. Mayor Gordby must have a big surprise," she said with a reassuring smile.

"Yes," I attempted to compose myself, trying to not stumble on the words. "It reminds me of when I arrived. Completely stunning." I threw a small smile at her that didn't reach my eyes.

She leaned in close and whispered, "It will be okay. He would *never* come here."

Selena was right, but that didn't stop the feeling of fear deep in me, like a rock was sinking into my stomach and pulling me down to the place I buried the memories of that day a decade ago. To the part of me that is not a princess nor a beast, but a terrified little girl.

I couldn't let myself fall there, I refused. I was not *her* and I had not been *her* in years. I took a deep breath and felt the air hit every part of my body before I looked down at Selena. This time, the look of resolve was not forced. I would survive this, whatever it was. Who knows, maybe whomever this envoy carried would be my easiest opponent yet, nothing more than a posh man who had never fought for anything in his life.

The crowd thickened as we moved towards the square. Citizens of Greydenn were taking in the decorations around them, openly wondering what was to come with much more excitement than I could muster. The happiness and excitement on their faces eased the pit in my stomach more than words ever could. These people accepted a cursed princess a decade ago, a gift I would never forget. No, whatever came today, I would deal with it for them. It is what they deserved.

And if it was necessary, I would be a beast for them. I would relish in my power to protect these people–my people.

Selena tapped my arm and pointed out the small form zipping around the crowd musing with flowers, donned in a purple cloak that matched the drapes.

"There's Gordby, let's go see if he will tell us what he has planned," Selena said.

Selena pulled me towards the man and as we walked, I made an effort to soften my sharp face, feeling the tension leave my face with every quickening step. By the time we pushed through the crowd, I was nothing more than the serene princess I was expected to be.

I tapped Gordby on the shoulder. "It looks like you have been so busy Mayor," I said with a genuine smile on my face. The work he had done was gorgeous, even if whatever reason behind it deeply unsettled me. "Please tell us what you have planned. We are dying to know!"

Selena grinned at the man as well. "I promise we can keep a secret," she said with an eager nod and a sweet smile. I mimicked her movements, hoping it was enough to get the information we wanted.

Gordby softened as his round cheeks grew red. "Oh, you girls tempt me, but where is the fun in that?" he said with the look akin to a child telling a friend they have a secret, "You will find out with everyone else!"

Selena and I shared a look. This was going to be more difficult than we thought. Gordby was a jovial man that was usually very easy to get information from. Luckily, I always carried a card in my hand that no one could refuse.

"Mayor, it's just I get so anxious about visitors in the last few months, and all this amazing decor makes me think there is a very important visitor coming today." I did my best to look as pathetic as possible. My shoulders slumped until the height difference between my companion and me was no longer as noticeable. I rubbed my hands together anxiously, hoping the motion would wring an answer out of the old man. To my joy, Selena noticed and instantly turned into the clucking maid assuring her poor lady in times of need. She started to rub my arm reassuringly while throwing concerned looks between Gordby and me. "Please, give me a hint to calm my worried mind," I begged him with my eyes, softening my features until I resembled the scared little girl he greeted all those years ago.

To my delight, Gordby visibly softened. "Aye princess, I will give you a hint, honestly it is all I know as well." Gordby stepped closer and waved for Selena and me to hunch down to his level. He glanced around before he continued. "Word was sent to me this morning by raven that a royal envoy carrying an important passenger and a letter to Greydenn directly from the King will arrive this afternoon. That is all I know, Princess." He moved forward and reached up to pat my shoulder. "I am sure whomever it is will bring good news, Princess. Maybe they have finally found a way to remove the malady from your life and you can return home?" He offered me a genuine smile of hope, one I knew he meant with every fiber of his being, as he squeezed my shoulder before returning his hand to his side.

But there was no home to return to. The closest I had known to a true home had been Greydenn. The only way I would return to High Castle is as a head on a spike if my brother had his way.

A commotion coming down the path pulled Gordby's attention from us. A gaggle of town children ran with grins on their faces, as they shouted at the growing crowd. It took a moment for them to get close enough to hear. "A royal chariot is coming!" the children yelled with glee.

A hollow chill rolled down my spine. Something was brewing, something that would change me forever. I could sense it in the air as surely as I could sense the town people's happiness.

A few moments later, the site of the dark purple carriage pulled by a team of all white horses broke the hill. Selena squeezed my arm, whispering one word so low that even I could barely hear. "Breathe."

Unaware I had been holding my breath, I sucked in air methodically–*in, hold, out, in, hold, out*. The routine of it calmed me and my heart rate slowed.

By the time the carriage arrived in front of the building, my breath had slowed and my spine had straightened. A small man with copper hair that peaked from under his feathered cap jumped from the carriage. His velvet uniform had the insignia of Albaria embossed in gold on his chest marked him as a royal herald. The herald moved through the crowd with an upturned nose as he unrolled a parchment. He cleared his throat and began speaking to no one in particular. "His royal highness, King Elrick Galterius, First of his Name, would like to thank the good people of Greydenn for welcoming his beloved sister ten years ago despite the malady it has brought your people. While the champion king was the princess's protector, he could not protect her from the curse laid on them both in the womb. Though the valiant king did try when the dragon first attached to his sister all those years ago. The young prince bravely fought to protect his sister, causing him to forever be scarred." Shocked looks marked the faces of the townspeople at this revelation. There was no scar in my brother's royal portrait.

The townspeople moved their heads as they muttered, obviously trying to find me in the crowd. Selena had pulled me towards the back, attempting to hide us both in the shadows. Knowing my height played against me in this, I slouched, hoping it was enough to keep prying eyes from me. It was so strange to hear someone speak of what happened. A feeling of euphoria and fear mixed in me. I wondered what the scar looked like. I hoped it was deep and gnarled. I hoped every time he looked in the mirror he was reminded of how I bested him. It felt good to know I was able to mark him like he marked me.

It also explained why he wanted me dead so badly. Elrick was always so conceited about his looks.

The herald began speaking again as the crowd quieted around him. "The good king has sent several prized fighters to slay this town's malady, the great beast that attaches itself to Princess Elora at night. As you are all aware, those great men have been mercilessly slain by the beast."

I did my best to suppress the scoff building in my throat. Those men were far from great, and for the most part, I gave them a more merciful death than they deserved. They rarely suffered, I always made sure of that. The herald paused and scanned the crowd as a hushed murmur broke out. "In an attempt to once again save the great people of Greydenn from the malady his parent's cursed them too, the late King Rainard Galterius and Queen Lilion Galterius, the King has sent his best champion to slay the beast once and for all," he said.

The crowd cheered as a shiver went down my spine. I was frozen in place. Breathing became very difficult, like all the air in the square had been removed. They did not know they were cheering for my death, I reminded myself. A thought haunted me–would they still cheer like this if they did know? Would they see me more as a princess or the beast?

Suddenly, the carriage door opened. I looked into the abyss, trying to get a glimpse of my next opponent while blending into the back. A tall form, with beautiful golden hair that touched his shoulders emerged. He was wearing a fine tunic embossed with the insignia of Albaria, matching the herald. He seemed familiar in a way I couldn't place. His eyes scanned the crowd, looking for something. He seemed to find what he was searching for when his eyes found mine. A jolt passed through my entire body as his blue eyes pierced mine. From the back I could see him mouth a single word: *Elora*.

I realized with a shock who this knight was. My ears started to ring and the ground felt uneven. Memories started flooding back to me, things I hadn't dared let cross my mind in a decade–bruises, laughs, and a golden-haired boy picking me yellow flowers. A boy who always knew how to dull the pain after my brother had his fun with me.

Percy.

"Oh my gods," a knowing Selena whispered.

"May I present, Sir Percival Alderius of Vinguarri, King Elrick's sworn protector," the herald said. He rolled the parchment up and bowed at the young knight.

My vision went black, the last thing I noticed was Selena's voice calling my name. The smell of leather and peppermint enveloped me as hands reached to grab me. I did not care who had me, as only one thought was playing on a loop in my mind as I drifted into a world of nothingness.

Percy had come to kill me.

Chapter Three

WARMTH held me in a soft caress that lulled me into a sense of unending peace. My eyes seemed glued shut, but I was so comfortable I did not mind. The lights danced behind my eyelids, and if it wasn't for the gentle mutterings around me, I would have been content to stay here, drifting for hours in a warm sea of nothingness.

A gentle hand, wrinkled with time, grabbed my cheek, pulling me from my drifting mind. "Elora, dearie, it's time to wake up."

I tried to fight it, but Olgara's spoken words jolted me awake, completely against my own will. It was like I no longer had control over my own body. The power my nanny had over me was astounding. I shot up, nearly bumping heads with Olgara as the shroud of darkness was ripped from my eyes. The old woman moved out of my trajectory with more elegance and skill then I would have ever assumed she was capable of.

"Aye, there's my girl," she said with a smile. "Ladies, she is awake," Olgara called over her shoulder, seeming to summon Selena and Katherine out of thin air. They both instantly appeared in the doorway of my chambers.

I smiled at my friends. The tension in their shoulders eased as they began to make their way to me. "How did I get here?" I asked no one in particular. Last I remembered, I was waiting for an announcement outside the town hall. Selena's face fell as her golden eyes turned sad. Suddenly, the memory came flooding back–the herald, the proclamation, the knight stepping out of the carriage. Before I could allow myself to think of his name, darkness crept over my vision once again, pulling me into nothingness.

"Here dearie, take a drink of this, It will help," said Olgara as she handed me a glass with a clear liquid inside.

Olgara was right, water was what I needed. I grabbed the cup and gulped. As the liquid passed my lips, I choked on what felt like the fire of a thousand suns. The liquid in my cup most definitely was *not* water. This was Olgara's *special* concoction that tasted like clear hellfire, her own special spirit.

Olgara laughed haughtily as I struggled to swallow the liquid in my mouth. "Aye, dearie. I knew that would bring you back to the land of the living," she said with a laugh and a pat on my back. She quickly replaced the glass in my hand with another cup, this one also full of clear liquid. I hesitantly sniffed the glass as my eyes narrowed at my former nanny.

"Stop being so dramatic, that one is nothing but spring water," she said.

"I am not dramatic, but shocked by the fact you thought giving someone who just awoke after fainting your homemade spirits," I said with venom before taking a gulp from the new cup. Thankfully, this was just water, rich and cool from the spring on top of the palace grounds. The water chased the burning in my body from the spirit and cooled the flame, leaving a path of serenity in its wake.

"How are you feeling?" asked Katherine, worry etched into her face. Her grey eyes were narrowed, searching, as she pursed her thin lips.

"I feel like the lights are too bright and the world is moving slower than normal, but also faster at the same time," I responded. I blinked, my own honesty shocking me. Clearly not all effects of the spirit were cleansed by the water.

Katherine snickered as she plopped down on the bed at my feet with Selena close behind. The worry from her face melted away and was replaced by an even smile. Selena walked up to me and sat next to me in bed, seeming to cradle me. Her golden eyes bore into me, searching for something, as she studied me. Clearly she was not as quickly put to ease as Katherine was.

I allowed myself a moment to sit in the luxury of my two friends' company. They grounded me. There were so many things left unspoken between us, so many things I could never share with them. But this moment, this they understood, or at least they believe they did. They believed I was reacting to seeing the childhood friend of my brother, the one who witnessed some of the abuse Elrick rained down on me. The one who would help brush me off when he could, the one who brought me pretty yellow flowers after witnessing the worst of it. Did they think the fear of his death is what sent me into this fit? They would never know why Elrick did the things he did to me, never understand that my brother thought he was punishing a beast sent to harm all of Albaria. I always wondered how the fates could smile so fondly on a creature that elated in the harm of his own kin. No, my friends would never fully understand the emotions I was feeling, and that broke my soul into thousands of pieces. I was unknowable.

"How did I get here?" I whispered to no one in particular.

Selena responded, more literally than I intended. "I was able to grab you when you fell without alerting anyone. Luckily, Dameon just appeared and helped me to get you to the alleyway and through the corridor. Then he thought I was slowing things down so he insisted on carrying you to the stables."

Heat rushed my cheeks. I would never hear the end of this from him.

I turned to Selena. "Oh, I'm sure he relished in the moment when he dropped me off to the stable master," I groaned. How could I let myself become such a damsel in distress?

Selena stifled a giggle as she pressed her hand to her full mouth. My face dropped and my mouth hung open. I knew I would not like whatever was coming.

"So, he knows how…private…you can be about things. So we actually snuck into the stables and grabbed two horses to take you back to the castle." Selena smiled awkwardly as she spoke, like she was trying to soften the embarrassment building in me.

"Two horses…for the three of us…when I was fully unconscious? Please don't tell me…" I trailed off, trying my best to delay the inevitable. Katherine giggled at my discomfort.

"Unfortunately for you, I will never lie." Selena paused and rubbed her hands together. She bit her lip, like she was trying to suppress a smile. "While I would have been honored to be the one to assist you on the horse, you are far taller than me and I am not as experienced with horses as the former stable boy."

"Selena…" I begged.

Suddenly, Katherine could not hold it in any longer as even Olgara was beginning to giggle, "Imagine my surprise when I open the doors and see you Elora, draped in his arms on horseback with your head on his chest," Katherine mimed fainting herself, causing my face to heat even more. No, I would never hear the end of this.

"Aye, girlies, leave her alone for now," Olgara hushed my giggling friends. "Why don't you both go to seeing a message delivered to the knight in Greydenn. He is welcome to join us all for dinner tonight at the castle at 5 o'clock. Inform him he will be making his leave from the grounds with the rest of the folk before sunset."

Olgara ushered Katherine and Selena out. Both my friends mimed fainting themselves and calling out for a big strong guard to save them as they left. Traitorous wenches. When the door finally shut behind them, I sank into my bed and threw the blankets over my head. I hoped that Olgara would join the others in exiting. I desperately needed a moment of peace to collect myself if I was to ever show my face to my friends again, but especially Dameon. We had not shared a horse since we were children, and he still gave me grief for it all these years later. My stomach dropped when I imagined the torment he was probably preparing.

The creak of the stool beside my bed quickly dashed my hope. A hand grabbed my blankets and slowly unveiled my head. "Do you want to tell me what really happened, dearie?" Olgara said with a knowing look. Ever since I could remember she had always seemed to know more than all those around her. She was aware of every twitch on my face and every thought I ever had, it seemed. As a child, I would try to sneak things past her, but it never worked. The only thing she never seemed to know about were my visits to the stables once she had long fallen asleep.

"Olgara, it's Percy. Elrick sent Percy to kill me." I whispered. My voice was smaller than I expected it to be.

Olgara stroked my hair away from my face. "I know dearie, but you need to remember something, something important."

"What could be so important now?" I said with an exasperated sigh.

Olgara's eyes softened. "Percy doesn't know he was sent to kill *you*. He thinks he is here to *save* you."

"What does that matter? He cannot do one without the other?" I said.

Olgara scoffed. "Since when have you needed saving, dearie?"

I huffed as I stared at my former nanny. "I have killed a dozen men, Olgara. Compared to Percy, maybe I am the beast."

"You have killed a dozen men, all who came here on their own accord to fight for what they thought they deserved." Olgara paused before continuing. "You gave the majority swift deaths and if I remember correctly, you also offered all but one of them a bargain–a chance to live."

"How do you know that?" I asked breathlessly. All my battles happened long after I thought Olgara was asleep.

Olgara scoffed. "Do you think I am so heartless as to sleep peacefully while you battle for your life? No, dearie, I watch from my window. Every time," she said with a soft smile.

I never knew that Olgara was aware of my bargains, that she watched the battles. The statement honestly left me in shock. All I could do was look her in the eyes, the same wrinkled face that had been with me my whole life, "What am I to do?"

"The same thing you have done the last three months—when the time comes, try to convince him to set down his sword," she said.

"What if he doesn't? What then?" I asked, hoping my all-knowing nanny would help me in this.

"Hope, dearie. That is all you can do."

*   *   *

MIRADOR Castle was not nearly as large as the High Castle in Vinguarii, more of a large keep carved into a mountain. The grounds of Mirador, however, rivaled those of High Castle in beauty. The comfort I felt here was so different than at High Castle. The marble floors there gleamed in a way that made stepping on them seem criminal. It was cold, and asture. Power emanated from the seat of Albaria. Mirador, however, was warm, decorated and built in a way that was meant to be lived in. The shadows of its former inhabitants were still seen in the worn down footfalls of the steps, or the grooves on the wall where some unknown person once hung something dear to them. I had always found in times of trouble that wandering the halls of Mirador with their stained glass windows or peering into the spring surrounded by tall trees soothed my very soul.

The traces of the past inhabitants felt like familiar ghosts to me. I did not tiptoe around Mirador, nor stomp to claim ownership. I walked just as the people before me did–assuredly.

After Olgara left me, my feet carried me to the long hallway of the North wing of the castle lined with stained glass on both sides. Gentle light seemed to always be drifting through, as if the sun herself wished to see her light changed by glass. The stone floors glowed with thousands of rainbows as the warm light passed through the glass. I was lost in the colors, attempting to pinpoint where one ended and another began when a gentle cough alerted me I wasn't alone. To my surprise, it wasn't a castle worker I saw, but Dameon, stretched long and tall leaning against the cool stone between window panes. The multicolored light seemed to glow from his tan skin, painting shadows and light across his cheekbones and full lips. The long lashes of his partially closed eyes rested gently on his face. The sight almost took my breath away, until I remembered *why* he was in the castle. Dameon coming to Mirador was such a rare occurrence. Blood rushed my cheeks.

Dameon pushed off the wall with the grace of a warrior. In two long strides, he stood before me, looking down at me with a strange look. His deep brown eyes were searching me. I felt bared open. I hated the vulnerability of it.

"What, have I grown horns?" I said, attempting to lighten the mood.

He took me in, and to my shock, wrapped his arms around me, pulling me to his chest into a deep hug. I was tall for a woman, but still did not even reach Dameon's chin. The smell of leather and saddle soap wrapped around me as tightly as his arms. "You scared the shit out of me," he whispered into my hair.

I froze. This was so unlike us. I placed my hands on his chest and pushed back to look at his face, the intensity of his eyes almost caused me to stutter out my next words. "Oh, we both know you are always looking for an excuse to play the hero."

Dameon studied my face and as quickly as his arms were thrown around me moments ago, they retracted. The worry on his face was pushed away for something I could not place.

"Are you going to tell me what happened?" Dameon asked. His face was neutral.

"Tell you what?" I asked. I threw my arms across my chest. "From what Selena has said, you know all too well what happened, I fainted."

Dameon threw me an incredulous look, and I threw my arms to my side. I felt bared open again, entirely too vulnerable. "Thank you," I muttered, "for helping to get me back here unseen. I greatly appreciate it."

Dameon was still looking at me as he crossed his arms, as if he was still waiting for something.

"I had such a tiring morning, maybe I did not eat enough at breakfast?" I finished, hoping that was enough for him. Judging by the fact he still has not moved or said anything, it wasn't. His silence ate at me. Each passing second I grew more irritated by it.

"Is there something more you need? If not, you may take your leave" I asked with more venom than necessary as I motioned for the door at the end of the corridor.

Dameon's eyes widened, anger apparent in his features. "What I need," he said, "is for you to stop bullshitting me and tell me what is *actually* going on. Who is that knight and why did the sight of him send such fear through you?"

His words shocked me as my stomach sank. "That does not concern you," I said between gritted teeth. This truth was held too close to the other things I was forced to keep from him.

"It became my concern when I had to carry your unconscious body!" Dameon threw his arms in the air before quickly crossing them back at his chest. "Did you know you weren't completely silent? The whole ride up the mountain you were muttering the same thing over and over," Dameon paused "*Please don't hurt me.*" He said each word like it opened a wound in him. I wondered if he knew that the words hit me like a knife against the skin.

I could feel the ghosts of hands around me, squeezing me. Memories I pushed down for so long clawed their way through my mind, each vying for the honor of sending me spiraling. I could hear the ghost of my brother's voice echoing in my ears. Color drained from my face as my skin tingled. Dameon softened at the sight of my distress as pity crept across his face.

"Lor, I'm sorry. I just...I just remember the marks on your skin when you first got here. Someone hurt you and if it is this knight I need to know," Dameon pleaded. His eyes were pained. He reached to touch me and I stepped away. His outstretched arm dangled in mid- air for a moment before falling to his side.

The realization that Dameon saw the things I tried to hide all those years ago hit me like cold water, completely taking my breath away. I couldn't speak.

"Why do you think you are entitled to know?" I whispered out before building the venom in my voice. How dare he bring up those things. I was filled with rage as I looked Dameon in the eye, my voice raised. "Why do you think you are entitled to know?"

Dameon was caught off guard by this. Rage mixed with pain filled his eyes as he threw his hands up in exasperation. "I don't know, Lor, maybe because we are friends. Maybe because I am a guard sworn to protect all in Greydenn and you count in that!"

"Of course, always looking for a reason to be the hero, aren't we?" I said.

Dameon's eyes turned pleading as he moved to grab my hand. "Please just tell me so I can help you. I just need to know you are safe before I go back down the path."

I threw his hand down. "I do not need saving, Dameon."

"Tell. Me." The words were ground out of his gritted teeth.

Any composure I had left flew out of my body. "Tell you what, Dameon? Tell you that I fainted at the mere sight of the knight not because he ever hurt me, but because he was kind to me? He was kind to me and now he has been sent to die for me! That he saw the things I endured and I will now watch him die? Is that what you want to hear?" Tears stung my eyes. *I would be the one to kill Percy. I am the beast*, I said to myself.

"If he stood by and watched whoever hurt you he deserves the death coming to him, be it by the dragon or by other means," Dameon growled. His face was steady, deadly calm hiding a storm underneath. He looked like an angry god preparing to smite down a lesser being.

I stopped. "We were kids, Dameon. There is nothing he could do that wouldn't have made him the next target." I couldn't tell Dameon the villain of my story is the new king, that it was my brother who left the majority of the marks on me in a desperate attempt to rid the country of the beast in me. Dameon saw me as a wounded princess–one he needed to save to remove the chip forever on his shoulder. I wasn't the damsel he saw me as. I was the beast in this story. It was treasonous to talk ill of the king and above all else, Dameon said an oath to Elrick when he swore to the crown. I couldn't bear to watch Dameon also choose my brother knowing the truth as all else had.

Dameon stared at me and his eyes softened as the tension left his shoulders. He took another step towards me and reached for my hand. I stepped back before he could grab it.

"If you will excuse me, I must go prepare myself for dinner," I said in the most formal voice I could muster. I never used this voice with Dameon in the decade of our friendship. It felt foreign on my tongue. "Stay if you would like, consider it a thanks for assisting me today." I hoped he would not.

I turned around and walked down the corridor before he could respond. I felt his eyes burning into the back of me, begging me to turn around. I did not, I *could not.* Tears streamed down my face silently.

I hoped he did not stay. It would be too much to have to eat dinner with him and Percy knowing they had both seen me at my weakest. I sent a silent prayer to the gods, pleading for this one thing.

A small voice reverberated in the back of my pleas, one I hoped the gods ignored as fervently as I tried to.

What if he leaves?

*   *   *

BY the time I made it back to my chambers, my eyes had long since dried as dread had built in my stomach. When I opened my chamber doors, I was surprised to find no one there, no Olgara, no Katherine, no Selena. The shock of this was soon abridged when I saw the note on my mattress and smelled the scent of lavender in the air–a bath had been drawn for me by Olgara and all three would be back in my chambers in an hour to prepare me for dinner.

Two baths in a day was a luxury I usually did not partake in, but today, it was needed. I slipped into the scented water and fully immersed myself, my hair forming a halo around me. As I held my breath, I tried to force the thoughts of today out of my mind by focusing on the burning in my chest. If I concentrated hard enough, maybe I could pretend that I was not in this tub, but my lake, I hoped. This proved futile and as I sat up, gasping for air. The memories of this day were still etched in my mind. How could I manage this? How could I kill Percy? The thought of doing so made me want to wretch. Beast or not, I did not know if I was capable of this.

A thought danced in the back of my mind, ever persistent, spoken in my mother's voice as it always was. *Give up the dragon*. It seemed easy. But pretending the scales did not lie beneath my skin would not remove them entirely. My parents hoped that if I just stopped changing, maybe I would one day forget how, maybe the dragon would disappear. I could do that now, just never turn again and pretend the dragon was defeated. The thought alone left me heaving until I once again slipped below the surface of the perfumed bath. More than just the dragon would die if I made that decision. I would sooner give up breathing than give up the sky. My other form was etched into me.

I opened my eyes under the water, a thought so profound hit me that I was able to ignore the stinging in my eyes as I sat up, splashing water all around. Maybe there was another way to defeat Percy, another trick up my sleeve that meant we both lived and the dragon in me was still free.

The realization sent me into a frenzy as I leapt from the bath and began drying off, almost slipping in the mess I had made. By the time a knock sounded at my door, I had already laid out my best dress and made plans. Tonight, I had to look my best. I had to be every bit the lost princess–regal, glowing, elegant–if my plan was to work, and it had to work. Our lives depended on it.

Selena and Katherine were already dressed, both in elegant but simple gowns of matching lilac. Selena's hugged her every curve while Katherine's accentuated her long, lean figure. They both eyed my dress, one I rarely deigned to wear because of the intricacies. The dress was stunning, a beautiful slate blue gauzy fabric covered in beading and metalwork. The neckline was much deeper than I usually wore, coming to a point below my breasts.

"I am surprised you chose this," Selena said while toying with the gauzy blue fabric.

"Tonight is a special occasion, ladies," I said. My voice was joyful as I sat at my vanity.

"Because Percival is joining us?" Katherine asked with a queer look on her face.

"Yes," I said, trying to hide the lie in my face. "He is an old friend we haven't seen in years. I want him to feel welcome in Greydenn, lest he report back to the King that we are unwelcoming hosts."

Selena sucked in a breath. "No, we certainly do not want that."

"We know what he is capable of when he is upset," Katherine whispered to herself while eyeing me in the suspicious way of hers.

I chose to ignore her. There was no time to get lost in memories tonight.

Selena started on my hair, adding intricate braids to the front and pulling the rest to cascade down my back. Her nimble fingers moved adeptly through my hair, expertly completing the vision I had to highlight my features and my crown. Katherine added rouge to my cheek and lips to accentuate my features, so faintly that no man would ever notice. She completed the effortless look with skill. Next, it was time for the dress. The dress that was to be my armor and weapon tonight. The dragon would not make an appearance tonight, but I was still going to battle. I stepped out of my dressing gown, baring it all to my friends as they moved to tie the dress around me. They adjusted the front and placed the golden metal caps sleeves on my shoulders, expertly draping the long gauzy sleeves around me.

Once they finished, I admired their handiwork in the mirror, I looked more beautiful than I remembered being. The dress was magnificent, the deep v hit just below my breast, framing my chest in light blue fabric with gold metal detailing.

My waist was cinched in a gold belt that connected to a strap down my spine along the open back. The cap sleeves were framed with metal and a strap went across my clavicle, connecting the shoulder cups to the dress as long flowing open sleeves cascaded down my arms to the floor. To a man, I would look beautiful, ethereal, and bared open. *Vulnerable.* But to a woman, it was apparent that a man's perception could not be further from the truth. This dress was my weapon. I was a woman dressed for battle.

A knock at the door startled me from my reflection. It appeared that Katherine and Selena were just as transfixed as me, both openly staring at their handiwork when Olgara entered. The old woman was carrying the tiara I so rarely wore on a white satin pillow. Golden vines interlooped with each other around small deep purple stones. The tiara rose to a slight apex in the middle. It was designed to mirror the crown of the queen, a daintier version of the crown that sat on my mother's brow in all my memories.

"Ladies, will you please excuse Elora and me? I must talk with the princess before dinner tonight," Olgara said.

I nodded at my friends that they were free to go and called out my thanks as they left the chambers. They had outdone themselves. Having them at the table with me on either side would give me the strength to pull off what I needed to do.

Once they were gone, Olgara turned me around to face her. "This is quite the dress for the occasion, dearie," she said with a knowing look.

"It is your best work, and you always complain that it never sees the light of day," I said, planting a sly smile on my face. Olgara was able to create the most beautiful clothes seemingly from thin air.

"Aye, I am very talented," she said with a wink, "but this isn't a dress for a random knight showing up, even one that was a childhood friend. You are dressed with a *purpose*."

"Of course I am, Olgara, there is to be a battle tonight." I turned around to face the mirror as Olgara stood behind me, gazing at the picture before her. We were total opposites. Where my skin was pink and smooth, Olgara's was sallow and wrinkled with time. My long, dark hair cascaded down my back while her silver tresses were tucked into a tight bun at the nape of her neck. Where my green eyes were clear and crisp, hers were milky with age. She was dressed demurely in a green linen frock. I looked every bit the princess, but I did not question who had the real power in this room.

"A battle? So rare for the dragon to show up two nights in a row," she said.

"This battle will not be between the dragon and the knight, Olgara, but between a *princess* and a knight," I said with a smile.

"What is your plan, girl?" Olgara eyes me quizzically.

My smile widened as I made eye contact with my old nanny in the mirror. "I am going to make Percy fall in love with me."

"So you can convince him to not fight the dragon, I am guessing?" Olgara's face was unreadable.

"Precisely."

Olgara let out a deep sigh before grabbing the crown. "Well I can't let any soldier go to battle without a proper helmet." As she placed the crown atop my head, she planted a kiss on my forehead. I surprised myself by closing my eyes and leaning into it.

I took one last look in the mirror before turning to Olgara. "Let's go to war."

Chapter Four

THE walk from my chambers to the dining hall on the main floor seemed to only strengthen my resolve. My footfalls were light but steady across the stone floors of the castle. I reached the top of the grand staircase unseen by the table below, ready to descend down to my unknown. As I moved to take a step into view, I was pulled to a stop. Olgara had grabbed the strap going down my spine. I looked down at my nanny only to meet milky blue eyes holding the resolve of steel. It seemed that I was not the only one plotting tonight.

Olgara took a measured step in front of me and straightened her back. She looked down at the table below like a god watching their people high from the sky. She cleared her throat, drawing attention to her before speaking. "May I present Princess Elora Adhelina Galterius, sister of the King, Keeper of Mirador Castle, Ward of Greydenn."

The use of my full title, with the added piece about being named Keeper of Mirador, a fallacy that everyone in this room but Percy would know is a lie, shocked me. This castle was not mine and I did not have any claim to being its keeper. I was sent here to be a prisoner, not a lord. Heat crept up my face. I quickly composed myself before stepping into view, embodying the serene princess my parents always hoped I would be. There were two surprises waiting for me when I looked down–the first being that an uncomfortable Dameon was seated next to Percy, the second being that everyone at the table, Dameon, Percy, Selena, and Katherine were all standing, looking up at me expectantly. To my utter shock, everyone in the room, including Olgara, bowed to me. I took this as my cue and glided down the stairs, making sure my eyes never left Percy's as Olgara followed closely behind. He had grown into a man, but the boy I knew was still evident in his soulful blue eyes and golden hair. He was strapping in his family's coat of arms. The dark blue fabric accentuated his eyes. His cheeks were painted with a dusting of pink as he gazed upon me. I smiled demurely as I descended. My battle had now begun.

I arrived at the head of the table and motioned for everyone to sit as I took my seat. Katherine was seated at my left while Selena was at my right. From the corner of my eye, I could see Selena's soft smile. I hoped Percy would not find it odd to have my maids in such a place of honor, so different from what was expected of us at High Castle. Regardless of my plans, this is one thing I would never give up. These women were given the free will they had always deserved when we arrived in Greydenn. I would never send them to the shadows again.

Olgara shuffled her way across the room and took the seat on the other side of Katherine, across from a sullen-looking Dameon. He was still in his dusty clothes from earlier, in such contrast to the exquisitely dressed Percy, who was situated directly across from me at the end of the table. The dress was working–Percy could not keep his eyes off of me. Heat crept across his face as he scanned my body. I stood tall, refusing to shrink from his gaze. He seemed lost in the moment when a scoff from Dameon broke his attention. The shuffling of feet was heard and Dameon flinched as Olgara sent him a warning look.

This would be an interesting dinner indeed.

"Sir Percival, it is my *honor* to welcome you to Mirador Castle," I fluttered my eyelashes demurely, hoping it would trap Percy in my gaze.

He took the bait, apparent with another flush on his pale skin. "Princess Elora, I am honored to be your guest," he stumbled on his words like he was unsure of what to say next. "I…I have missed you greatly." His reddening cheeks mirrored my own.

The admittance shocked me. I honestly did not expect him to have thought about me the last ten years. Maybe this would be easier than I previously thought.

Someone putting down their goblet harder than necessary startled me from my thoughts, and I looked down to see bits of red wine splashed on the white table cloth next to Dameon, like blood spilled on fallen snow. Dameon's brown eyes were waxy as he stared at the cup. His hands were still wrapped around the goblet, white-knuckled.

I could not believe what I was seeing. Was Dameon *drunk*? He had never been known to lose himself in wine, but maybe I only knew as much about him as he knew of me. The idea of him keeping a secret from me soured my stomach, even if I kept them from him.

Selena, ever the hero, spoke up, drawing the attention to herself instead of the person seated next to her. "Shall we eat? It smells amazing."

Selena was right, the feast before us did smell amazing. It was humble compared to what Percy was used to, I was sure, but much fancier than we usually had at Mirador. The table was covered in dishes, roast duck with a blackberry reduction, vegetables cooked in butter, pillowy rolls, and a sweet cake covered in fruit and cream for dessert. Chef had outdone himself today.

I began loading my plate with the passed dishes moving in a circle around the table. Katherine handed me a dish while I passed one to Selena absentmindedly. Everyone at the table was doing the same with little thought, even Dameon who so rarely dined here was doing it in his drunken haze, all except Percy. He seemed flummoxed by what was happening around him, unsure of what to do. A realization hit suddenly–this behavior was not normal at a royal table.

"Sorry, Sir Percival, I know this is not what you are used to. We do not have anyone serve us our meals to allow the castle workers more time to finish their duties before heading down the mountain for the night," I said as I motioned to the table.

Percy looked up at me. "Please Princess, call me Percy as you used to. My title from your lips is shocking to me," he said with a smile that made his blue eyes crinkle.

I smiled. "Call me Elora, then, as you once did as well," I said. I could see Dameon taking yet another long pull from his goblet.

Percy relaxed into the meal from there. He loaded his plate awkwardly–clearly this was something he had never had to do before. Every dish handed to him ended up clanking together with his own plateware. When it came time for him to cut his portion of the duck, it was like watching a newborn babe use a knife for the first time. *Everything* was done for those who reside in High Castle. I saw the lack of agency as shackles and relished in the freedom and normalcy I was able to cultivate in Mirador. I sent a silent prayer to the gods that Percy would feel the same.

"So tell me," Katherine said breaking the silence, "how did you earn your title?"

"Yes," echoed an excited Selena, "tell us of your life, it has been so long since we have all seen each other."

Percy raised his eyebrows in confusion. He looked at Katherine and Selena as if he had never seen them before in his life. We were all children together in the castle, even if they were my servants. A thought stopped me. He did not recognize them not in spite of them being my servants even then, but *because* of it. I took a deep breath. This would be more difficult than I thought.

"If you recall, Percy, Selena and Katherine were my servants at High Castle," I said, hoping to jog his memory.

"Ah yes," he said with an awkward smile, "how could I forget. It is nice to see you two again, it appears life at Mirador has suited you well." He smiled at them both genuinely.

"But I agree with my ladies. I would love to hear how you earned your title," I said expectantly. Earning the title of knight was seen as an utmost honor in Albaria, something only the most courageous of men are able to do. The title and the lands that come with it are a gift from the king as thanks for a great heroic act.

Percy's skin reddened as he looked down at his plate. "Oh, my title is nothing," he said demurely.

"I am sure it is a great story, Sir Percival," Selena said with a smile. I nodded along, hoping it would be enough to pull the story from him.

"I have always loved the stories of the great Knights of the past," Katherine said. "It would be such a treat to hear from one personally." Katherine had always been a bookworm. While Selena excelled in knowledge of people, Katherine preferred the information she could get from the great tomes in the library.

Percy's eyes widened. I had never seen anyone act with such embarrassment when it came to their title. Clearly he did not want to boast. He opened his mouth and closed it several times, like he was trying to find his words. After several silent moments, he took a deep breath and focused his eyes on mine. He smiled and huffed a laugh before taking a drink from his cup.

"Alright, you have won. I will tell you the story of how I," Percy paused, like he needed to beg the next words from his mouth, *"earned* my title." He stressed the word and smiled awkwardly before beginning again.

Before he could continue, a laugh cut him short. Dameon's dark chuckle made my blood boil. A confused Percy glanced at him. "Is something the matter? Did I also know you in the past? I am so bad with faces." Percy chuckled awkwardly as he spoke.

Dameon looked up at Percy. "No, we have never had the *pleasure* of meeting. I am Captain Dameon Grey, of the Greydenn Guard." He grabbed his cup and brought it to his lips quickly before pointing at Percy with the same hand. My heart stopped beating for the split second Dameon drank deeply from the cup. His deep brown eyes did not stray from Percy the whole time. Wine sloshed from the outstretched cup onto a horrified Percy. "And I think you are full of shit."

"Dameon," I yelled as I threw my hands on the table.

"I beg your pardon," asked Percy. His brows furrowed as he balled his fists together.

"Sorry, let me be more clear. I think you are a spoiled boy who bought your title and has his nose so far up his own ass that he never notices those around him, especially the 'small folk' who help you." Dameon paused and looked at Selena and Katherine for reassurance. He found only shocked expressions, but this did not seem to deter him. "Tell me, how can someone see people around for years and never notice them? Do you think you are better than us?"

Within an instant I was out of my chair and behind Dameon. I grabbed his arm and tugged, preparing myself for a fight. Dameon was much taller than me and strong. The muscles of his arm flexed under my touch. He willingly went, stumbling a bit with drink. Without a word, I dragged him to the front of the corridor and to the door, thankfully, without much fuss until we arrived. Dameon turned to me. "Sweet princess," his words slurred, "are you to put out the poor bastard guard with no dinner? Not even the scraps," he said with the most pitiful face he could muster, jutting out his bottom lip like a scolded child.

I growled at him before stomping back, grabbing his plate. I marched back to the place I left him and shoved it into his hands. "Here you go, Dameon. Enjoy your fucking meal with the dogs." I slammed the heavy front door as hard as I could, which unfortunately took several seconds. Dameon stood there and watched as he drunkenly snorted at my effort. The last thing I saw was his smirk, a smirk that caused so much rage to build into me that I had to steady my breathing before walking back to the table. When I arrived, the silence was so tense and awkward that I feared it would last forever. Then the unthinkable happened–Olgara laughed. Katherine and Selena both soon lost it as well, leaving a befuddled Percy and me the only ones not breaking a rib.

"Please, enlighten me, what is so funny?" I asked with venom dripping from every word as my eyes scanned between the three traitors.

Olgara's smile widened. "So much dearie," she said with a shake of her head, "so so much."

*   *   *

THE rest of dinner was spent in awkward silence until the stroke of a bell tower instructed the guests it was nearly time to leave. Percy, unused to this turn of events, seemed shocked by the shuffling, people leaving the castle like a well-oiled machine.

"Have I missed something?" he asked. My face drained of color.

"Oh my gods, my apologies," I said. "No one is allowed on castle grounds after sunset except Olgara and me. If the dragon shows tonight, it does not take kindly to visitors."

Percy nodded his head. "Ah yes I had been told that. The Mayor said I would be staying in Greydenn."

Percy moved to leave with a queer look on his face. I stood up, hoping I could salvage this wreck of a night. Percy's life depended on it.

"Here, let me walk you to the door," I said as I walked towards him. To my surprise he offered me his arm with a shy smile. I took it dutifully, draping my hand across the crisp blue fabric of his coat.

"I want to offer my sincerest apologies for dinner tonight. I did not hope your first dinner at Mirador to end like this," I said, looking up into his eyes.

Percy blushed. "To be perfectly honest Elora, nothing could go wrong any night where I am lucky enough to see you. I have missed you so." Heat crept into my face and I averted my eyes, only to have Percy grab my chin and gently bring them back to his own. "You have grown so beautiful," he whispered.

"You flatter me," I said with a breath.

"It is not flattery when it is a fact, Elora," he said leaning closer.

Before I could stop myself, I stepped away from him, ending the moment. "You should leave now, Percy. It isn't safe."

A saddened look swept quickly across his face. "You're right," he grabbed my hand, "but I promise you, Elora, I will not be leaving this place until you are safe at last." The earnesty in his eyes terrified me.

A shutter went down my spine. If I failed, the only way Percy would be leaving Greydenn was in a box. His death would kill any hope I had of being good, regardless of prophecy. I could not allow that to happen.

Percy placed a soft kiss on my hand before departing. As the door shut behind him, I hoped I had not already ruined things. Why didn't I let him kiss me? Why was I standing in my own way?

Katherine and Selena both departed soon after Percy. After helping Olgara clean the table, I made my way up to my chambers, exhaustion hitting me with each step. No, the dragon would definitely not be making an appearance tonight. I quickly undressed and lay on my bed, falling into a deep sleep nearly instantly. I dreamt of a world where I could fly in the light without fears of my own shadows.

Chapter Five

THE bell tower rang once in the distance. I had been lying here awake for two hours. I longed for the deep sleep I had, for the peaceful dreams of flight. But each time I closed my eyes, I was not met with sweetness, but a new fear or horror about my current situation. If I messed things up at dinner I had doomed both Percy and me.

I whirred from my bed as realization struck. No, *I* did not cause this, *I* did not damn this plan. That blame lay with one person only.

Before I could stop myself, I was digging into the back of my wardrobe. Tucked safely behind my gowns was a plain brown tunic and breeches I kept hidden there for nights like this. I quickly dressed and carefully tucked my hair into the matching cap. I tiptoed through my chambers to my door, which I slipped through silently and made it to the stairs. I held my breath as I made my way down the staircase. Each footfall was carefully planned. The creaking old steps were a challenge I had long ago beaten. I had memorized the safe places to step so I could move silently. There was no need for all of this, honestly. Sneaking out of a castle was much easier when the only other occupant was an old woman who slept like the dead.

Olgara never left her chambers at night, *ever*. Even when she needed moon-blooming flowers and herbs for her latest concoction, she sent Katherine or me for it. The number of times I had been instructed to fly to areas too difficult for a person to reach to gather flowers described to me by Olgara was too numerous to count.

I walked through the door of the castle, slipping through silently. It did not matter though–I could have slammed it and Olgara would not have awoken, let alone stopped me. I had a mission to complete, fueled by spite. Not even the fear of Olgara's wrath could stop me. I made my way down the path, slipping through the tree-lined switchbacks as quiet and low as a mouse. The shadows of the trees kept me completely concealed. The likelihood of anyone from town seeing me was low, but I could not bear the questions asked if someone did ever find me doing this. I made it to the stables at the base of the path in record time, powered by anger and spite for one person and one person only: Dameon.

The familiar scent of leather and horses hit me like a wave as I opened the barn door. My tense shoulders dropped. I stopped myself and grasped at the anger that drove me here with the desperation of a child holding on to their favorite toy. I climbed the ladder to the hayloft instinctively and as silently as possible. I crept up slowly, using the sounds of stomping horses to cover my footfalls. As soon as I could see above the lip, I scanned the dark hayloft, looking for my adversary. My breath caught in my throat as I crested the ladder and stepped into the empty hayloft. Realization hit me a moment later–why would Dameon be here? He had been a guard for years now, he surely had a beĖer bed in the guard dormitories than the hay of the loft. I turned around, shocked by my own stupidity and disappointment. I wanted to yell at him and I needed him to yell back, but not as badly as I wanted things to return to how they were. So many times this loft was a haven for me as a child. Dameon's stories when I couldn't sleep eased something in me. The number of times he had soothed me to sleep only to gently wake me up and tell me it was time to return to the castle was unknowable. On the nights when we both were restless though, that was the real fun. We always picked the fastest horses and rode out into the forest under the light of the moon, me holding on to him with all my might as childlike giggles emerged from us both. He eventually taught me to ride and then the game became racing. I smiled as I remembered his boyish grin when he inevitably won.

Finding the loft empty felt like closing a chapter in a way I couldn't explain. I turned to go back down the rickety ladder when movement caught my eye. In the corner of the loft, I found a letter nailed to the wall of the barn with a familiar pouch. I pocketed the bag full of peppermints and brought the letter close to me to read in the low light:

> *Lor, If you're reading this, it's probably because you're too angry to sleep. I'm sorry for ruining dinner. I know you probably need some space so I requested to be sent out on a forest mission for a few days. When I come back, come see me when you are ready to talk, if you want to.*
>
> *I promise to ride fast and think of you.*

I crumpled the leter in anger. Before I could toss it away, for a reason I could not explain, I stopped myself. I gently unfurled the crumpled paper before neatly folding it and placing it in my pocket. How like Dameon to run away at the first sign of trouble. I left the loft, stopping in the stables to give each horse a few of the treats. The new foals, all long limbs with no coordination, warmed something in me. As I left , I placed one of the peppermints in my own mouth, letting the sweet sugar melt away my anger as I walked back up the path to Mirador.

*   *   *

SPITE drove me to an early rise. I was determined for this plan to work and too anxious to sleep. When Katherine and Selena opened my chambers, shock colored both their faces to see me sitting on the edge of my bed fully dressed in a lilac satin gown with beading along the scoop neckline and the hem. By that point, I had been ready for hours.

"Well, isn't this surprising?" Katherine said with a smirk.

"Oh yes, I wonder what could ever be driving this sudden morning preparedness?" Selena gave me a look that made me think she could sense my every thought.

I quickly stood up and brushed non-existent dust from my lap before clapping my hands together. "What can I say, ladies. I just feel today will be a *brilliant* day," I said with the most winning smile I could muster. Equally luminous smiles were mirrored back to me from the faces of my friends. We made our way down to breakfast quickly, stopping only to thank Chef for his meal the night before as he handed us our breakfast for the morning–fresh bread, butter, cured meats, and berries. Olgara was already at the table when we arrived, instinctively pouring us all cups of tea to our own personal preferences. The bread was still warm, melting the butter I slathered on almost instantly. A knock was heard at the door, alarming me. I looked around the room, to see Katherine and Selena as equally startled as me. No one knocked at Mirador, especially not on the front door. Most people strolled in if they had a reason to be here so early in the morning. Olgara, though, was unsurprisingly nonchalant about the noise as she ate her breakfast without notice.

I shot out of my seat and hurried to the door. There was only one person in all of Greydenn who would knock on Mirador Castle doors. I did my best to compose myself as I opened the door slowly, trying to appear as though nothing is out of the ordinary. Percy greeted me at the door with a smile. He was dressed more casually than last night, in a dark blue tunic with gold thread and matching breeches. His sword sheathed at his side. A bouquet of purple, white, and pink flowers were held tightly in his hands.

"Princess Elora," he said with a breath out, "you look absolutely beautiful today."

I blushed at his words. "Thank you, Percy. But just Elora will do."

Percy let out a nervous laugh. "Yes, please forgive me, Elora." He paused before extending the flowers out. "These are for you," he said with a nervous smile. Heat crept across his cheekbones, mirrored by my own.

I took the flowers and marveled at their beauty. I recognized them at once as the ones that bloom along the mountain this time of year, lupines. He must have cut them on his walk, a mix of purple, pink, and white blooms. They smelled heavenly as I buried my face in them. I smiled, so big it made my cheeks hurt. "Thank you," I said, "these are absolutely beautiful, Percy."

Suddenly, Olgara appeared behind me, moving almost silently. "It appears the beauty has caused Princess Elora to forget her manners, Sir Alderius. Please come in."

"Yes! Chef just made breakfast, would you like some?" I asked as he was ushered inside by my old nanny.

"Oh, how kind of you," he said awkwardly as his eyes darted about. "I ate this morning at my lodgings, but it is so kind of you to offer," he said, finally meeting my eyes again.

"Of course you did," I moved in to whisper, "I would never tell Chef this, but BridgeĖe might be an even beĖer cook than him."

Percy gave me a queer look, like he was struggling to put pieces of a puzzle together. "BridgeĖe?" He tilted his head to the side as he said her name, as if it was a strange new dialect.

"The boarding house owner," I said slowly. "Short, plump, amazing cook? Probably the one you received a key from when you arrived?" I stopped, maybe he wasn't staying there? There was only one boarding house in Greydenn, conveniently located next door to Shady Pint, the town tavern that housed a small brothel on the second floor. Surely, Percy couldn't be renting one of *those* rooms.

Percy's deep blue eyes lit up with recognition. "Oh yes, how embarrassing. Now that you mention it, I guess it was the same woman who checked me in and served me breakfast." His smile was strained and did not meet his eyes.

"It is so hard to remember names. I should have prefaced the information for you!" I said with an equally forced smile. It was never hard for me to remember the name, face, and story of every person in Greydenn, but I had been here for a decade. Just one year shy of the amount of time I spent in High Castle.

The conversation paused awkwardly. Percy and I both seemed more intrigued by our own shoes than by each other. Katherine snickered softly. Selena, ever the hero, did her best to cover the noise as she spoke. "So, Sir Alderius, what brings you to Mirador this morning?" She smiled softly as she spoke. Her golden eyes were warm as she looked at him expectantly.

I scoffed. "Selena, please call him Percy. Whenever you say Sir Alderius, I only picture his father." I turned around to look at Percy, stunned to see the smile on my own face not mirrored on his own. "Is…is that okay? I mean no offense, I am sure you worked very hard for that title." I stumbled on my words. "Sorry, we have just moved long past titles here in Mirador. Seemed rather pointless," I said with a shrug.

"Oh, yes…it is…completely fine." Percy looked at me before turning to the other women. "Please, feel free to call me Percy."

Another silence ensued where everyone in the room was once again enamored with our shoes. In truth, I had not felt this awkward since before I grew into my womanhood, when I was just a gaggle of limbs and blemished skin.

"Why don't I place these in some water in your chambers," Olgara said as she grabbed the bouquet from my hands. As soon as they were gone, I missed the weight of them.

I had never felt so aware of my hands in my life. Everything felt empty. What did I do with them? I moved to cross them before I remembered the talks from my mother in my youth about how unladylike that was. Quickly, I put them down on my sides, trying to seem relaxed.

"So Percy, were you just coming to drop off the flowers?" My words seemed to register something in Percy's head–he clearly did have another purpose.

"Yes, I mean no, it was not my only purpose." He reddened as his words sped up. "I was hoping to ask you to accompany me to town today. You seem well versed in the ways here and I would love to learn from you. To see how you have spent your time all these years." Percy stopped, reddening more. "But I know it is unbecoming of a lady to be seen alone with a suitor, perhaps Olgara can escort us?"

A deep scoff emanated from the small form of Olgara, luckily giving me time to suppress my own giggle at the idea of a chaperon. "I'd rather polish all the silver in Albaria by hand." Olgara looked up at us, seemingly just now realizing those words did not stay in her head.

Selena, ever the hero, spoke up as she from the table toward us. "Sorry, Olgara has a hard time getting up and down the mountain is all." This was a lie, as Olgara could definitely outpace all of us when she felt there was a purpose to. Today, she clearly did not see a purpose. "I would be more than happy to join you, perhaps Katherine can come as well?" Selena looked expectantly back at our friend.

"Sorry," Katherine said as she leaned onto her elbows on the table. "I promised Olgara I would help with the silver." She winked at us. I fought the urge to stick my tongue out at her, but that was very unladylike and sweet Percy would most likely not recover from the sight.

"Understood, thank you for the clarification, Selena. It would be an honor to have you act as our chaperone." Percy gave Selena a small head nod as a scoff–turned cough is heard from Katherine.

"So sorry, hayfever. Another reason for me to stay back." I turned my back to Katherine and adeptly twisted my arm behind to give her an indecent gesture out of Percy's line of sight.

"Is there anything in particular you would like to see today? The town shop district is not nearly as bustling as you are used to in Vinguarii, really more of a street corner than a district, but there is an amazing tailor, bakery, and a few other things. Or the stables, perhaps? I heard there are some new foals which just dropped." I was fully aware that I was rambling at this point, but couldn't stop. I looked at Selena expectantly, hoping she would save me as she always did.

She took the bait. "We can take a stroll through the town proper and head off into the farmlands! There are so many beautiful sights this time of year in the valley."

Percy looked at us with a queer expression and a smile, seemingly overwhelmed by us. "Um…sure. Why don't we just stroll down the mountain and see where the day takes us. Mayhaps we can go to the library? I've heard tea rooms are all the rage with young ladies of higher standard like yourselves." Percy motioned to me before turning to Selena and trailing off.

"There is no library in Greydenn–the library in Mirador functions as such. Nor a tea room," I said with a blush. He must think us backwards from what he was used to. I tried to remember if I was like this–so stiff and uptight–when I first arrived in Greydenn.

Percy chuckled. "Okay, why don't we just head down the mountain and you can show me whatever you like, or whatever there is to show me." Percy offered me his arm and I quickly grabbed his, all but pulling him to the door.

The walk down the mountain was uneventful. I pointed out the types of trees lining the path and Percy dutifully listened. About halfway down I noticed something strange–Selena was staying a few paces behind us, just like she had to do in Vinguarrii. A feeling like a rock being thrown into water hit–if my plan worked, I'd still have to marry Percy. How would I hide the dragon from a husband? More importantly, how would I convince Percy to adopt the customs of Greydenn? I refused to cast my friends out just because of a matter of birth. Would that also mean no more night rides with Dameon? My thoughts were moving so fast in my head that I stumbled, righting myself before Percy noticed.

No, I can't think of this now. I *needed* Percy to fall in love with me because I could not kill him. It was not in me. I refused to become the monster in my story, prophecy be damned.

We made it to the bottom of the mountain without further incident. The beauty of Greydenn this time of year, when Spring was slowly giving way to summer, astounded me. I paused to take it in. The lush green hills around us were dotted with wildflowers. Green fields stretched in every flat space seen in the distance. Children ran around without a care, their musical laughter carried by the soft summer breeze. I pulled Percy to a stop with me. If anything could change his perspective on things, it was this image. "Isn't it beautiful?" I said wistfully. I looked up at Percy only to find him looking at me.

"Yes, it is," he said without averting his eyes.

Selena walked up beside me, her eyes shining with glee. "Elora, do you smell that?" I looked at her inquisitively before sniffing the air, only to find the usual scents of Greydenn—flowers, rich earth, the usual scents of Greydenn. The faint smell of raspberries and baked goods hit me. Selena and I exchanged excited expressions before she grabbed her skirts and darted down the street. I moved to follow her when a sudden tugging reminded me I was still attached to Percy. His face was bewildered as he looked between me and Selena's fast-moving frame.

"Why such haste, Elora? What is going on?" I pulled him to a trot, hoping he would follow as I explained. "The smell of raspberries can mean only one thing," I said as I pulled. "The bakery is making their famous raspberry white chocolate scones." I was grateful we were near the same size at this moment. I looked up into his face, seeing a faint smile creep across his lips. "These scones are *coveted* by all in Greydenn. If we do not move quickly, we will not get one."

Percy looked over at me as the smile faded from his lips. "Surely they will save one for you, you are the Princess. If you want them, they should be made at your behest."

My back stiffened at the thought. I pulled my arm from his so I could turn and fully address him. "I cannot force things just because I want them, Percy. Half the fun of a scone day is the rarity of it. They take so much work to get right—so much time. Who am I to tell the baker, the one actually doing the work, running their business, when to make and what to make?

What happens to the bakery if we have scones every day and they no longer sell?"

Percy considered this, taking a few seconds to mull over his thoughts before speaking. Suddenly, he darted ahead of me into the direction Selena was still running. He turned around, yelling at me. "Elora, I thought this was a matter of urgency?"

I laughed as I hoisted my skirts and ran to join him. We ran together the rest of the way to the bakery only to find Selena in the back of the forming line. Percy looked amused. "I am assuming it is not customary for the princess to cut in line in Greydenn either?"

"No, not customary," I said with a chuckle.

"I fear for the safety of whatever princess who tried," Selena said with a wicked smile as she wagged her finger at me.

I laughed at Selena's words. I turned to Percy expectantly. To my surprise, Percy seemed to take offense to this and his jovial smile disappeared. "Surely you cannot mean that anyone in this town would move to hurt Elora?" he said with more force than necessary. He towered over Selena, her short frame barely hitting his shoulder.

"No, of course not. It was merely a jest." Selena shifted her golden eyes downward. Gone was the glint from just a few moments ago. I stepped between them, putting Selena firmly behind me.

"Percy, I am safe here. These are my people. It was merely a joke." Each word fell from my lips with the force of a command as Selena shrunk behind me. Percy considered my words for a moment before a smile appeared on his lips, one that did not quite reach his eyes.

"Sorry to overreact. I am sure that you are completely safe." He paused before continuing. "Who was it that taught you to defend yourself? I am sure your late parents would not allow the princess such freedoms until it was determined she could protect herself."

I scoffed before I could stop it and my eyes narrowed. My spine straightened. "I have not been formally trained because I never needed to be, Percy." I was a dragon. I proved years ago that I could defend myself when necessary. Anger rose in my body as my scales shifted beneath my skin. I. Was. Powerful. I had ended all those who came to slay me.

But Percy didn't know that, he *could not* know that. Suddenly, Selena ducked out from behind me.

"Greydenn is safe, much safer than Vinguarii. But your determination to protect Elora is very admirable, Percy," Selena said. Foolish of me to think she needed protecting when she was always the one to save me, rather she knew it or not. Selena turned to me. "But I do agree with Percy, Elora. I think it is high time you learn how to protect yourself."

I take it back. Selena was traitorous.

"I do not need to learn anything. I am safe here."

"May I remind you that you are besieged by a dragon?" Percy said with a huff as he threw his arms in the air.

I looked at Selena, then Percy before I realized the opportunity I had been given. This could be the perfect way to get some alone time with Percy. "Okay, I'll relent. Percy, I would love for you to train me to defend myself." Percy's eyebrows rose in shock as his mouth fell open. Heat crept across his face.

"Oh, that is not what I was hinting at in this conversation. I do not want you to get the wrong idea. I am not sure I am qualified to train you," he said.

"Nonsense, I say. You are a knight. Who better to train me?" I smiled at him expectantly.

Percy's blush intensified. "I would love to, but the training would most likely require touching, being very close. I wish not to compromise your reputation."

If only he knew he was a few years too late for that. I was struggling to find a proper way to respond when Selena surprised me. "I would love to learn as well. Perhaps I can act as a chaperone and a pupil as well?" She planted a serene smile on her face before widening her brown eyes. She looked absolutely innocent–the kind of person it is impossible to say no to. Her halo of curls only added to the image she was conveying.

Percy paused and looked around, as if a stranger on the street could save him. He left out a huff of air. "Okay, I'll relent. It will be an honor to train you both. I will need to gather supplies for this, I confess I am not sure where to start."

Suddenly, I remembered the few stories Dameon had told me when he first joined the guards. "I believe the guardhouse has training supplies. Perhaps I can send down for spare training supplies?"

"Nonsense," Percy said. "I am the trainer, I will acquire the supplies, but thank you for giving me an idea on where to start." Percy took my hand in his. "You truly are remarkable, Elora. I have missed that about you all these years."

Heat rose from my neck coloring my face. "You are too kind, Percy. I have missed that about you."

Selena chimed in, pulling our eyes from each other. "When shall training start?"

Percy pondered this for a moment. "If I am able to acquire the necessary supplies from the guardhouse, I do not see a reason we cannot start this afternoon."

"Sounds perfect," I said.

Before we knew it, it was our turn to get our sweet treats. "Five scones, please," I said to the flour-covered baker behind the counter. Gretchen smiled at me. "Of course, milady. Anything else?"

"No, that will be all." I handed her more coins than I knew it cost. Gretchen smiled. Luckily, after ten years, she was used to me giving her more than she thought she deserved, but I knew that the coin I gave her was just what she could be selling her wares for with her talent. I distributed three of the scones among us, saving one for Olgara and Katherine each. If I returned to Mirador on a scone day empty handed, the self-defense classes from Percy would come too late. We all ate in silence, relishing the flavor of the still warm scones when Percy spoke.

"These are simply marvelous," he said around a mouth full of scone. "I have never had something like this." Selena and I nodded in agreement, our mouths both too full to speak. "It really is a pity such a beautiful town is beseeched with such a terrible beast," he spoke absentmindedly as he took another bite.

My scone turned dry in my mouth and I had to force the once delectable pastry down my throat, using the time to steady the words on my tongue. "Yes, it is such a shame." I tried to not think about myself as a beast descending on Greydenn. A thought crept up in my brain, one that oftentimes was there and

I repeatedly had to silence–was I just a monster that Greydenn had to endure? What would happen if they found out? Would they see me only as the beast, ignoring the decade of relationships I had built with the townsfolk? Would they desert me too? I worried that I was nothing more than a curse to all of Greydenn–the same way my parents saw me.

Selena spoke up. "That reminds me. Percy, what are your plans regarding the dragon? I have not heard you mention anything."

Percy pondered this, seeming to weigh his every word. "The dragon has taken the lives of twelve knights now, according to the numbers by the mayor, but never a person from the town." Percy looked at me. "Is that correct?"

"Yes," I said with a weighted breath.

"I believe those other great men had a similar flaw–a lack of planning. Clearly, the dragon does not atack unless provoked. I plan to not provoke it until I have learned enough about it that I am sure I can defeat the beast."

A shaky breath left me. "That seems like a great plan." Maybe since he was already planning to take some time, I could use it to my advantage. I needed time to truly make him fall for me so I could talk him out of the dragon-slaying nonsense. I took another bite of my scone and it tasted of hope.

Chapter Six

PERCY departed to gather supplies while Selena and I made our way back up to Mirador. We agreed to meet in the great hall of Mirador in a few hours. By the time we arrived, we were both damp with the effort of walking up the hill in the building summer heat.

"Maybe we should have sprung for the carriage," I muttered as I wiped the sweat from my brow.

"It just seemed so frivolous," Selena huffed as we stepped from the path onto the stone bridge that led from the path to Mirador.

I laughed weakly. "Interesting how things that seem frivolous at the bottom of the mountain become the right choice by the time we make it to the top." I turned and smiled at Selena. The summer sun shined down on her like a blessing. Her dark brown curls framed her glowing face as her golden eyes crinkled with a smile.

I grabbed the ancient wooden door of the castle and pulled. The air was always much cooler behind the stone walls of Mirador. Much to my dismay, both Olgara and Katherine greeted us at the door, expectant as children.

"Tell me, sweet Princess, did your stroll with the handsome knight go well?" Katherine mocked. She pressed her wrist to her forehead, fending fainting.

"You are insufferable," I said as I pushed past her.

Katherine grew quiet. "Oh no, did he take advantage of our virtuous princess?" Katherine turned to Selena and grabbed her shoulders, shaking them gently. "It was your duty, Selena, to keep our sweet princess pure!" Selena looked at Katherine flatly and Katherine's smile grew.

"You seem so curious as to what happened when you were the one who refused to come," I replied flatly. Katherine let go of Selena and turned her attention fully to me again before placing a hand on her hip. Her fingers were long and thin, just like the rest of her.

"Do you really think it would have been a good idea for me of all people to attend?" She paused and raised an eyebrow.

Though I hated to admit it, she did have a point. Percy was not yet ready to endure Katherine's sense of humor.

"The poor boy would not last five minutes in this creature's presence," Olgara motioned to Katherine. She shook her head. "A moment with her would probably have him looking forward to running straight for the dragon."

I held the bag of scones above my head as I motioned to Katherine and Olgara. "I got these for you, but in return, you must leave me alone about this." I was so tired after my night and the morning stroll with Percy. I needed peace and quiet. Katherine and Olgara both nodded their agreement before taking their scones. With four hours until Percy arrived, I decide to retire to my chambers and try to recover some of the sleep lost the previous night.

As I made my way up the stairs, Katherine followed me. "Wait, I really do want to know how it went," she said around a mouthful of scone. I paused and turned around, giving her an incredulous look. Her steel eyes were expectant and her face soft. Crumbs dusted her cheeks, mixing in with her copious amount of freckles. Any hardness in my heart at her jokes instantly melted away. But I still did not wish to speak of these things.

"Can we talk of anything else," I asked. Katherine walked up the stairs and laced her arm through mine.

"Always," she said as we made the way to my chambers, talking about everything and nothing at all.

*   *   *

AFTER a few hours, I was roused by a hand gently stroking my hair and a feeling of warmth in front of me and behind. My eyes felt heavy as lead. I relished in the warmth and touch for a moment before prying my eyes open. Once I did, the sight before me caused a sleepy smile to spread across my face, both Katherine and Selena lying with me. Katherine's willowy form was behind me while Selena was in front. She was facing me as she gently stroked my hair.

"Sorry, ladies," I murmured with sleep still on my breath, "but I am soon to be a taken woman." Katherine laughed wildly as Selena moved to open her mouth.

"As if," she said with an affronted laugh.

Katherine lifted her head to face Selena. "The princess is truly so presumptuous."

"Must be because it has been so long since anyone has graced her bed," Selena responded.

"Your words hurt me," I said with a pained expression on my face that quickly melted to laughter. The joyous sound of my friends laughing filled my chambers and my heart. Once I was able to catch my breath, I sat up, eyeing them both suspiciously. By the clock on the wall I knew I still had well over two hours before Percy would arrive. "So what brings you two here to my bed?" I raised my eyebrows at my friends.

Selena and Katherine shared a knowing look, like they were having an entire conversation silently. "Honestly," Selena said as she sat up, "this just feels like the first relatively normal moment in *months*."

Katherine nodded. "It has been so long since we could breathe together, to think about something besides the dragon and the knights."

Selena reached for both of our hands. "I think we have just missed you. You have been so down since the king's proclamation." Her words were careful. Measured.

I reached for Katherines's hand with the one not occupied by Selena's and gave both a gentle squeeze. "I have missed you two dearly, which feels odd since I still have seen you both every day." I hesitated to continue, stumbling on my words, on the emotions I felt for these two women. But they just nodded, knowing what I meant. Speaking of such things has always been so hard for me.

Both of my friends looked me in the eyes, seeming to know what I wished to say but couldn't find the words for. A few seconds passed like this, three women lost in thought and love for one another. Perfect understanding.

"So," Katherine said as she flipped onto her back and absentmindedly stared at the ceiling of my chambers. "How did your stroll with *Sir Percival* go this morning? Did Selena's presence stop you from fornicating on the streets and ruining your sweet and pure reputation?" Katherine faked swooning and to my surprise, before I could react, Selena whacked her in the face with a pillow.

"*Our* walk with Percy," Selena said while stressing the first word, "went wonderfully, in my opinion, of course." She looked to me as she finished, eyes searching mine for confirmation. I nodded my agreement and Selena beamed at the reassurance.

"It did go well," I stopped for a moment. "I think." Did it go well? Percy had seemed so shocked by the way I carried myself in Greydenn, the informality with the people. The rules of High Castle never came naturally to me. The way I had to carry myself and act never seemed to *fit*. Thinking about myself as higher than someone else, something my brother had no issue doing, always felt wrong. He had always seen himself as greater than all, destined for the crown. What came naturally to him took force from me, just another one of my failings in the eyes of my family. When I arrived in Greydenn, I felt free for the first time. The days it took to reach the far away village from Vinguarii, from the constraints of High Castle were when I allowed myself to mourn my previous life, to mourn the connection I could have had with my family. Within my first month here, I felt at home for the first time, truly at peace. The nights of flying combined with the relationships I was building brought color to my face and joy to my life. I would never forget my first summer here–Katherine, Selena and I filling our days with running through the meadows surrounding Greydenn, placing wildflowers in our hair and swimming in the river. My nights were filled with flying and Dameon. The freedom I found here fit me as well as my dragon wings.

But would Percy adjust? If my plan was to work, his love for me had to outweigh his love for the structure and order of High Castle. Would he feel at home in these mountains or stifled by the distance between the only world he had ever known?

"Elora," Selena's calm voice called me back from my thoughts. "Are you okay?" Her eyebrows were drawn in concern as her eyes searched my face.

"Yes," I answered, unsure of the truth in my own words. "I just…" my words trailed off as I became transfixed with a pull in the fabric on my bed, absentmindedly twirling the loose thread in my fingers. A hand covered mine, and to my surprise, it was not Selena's rich brown skin covering mine, but Katherine's, just a shade off from my own and covered in a constellation of freckles.

"I can't imagine what you are feeling right now, but we are both here for you, always." For once, her voice was not hiding a jest, her sincerity written on her freckle-covered face as her grey eyes stared intently into my own. "Let us in, Elora. We are here for you."

I took a deep breath and considered telling them my plan. This secret danced terrifyingly close to the dragon. I wondered if it would be worth it. Would letting them in lead to my undoing? Surely they would abandon me the same way my parents did. That is the fate of a monster, after all.

"I care about Percy, and I do not want him to be killed by the dragon. But I know in my heart that if he tries to slay the dragon, it will not be the beast who dies that night." A single tear fell down my face because of the secret I could never share with my friends. The curse of being unknowable weighed on me. A pit fell in my stomach and I could not imagine a *me* that was capable of killing Percy where I would not be a monster–the beast my parents, the prophecy, my brother, all think me to be. Did they know me better than myself? Did my brother do all those things to me because he saw the monster I hid?

"You can't know that," Katherine said gently.

I took a deep breath, steadying myself for what I was about to share. "I am fully confident in it. Which is why I have a plan–I am going to make Percy fall in love with me and say I will only marry him if he agrees to live with the dragon as those in Greydenn have done the last decade."

Selena leaned forward, stroking the tear from my cheek. "But what about you, Elora? Do you love him? Is this the future you want?"

I was a royal–a royal woman at that. My ancestors had routinely married without love, usually hating their partner. My own parents had never even met before their wedding. The young king needed a queen and a neighboring country was more than happy to send a princess for an alliance.I was luckier than those women who came before me for I at least had care in my heart for Percy, a care that I was certain could grow to love. "I believe I can grow to love him easily. I care for him so deeply," I said earnestly while looking at my friends.

Katherine looked at me, then Selena. "Are you sure there is not someone else who you might care *more* deeply for? Someone else you would wish to marry?"

I furrowed my brow. Both of them were fully aware that my previous trysts have been just that, trysts that had no emotion attached to them, just want of the body. "No? You both know I have never had true feelings for the people I have bedded in the past. What are you hinting at?"

Selena let out a sigh that Katherine talked over, the unusual sweetness from a few moments ago now gone. "Look, do you think we haven't noticed your frequent trips to the stables the last decade? Or the way a certain former stable boy always seems to be a step behind you when needed?"

"And a drunken tirade at dinner," muttered Selena.

Traitors.

I was in total shock for a split second, shock that turned to a feeling I can only describe as anger, but didn't seem to quite fit. "Are you insinuating that I am in love with *Dameon*? That I would wish to wed him? He is a thorn in my side!" Katherine and Selena both gave me a look, a look like they thought I was more full of horse shit than the stables. They were so synchronized that I wondered if they had practiced for this very moment.

It was true, I did care about Dameon deeply. He had been as consistent as the friends now in my chamber. I would be lying to say that young me didn't sometimes blush when thinking of him, or hold on tighter than necessary on our evening rides before I was confident to mount my own horse. But love? It was not something I had ever considered.

I took a deep breath before continuing. "I care deeply for him, in the same way I care deeply for you both. I will admit there was something there as children, but I feel that ship has long sailed."

Selena gave me an odd look before slapping her arms down on her legs. "Well that settles it, then. Katherine, it appears we have our work cut out for us."

"Whatever could you mean?" I asked, completely bewildered by the turn of events.

Katherine eyed Selena, seeming to have a conversion with her without words. "It really is obvious, Elora. You can be so dense sometimes."

"Maybe the tiara last night was too tight," Selena said with a laugh.

Both of the ladies jumped from my bed and reached for me. I hesitantly offered a hand to both when they pulled me off the bed and onto my feet.

"What is going on?" It wasn't yet time to leave. Why did these two seem to always communicate without including me? More importantly, *how* did they do it when I was in the room with them?

"We are going to make Percy fall in love with you, of course." Selena smiled, her golden eyes shining.

*   *   *

WALKING through the halls of Mirador in breeches wasn't a new experience for me, but doing so under the light of day, in full view of others *was*. Selena had found us both training blouses that clung to our skin, apparently the recommended attire for training so as to not catch on anything. The feeling was so different from the oversized tunic I had hidden in my armoire for my late-night escapes. As we passed the rare person in the hallways, I did my best to not avoid eye contact. Selena wilted under attention, seemingly too embarrassed of her change in appearance.

I do not know why she was acting this way when it looked as if these clothes were made for her. The breeches and top clung to her ample curves in a way that made it hard to pay attention when she spoke to me. Selena had braided her curls back into neat rows before we left, giving full view of her beautiful face. "Why are you cowering?" I asked. She was truly radiant.

"I have never worn breeches before," she whispered to me like it was a dangerous secret. "I feel so exposed."

"Well you look absolutely *radiant*." I craned my neck to eye her curves fully. "And that," I pointed to her behind, "that should be considered the most valuable asset of Mirador Castle—no, of all of Greydenn, perhaps all of Albaria." I threw her a wink as heat crept up her face.

"You are worse than a man," she said with a shy laugh. My words worked and her shoulders relaxed as she strutted down the hall.

"No, I am just honest. It is an honest fact that my best friend looks attractive in the clothing she is currently wearing." A sly smile crept up my face, one reflected on Selena's own. Before Selena could respond, we rounded the corner of the hallway and saw Percy looking out of one of the many windows of the corridor. He looked otherworldly in his sparring clothes, the light beaming from the stained glass window causing him to glow. His blue eyes and pale hair danced in the rainbow light. The light bounced off him, as if emanated from his skin. He was dressed similarly to us, a tight tunic and slim breeches showing off his muscular frame, his wide chest stretching against the fabric of the top. As always, his sword and scabbard were at his side, the gold hilt playing in the light as if it were magic.

My breath caught in my throat at the sight of him. When did I stop walking? I was completely unaware of my lack of movement, as if I had lost control of my limbs. I felt a nudge from my side as Selena whispered, "Stop drooling." I cast an irritated look at her before clearing my throat, alerting Percy to our presence. Percy turned to greet us, mouth beginning to move when heat crept up his face. His skin was bright red, darker than I had ever seen before, and he quickly cast his eyes on the ground at our feet.

"H..hello, erm, ladies." Percy was more flustered than I ever thought possible for a man to be. I could not fathom how these clothes left him so vulnerable. Surely the dress he saw me in last night left less to the imagination when it came to the plunging top. Selena snickered softly, so low only I could hear it.

"Is there a problem, Percy?" I spoke evenly, hoping to not embarrass him further.

"No," he cleared his throat. "No problem at all, Elora."

"This might be my ineptness talking, but surely it would be nearly impossible to train us if your eyes are only transfixed on our feet." Selena's voice was soft, like how one spoke to a scared animal or a fussing child.

Percy's throat bobbed as he slowly raised his head. I noted how his eyes lingered on me, but I willed a blush to not form on my face–I did not believe he would survive if he thought I noticed. Was this his first time seeing women dressed in such a way? I admit, I never saw any woman in breeches in all my time in Vinguarii, let alone in High Castle, but I assume he had seen ladies in various stages of undress at this point? Surely Percy had in his twenty-three years of life. Noble men had more options than women. The brothels of Vinguarii were numerous. A man of his standing could have his pick of women to enjoy.

"My apologies, ladies," he said when his eyes finally reached my own. "It was just a bit of a shock to see you dressed in such a way. You both look beautiful in your fighting clothes. High Castle, as I am sure you both remember, is very much more rigid in its expectations for the fairer sex."

As soon as those last two words were spoken, I tensed. Memories of High Castle, of the expectations thrown upon me hit me like frozen water, removing any lust from my eyes. I shook away the feeling as quickly as possible before speaking. I could not afford to mess this up. Percy could not afford for me to mess this up. "Ah yes, I imagine this is a shock to you." I laughed as sweetly as I could muster before looking him back in the eye.

"Well, I imagine my shock is mirrored by your own," he said with a shy smile.

"What do you mean?" I said. I was unsure what he was referring to. Though he did look impeccable in his training clothes, they really weren't much different than his daily clothes, or the clothes I saw men wear in Greydenn every day. Dameon's uniform wasn't much different than what Percy currently wore.

Percy's brows narrowed quizzically. "Wearing breeches," he said. His voice trailed off in such a way that I was unsure if it was a statement or a question.

Oh fuck. That question opened a whole world of others. Of course in his eyes, in everyone's eyes, the answer from me should be a resounding no. The trousers that felt like second skin a minute ago suddenly felt too tight, too exposing, like my every sin was written on the fabric wrapping my body. Truly, I only wore them when visiting the stables or Dameon–sneaking down a mountain in a full skirt was much harder than it sounded. Both Selena and Percy were looking at me, faces expectant. If I answered incorrectly, would he know more than he should? Percy was much too proper to understand my time with Dameon. Would he know I long ago lost the image of the pure princess, and the habits that matched? This question could lead to others. Questions were dangerous when there was so much to hide. Surely my comfort in trousers would not be what landed my head on a spike.

"Elora?" Concern was written on Selena's face, her golden brown eyes searched mine. A silent pleading for me to come back to the world in front of me and away from the prison of my thoughts, of my fears.

I took a steadying breath. I had lasted too long for breeches to be my undoing. "Yes," I said with an embarrassed laugh, "this is our first time in these types of clothes." I forced blush to appear on my cheeks, demurely avoiding eye contact with Percy. "I feel both more exposed and more comfortable than ever before. It is quite the sensation." I let out my best rendition of a giggle, the one that had landed others in my bed. To my surprise, Selena joined me, the same noise escaping her full lips.

Percy's face softened and he laughed, musical and pure in sound. "I imagine it is a wholly different sensation," he said with a grin.

"So," Selena broke the silence after the laughing ceased. "Shall we go in? I am dying to learn from you."

"Oh, yes. I hope my training lives up to both of your expectations." Percy opened the door to the ballroom. It was a grand room, with high vaulted ceilings and a mix of stained and clear glass windows. Dust floated in the air of the long abandoned room. Black and grey stone tiles lined the floors. It looked the same as it always had, just with the addition of wooden swords, targets, and a straw mannequin covered in burlap. "Ladies first," he said as he ushered us through the double doors.

Selena walked in first with me close behind her. My hand brushed Percy's as I walked past, sending a shiver up my spine. Percy walked in behind me, letting the door click shut as he walked past us and to the center of the room.

"Okay," he said to himself more than us. "I have not trained anyone before, and to be honest, I fear I am not the best at the job."

"Nonsense, Percy," I said. "You are a knight, there is no one better suited for this than you."

Percy let out an embarrassed laugh, more of a huff of air, devoid of joy. "That is very kind of you, Elora. I hope to live up to your expectations."

"You will make a lovely teacher, Percy." Selena offered him a reassuring nod. Percy straightened his spine and marched to the side of the room where a pile of supplies lay. He grabbed three wooden swords before striding back to stand in the middle of us. He motioned for us to pick up the shields at our feet.

"I thought long and hard this morning about where to start. I decided to start with you both as the King and I began our instruction fifteen years ago, the most basic steps I can think of."

My spine stiffened at the mention of my brother. When I left, he was becoming handy with weapons, something he so often used to inflict pain on me. I used to hide and observe their training, trying to find a weakness in his movements to use against him whenever he turned his sights on me. Percy dropped a sword in each of our hands, his hand lingering on mine for a second longer than necessary. The sword felt solid in my hands. The well-worn wooden handle grounded me, pulling me away from the thoughts of the past. I took a deep, centering breath, reminding myself to listen as Percy began.

"Okay, so I want you both to face me. I am going to teach you the most basic block and thrust combo." Percy picked up his own shield before facing me again. "Hold the sword in your right hand, firmly yet gently. With your left, hold the shield." Selena and I followed his instruction, but Percy still sat down his sparring gear and helped us individually set our stance and our hands correctly. "Now, Elora, I am going to strike you slowly. I want you to block with your shield and use that second of pause to thrust your sword underneath, hit me, and retract." He modeled the movements for me as he spoke.

I took a deep breath and nodded. Percy arced his sword above me with grace. I put my shield up, blocking myself but not my vision, the way I saw my brother do dozens of times when I spied. When Percy's sword hit, the softness of the blow surprised me. He was clearly holding back. I struck before I realized, hitting him in the stomach with such force that a grunt came from his lips. I quickly dropped my equipment and ran up to him and placed my hands on his side.

"Oh Percy, I am so sorry. I did not mean to hurt you." A forced grin took over his face, like a city falling to an army.

"No apology necessary, Elora," he grunted before sucking in a breath. "It is me who should apologize. Clearly my instructions lacked information on force. I will admit, you are surprisingly strong."

I blushed. "You are too kind, Percy." He righted himself before continuing. I expected him to do a practice round with Selena, but he seemed to ignore her, looking directly at me. "I want you to practice more with her."

For the next hour, Selena and I took turns doing the same block and thrust move over and over. Percy offered coaching and help when necessary, but after the first few minutes, our movements became fluid. The push and pull of our strikes were ingrained in my head by the end, when my arms were so tired I could barely hold my sword. Selena was stronger than me–she was barely shaking at the end. But I was quicker, my movements more fluid. By the end, we were both slightly more aggressive than need be, having fun pushing each other more and more when Percy finally stopped us. Sweat was dripping down both our faces. There was a hunger in Selena's eyes that felt animalistic, a wildness I knew was mirrored in my own.

"Okay, that is enough for now. Get some rest tonight and we shall resume at the same time tomorrow, provided you still both wish," he said.

"That would be splendid," I answered for both of us. "Would you like to stay for dinner, Percy?"

Percy smiled. "Thank you for the offer, Elora, but I have some business to attend to and fear I will not make it back in time."

My nose wrinkled, what business could he have? Selena seemed to have the same question, "What business? Is there something else that pulls you to Greydenn?" she asked.

Percy stiffened, seemingly irritated to be questioned by Selena. "I mean no offense," she said. "I am only curious."

Percy looked at me. "I need to write to King Elrick to let him know I arrived safely yesterday and met with you. I did not have time yesterday with getting settled, so I feel it is imperative to do it now that I have a moment."

I plastered a smile on my face, one I hoped Percy couldn't see right through. "Oh, of course. Please wish my brother well for me." I wanted the bastard to know I was still breathing. "May I at least escort you out of Mirador?"

Percy's face softened. "It will be an honor." I turned to Selena. "Please use my bathing chambers to freshen up before dinner. I will be up shortly." Selena gave me a nod and offered her thanks to Percy for the lesson before leaving us, heading in the opposite direction to my chambers. When I turned around, the look of shock on Percy's face took me by surprise. "What?" I asked as sweetly as I could muster.

"Nothing, I just do not know many ladies who would deign to allow their maids use of their private bathing chambers," he huffed.

My brows furrowed. "Well, her quarters are at the bottom of the mountain. It seems foolish to tell her to put her dress back on when sweaty and walk down the mountain for a bath, only to return for dinner," I said.

"Surely there is another chamber she could use, Elora. I am sure she wouldn't mind."

A snarl formed on my lips. I bit my tongue and did my best to turn it into a smile before he noticed. "Percy, Selena and Katherine are my friends. They chose to leave High Castle with me as girls and come to this place. They are more than their job, more than their lack of title. They are pieces of my own heart—my sisters in every way that counts. My companions. I see no issue with allowing my sisters to use my chamber when necessary for their own comfort. Do you?"

Percy softened. "I imagine you were so lonely when sent here."

"I was." My honesty shocked me as my voice caught in my throat.

"I apologize for being gruff. There is much to learn about the life you built here. The resilience it must have taken is admirable, Elora." Percy grabbed my hand. "I hope to learn more, to make a home with you here." I blushed, and to my shock, Percy didn't drop my hand.

"I wish that too," I said honestly. We started to walk down the corridor that led to the front door hand in hand. By the time he left, I felt blissful, as if I was walking on the clouds surrounding Mirador.

*   *   *

MY mind was reeling after dinner, too wired, too fast moving to even consider sleep yet. I felt a familiar itching in my muscles, in my bones–I *needed* to fly. Flying was the one thing that could make my heart sing the way Percy's words did earlier–the one thing that could cement the faint hope I felt in my soul into the real thing.

As soon as the sun set and the castle emptied, I ran up the stairs to my chambers. By the time I wrapped my fingers around the side of the painting, I was panting. I opened the secret passage and flung myself into the darkness as the door shut behind me. I ran down the path as I let memory guide me. With each beat of my heart, I could feel the dragon more and more. As twilight took hold of the sky, I ran through the cave and jumped. I extended my arms as I fell head first in my human form before I called on the dragon. My heart was pumping furiously in my chest as the pain set in, overshadowed by the joy and excitement in my bones. Right before I crashed into the forest below, my wings began to pump, pushing my great purple body into the sky. I let out a roar of pure joy, an alert to all those around that it was my time—a dragon's night.

I flew for hours before deciding to head to my lake. The wind had been singing in my wings all night as I sailed through the clouds. I was high above a long clearing when I saw movement below me, something too big to be a deer or elk that are often found in the forest. I dove down and leveled out to get a better view. To my surprise, it was a cloaked rider on horseback, using the glow of the moon to light their way on the path. I was close enough that the rhythmic hoofbeats sounded like a heartbeat. Strangely, neither the horse nor rider seemed to be startled by me. Surely they know I was here. I let out a noise to alert them of my presence, a low growl that neither reacted to. Suddenly, the rider threw up a single arm, pointing to the edge of the clearing far out. I had seen riders in Greydenn do a similar motion to request a race.

Not one to say no to a challenge, I let out a noise of agreement and began to fly as hard as I could. There was no way this horse would beat me. Shockingly, the horse and rider kept up, the horse unbelievably fast. Still, I made it to the edge of the clearing first and began to circle the edge of the clearing as I blew fire in the air. The horse and rider made it to the edge of the clearing a moment later. I flew lower to get a closer look—it was so rare to see a person this far out of Greydenn in the forest. As I did so, the horse reared on its hind legs on the rider's command as he removed his hood at the same moment. When the horse returned to all fours, I saw the face of my challenger–all dark hair and a boyish grin gazing up at me, brown eyes I would recognize anywhere.

I shot into the sky as fast as possible. The sight of Dameon bowing to me from atop his mount burned into my memory.

Chapter Seven

THE next two days passed in a blur of training, stolen moments with Percy, and flying away my anxieties. To my horror and delight, I never saw Dameon again on my flights. These stolen moments in the sky were for me– to think, to plan, to analyze every touch and word shared with Percy. The open, unending sky gave me the space I needed to think. If the poets had taught me anything, it was that love is a battle, and neither Percy nor I could afford for me to lose this war.

My hours of plotting and formulating a plan culminated into this moment. Training was about to end and it was time to see if my work had been in vain. I needed to find a way to get Percy alone. If I was to try and build a real connection with him it had to be without a chaperone. Percy did not open himself up enough around others. For my plan to work, I needed something more substantial than the few moments we stole after training, which had not progressed past the occasional touch or lingering stare. His lack of action was driving me mad– the type of mad I had not been since I was a young teenager, first in the thralls of young love. I had not been so unsure of myself since I really was the maiden Percy viewed me as.

I was completely lost in thought when a sudden noise drew me from my brain, accompanied by a thump against my arm–I was still in training. I was supposed to be actively sparring with Selena again, not dwelling in the confines of my own thoughts rattling against the cell bars I built for myself. I came back to reality and nodded at a worried Selena, letting her know I was back in this world. She attacked with lightning speed, the wooden sword in her hand seemingly invisible. I blocked and prevented her from hitting my face. Selena smiled up at me as she prepared her stance for her next attack. She was out for blood.

I loved it.

I lunged, using our height difference to my advantage. My longer limbs helped me reach her before she could prepare. To my surprise, she parried and thrusted at me again. It was all too quick for me and I stumbled, falling back into the hard body that had suddenly materialized behind me. Percy's hands gently grabbed my shoulders.

"Are you okay?" Percy's breath was hot on my neck and caused my skin to prickle.

I pushed my head back, further planting myself against him and looked to the side. "Never better," I breathed out, more full of want than I intended. He looked over at me and I saw a fire in his blue eyes, that was gone in an instant. I worried I was reading too much into it, but for a fleeting moment, the want was palpable. I arched my back into him when suddenly, the hands pulling me close pushed away instead. A thought ran across my mind that chilled me to the bone–has this all been one sided?

Percy adjusted his tunic, pulling it down to hide what I could plainly see–his obvious desire for me. He looked around, seeming to notice everything but me.

"Well, I think that is enough training for today, ladies. Great work." Percy clapped his hands together and quickly ushered himself out of the room. He did not wait for me to escort him to the entrance as I had every other training session before this. Selena threw me a knowing look, a full conversation written plainly on her face. Heat crept up my own as I picked up my feet. This moment was the best confirmation I had been given that my plan was working and I would *not* let this opportunity pass me by.

By the time I made it through the door, Percy was a considerable way down the hallway. He walked fast with his hands pumping at his side.

"Percy, why do you move with such haste?" I cried out. He halted and I walked quickly, closing the gap between us.

"So sorry, Elora. I just suddenly remembered I have a meeting in town." His blue eyes were downcast as he spoke.

I knew by the blush creeping up his face that there was no meeting in town. The only meeting at this point he would be heading to with such haste is one designed to dispel what I felt growing in him. Percy did not seem the kind to look to a brothel in his time of need, so I expected he was hoping for privacy in his chambers at the inn. I couldn't stop myself from wondering if he would think about me as he pumped his hand against the length I felt against myself just moments ago. Heat settled against my core at the thought, clouding my mind. Before I could stop myself my mouth was moving, the words shocking me. "Meet me at the tavern tonight?" The words came out as a mixture of a request and a question, causing a stunned Percy to turn and meet me.

"What?"

"Will you meet me at the tavern tonight?" Percy was eyeing me with a shocked look. Hoping to dissuade suspicion, I quickly continued. "Provided there is no dragon sighting tonight, of course. I think I can sneak out without notice and down the path."

"Elora, is that safe? I do not want you hurt or in danger," he said.

I moved forward. "Yes, I think so." The lie flowed from my mouth effortlessly.

He grabbed my hand, concern written on his face. "Why would you take that risk?" His eyes seemed to plead for my answer, for proof of what I was saying. He needed to know my purpose.

I took a step closer, our bodies mere inches from each other. "To be with you, Percy. I would risk anything to be with you."

Percy's eyes showed me that my words hit home. It was confirmation that the feelings growing in me for him were not one sided. "It would be an honor to meet you there."

"Then it is a date." I kissed his cheek before turning away, sauntering off slowly, hoping these breeches did as much for my backside as they did for Selena.

*   *   *

THE rest of the day passed slowly, dragging on like honey dripping off a spoon. By the time everyone finally left the castle, I was so restless that I could feel the scales shifting beneath my skin as my muscles begged for release. There was no flying tonight, though. If the dragon was spotted and I made my way to Greydenn without issue, people might start asking questions I could not afford to have spoken aloud. Percy's life, *my life*, depended on it.

I had to calm myself. It would be at least another two hours before it would be safe for me to sneak down the passage under the cover of darkness. My bones begged to melt, to lengthen, for my beautiful wings to take me soaring through the sky. Desperate for release, for comfort, I did the only thing I could think of to help. Something I dreaded doing to my very core–asking Olgara for help.

Within moments I was outside her door, listening to make sure I did not hear her rhythmic snoring. Princess or not, waking a sleeping Olgara for any reason that wasn't life threatening would probably end with me on the receiving end of her slipper. The old bat was deadly with her weapon of choice, a precise arm that even the bravest knights would cower from. I pressed my ear to the door, quieting my own breathing in order to hear anything from the other side.

"Dearie, I heard you coming from a flight away. Stop the charade and tell me what you want so I can get some peace and quiet." The familiar lilt of her voice caused my beating heart to steady as I opened the door.

"How is it your ears can hear me coming but you are able to feign deafness around everyone else?" I said as I strolled in, taking in the sight of my former nanny sitting at her desk, paper and ink neatly under sun-spotted hands. To her right was her mortar and pestle, the same one she had used to grind everything I have ever needed, from bath oils and herbs to the weekly tea that kept my past trysts from leading to unwelcome proof of my indiscretions. All the herbs that Katherine and I collected for her were neatly labeled in jars along the shelves above her. A small fire burned in the hearth in the far right wall.

"I have heard your heart since the moment I met you, your footfalls since you started to walk. I can hear you coming before you even realize where your feet lead you." I smiled at her unusually kind words. Clearly, I had caught her in a rare good mood tonight.

"Don't tell me you have gone soft in your old age, Olgara. No one would believe me." The small smile turned to smirk when I saw the scowl on her face at my words.

A sigh that can only come from someone of considerable age escaped her withered lips. "What do you want, dearie? You are nearly shaking with either excitement, restlessness, or fear, and I have never known you to be afraid of anything, even things you should be. And if it is restlessness, you would have already shed this skin for scales the second the sun dipped below the horizon, so it has to be excitement." She raised her eyebrows. "So I take it this has to do with your plan to save the boy."

In the middle of her chambers was a beautiful rug with intricate vine patterns. As I did when I was a child, I began to walk on the vines as if it was a path high in the air, arms outstretched to give me balance. "I am going to meet him at the tavern tonight," I said as I was rounding the first twist in the vines.

Olgara scoffed, at my words or the childish spectacle I was making of myself I did not know. "So what does that have to do with me, dearie?"

I turned around to look at her. "I am so restless I can feel the dragon begging to come out, like I could fly the entire length of the world in one night and it still not be enough, like it wouldn't even begin to quench my thirst for the sky."

"So why not fly? Meet with the boy another night, or still go tonight, just later."

"Percy is too cautious to meet me on a night when the dragon is spotted." I paused, a somber look spreading on my face as I met her eyes. "And I fear what questions he might ask if he spotted me out on a dragon night."

Olgara softened, beckoning me towards her. I suddenly wished I was a small child again, able to crawl in her lap and sit, to have those hands that adeptly mix and grind herbs to stroke my hair. "Do you want me to brew you a tea to help you calm down for the time being?"

I nodded fervently.

"Very well," she said as she stood. She placed her metal tea pot on the fire and began going through her collection and picking various bottles, some with names I recognized, others I did not. As the water heated, I watched her expertly grind the herbs with determined hands that had done this thousands of times. The smell of chamomile and lemon balm filled the room. The water was boiling by the time she expertly packed her concoction in a small cloth bag. She dropped it into the water and patted the seat at the small table in her chambers. I sat down and she filled a tea cup, the smell instantly calming me. I moved to take the cup when she swatted my hand. "Not yet," she said as she reached for the final ingredient, dropping a heaping spoon of honey into my cup. I smiled, she always knew just how I liked it.

"Thank you, Olgie," I said, letting the nickname I had for her as a child, when saying her full name was too difficult, roll off my tongue. A wrinkled hand ran through my hair just once.

"Anything for you, dearie."

I took a sip and the combination of the warmth of the cup, the smells, and the familiar taste instantly calmed me. By the time I drained the cup, my muscles no longer screamed and my bones were content with their current size. I took a deep breath, my first calm, steady one in hours. I placed the drained cup down, noting the odd shapes the tea remnants left in the bottom. Olgara was intently staring at the dregs as well, her face unreadable.

She looked up at me, eyes seeming to look right through me, to my very heart. "Do you love him?" Her voice had the faintest hint of shake. A feeling I couldn't place rushed through me like cold air.

"I think I could."

A soft smile appeared on her lips but did not reach her eyes. "Then let's hope that is enough."

As I got up to leave, I turned back to say my thanks, only to find Olgara looking at me as a single tear fell down her face. "What's wrong?" I moved back to grab her hand.

She moved away and shoos me out halfheartedly. "Nothing, dearie. I just wish for you to be happy and safe. That is all."

I planted my lips softly on her forehead before standing to my full height. "Don't turn soft on me now, old bat."

Olgara laughed as she grabbed my hand in hers. "Go. Be young tonight. Have the fun you have always deserved. Good memories can help us through the darkest times ahead." Her eyes gleamed in the fire-light.

I cocked my head to the side, unsure of the meaning of the words before saying my goodbyes and heading out. I was hopeful that tonight was one I would remember for the rest of my days.

*   *   *

THE tavern was busier than I expected it to be. Men and women alike filled the space, tankards of mead and ale lifted in the air as laughter filled the room. The bar to the right of the entrance was packed with familiar faces. A staircase leading to the second floor was hidden behind a curtain next to the bar. Wenches milled about, tankards in hand. Wooden tables with long benches filled the rest of the space. I hovered in the doorway and planned my route. This was not my first time sneaking in here–I had a routine. In the simple clothes I kept hidden in my armoire and my hair tucked into a cap, I shouldn't be recognized as long as I kept my eyes down. In the past, the same people who had seen me since a child took my tall slender frame and downcast eyes as a boy on the cusp of manhood, embarrassed to be in the tavern for the first time. The most attention I would get would be from the working women, but the state of my clothes implied I had no coin for the services, keeping all but the most desperate from engaging me.

I moved through the crowd, only taking my eyes off the floor when I could chance it to try and spot Percy. Minutes passed and to no avail, leading me to worry he had stood me up. As this fear took hold, I spotted him sitting in the corner alone, his back to the door. His pale yellow hair shone in the candle light.

I made my way over, placing my hand on his shoulder before sliding it down his strong arms. I lowered my voice until it dripped of honey, like I had seen the women here do so many times. "Lonely, good sir? Care for some company."

Percy tensed under my hand and moved his head to look up. "Your type of company is not req…" The words died on his lips as soon as we made eye contact, his face relaxing. I smiled, walking over to the seat across from him. "Can I sit?"

"Pl..Please," he stuttered as the shocked look left his face. It was replaced by a soft smile, one that resembled the boy I remembered. I took the seat, the smile on my face so wide my cheeks began to hurt. Percy and I sat there, lost in each other's eyes, the blue of his the same color as an icy stream, until the bar wench, Rachel, appeared to take my order. She was a middle-aged woman, long aged out of the business found on the second floor of the tavern, but still making her living within its walls. I avoided eye contact and did my best to alter my voice as I asked for a tankard of mead, dropping my coin on the table for her. Within seconds, a full tankard brimming with the delicious beverage was before me, causing my mouth to water. Mead was often served at Mirador, but never of the same quality as found in the tavern. I said a gruff thanks and took a gulp, letting the sweet bubbles dance across my tongue.

Percy eyed me strangely as I did so. As I put down the glass, he spoke again at last, his words dancing with laughter. "I take it that it is not your first time here." A grin spread across his face.

"No, I have been able to sneak down here in the past, but never for long." I paused, letting some of the honey drip back into my voice, the mead hitting my bloodstream and giving me more courage than usual. "And never with such great company." In truth, I had only been here a few times, usually alone, sitting in the corner observing others. In recent months I had used this time to learn as much about the knights sent for me as possible, spotting weaknesses in them to be used during battle. Dameon was the first person to ever convince me to come here when we were much too young to get in, but we found a few coins to the right person meant that two tankards of ale or mead would appear in our hands as we dashed out, content to drink our reward in the loft of the stable together. When the drink would make the world spin, we would lay beside each other in the hay as we lost ourselves in laughter.

Percy laughed. "It is an honor to drink with you, Elora." He raised his cup and I diligently clinked mine to his. Amber liquid sloshed from both our glasses onto the table.

"I am honestly shocked you agreed to meet me. You were always such a rule follower as kids," I said with a sly smile on my lips. Percy always followed every spoken and unspoken rule dutifully at High Castle. He had the honor and code of a knight in his very blood.

He snickered and the combination of the sound and the drink made me feel like it was floating. "Compared to you and Elrick, I definitely was," he said.

The mention of my brother sent a chill down my spine, but I pushed the grimace from my face. I refused to allow my feelings for that beast prevent me from saving Percy or myself.

"My brother's antics made me look like a saint, but my father never saw it that way." It always made me laugh in a dark way how my father seemed to notice my every stumble, but ignored the bruises left on me from my brother's hand.

Percy stopped, taking me in. He eyed me like he could see the darkness of my soul, the reasons my parents did not care for me as they did Elrick. My skin prickled under his gaze when he opened his mouth. "The castle lost its greatest joy when you were sent away." His words stunned me, but not as much as Percy reaching across to grab my hand. "I lost my greatest joy when you were sent away."

I squeezed his hand, warm and soft in mine, when I noticed the door open. A tall, cloaked figure walked in, sending my stomach to my knees and my breath to stop. Percy looked over as Dameon removed his cloak. A toothy grin spread across his dirty face when our eyes met. Within a moment, he was bounding over to our table and making himself comfortable in the seat next to me. Looking at Percy, he smiled and whispered so only we would hear. "It looks like someone convinced our beloved princess to sneak out of her castle for a night of fun?"

Percy stiffened, eyes wide at the declaration. Before I could stop myself, I opened my mouth. "I wanted to spend more time with Percy." I drew out the last word, hoping that Dameon would get the hint. Judging by the fact that he settled more into his seat and beckoned over Rachel, my words fell on deaf ears.

"A round of drinks for my friends here." Dameon threw double the amount of coin necessary on the table and Rachel's eyes widened. She quickly sat down fresh tankards next to our still full cups, giving Dameon a wink as she walked away. Dameon picked up the cup and propped his muddy boots on the table. Percy fumed as he eyed the dirty boots. He threw daggers at Dameon with his eyes as he took a heady chug from his tankard.

I needed to do something to ease the tension before all was lost. I turned to Dameon, "Thank you for the drinks. It was not necessary, but appreciated." Percy grunted his thank you and a smile spread across Dameon's face. He had always loved causing trouble. In all the commotion of Dameon and Percy meeting again after the dinner, I almost forgot about the night ride and about the conversation I needed to have with Dameon, the one that could only be done in private. My breath caught in my throat. Did he know? Is that why he bowed to the dragon? Is he so giddy to start drama right now not with Percy, but with me? Dameon had always been someone I trusted, but I feared him using this knowledge against me. I took a deep breath. I couldn't let myself spiral, not here.

"So, Dameon. How was your expedition into the forest?" I eyed him carefully. "Anything interesting happen?"

"Oh, not a single thing of note." The smile on his lips broadened as he looked at me. His eyes gleamed with feral intent. He took a deep drink from his cup, never breaking eye contact with me. His dark brown eyes shone with something— something I hoped my paranoia was adding. He saw the dragon, that much I knew. So either he knew it was me and was keeping the secret, or he did not but still wished to keep what he saw to himself. Why?

"Well that is very good," I said through gritted teeth before turning to Percy, adding a smile to my lips as I looked at his cold expression. His eyes were glued to Dameon.

"Percy, Dameon was once the stable hand in Greydenn but a few years ago, joined the guard." I turned to look at Dameon. "He has grown so much since then. Dameon has always been helpful to me, a true friend." A look I could not place flew across Dameon's face at the last word, but vanished.

"It's funny you mention, the stables, Lor." Percy stiffened even more at the sound of the nickname that so easily rolled off of Dameon's lips. "It appears someone rifled through my belongings there while I was gone." His smile turned devious.

"Funny, I would figure you kept your things in the guardhouse now?" I said through gritted teeth. To my horror, this conversation seemed to pique Percy's interest as he sat forward.

"Is it normal in Greydenn for items to be tampered with?" Percy looked to Dameon, his eyes still full of venom but now clouded over with something else.

"No—" I began to say, only to be cut off by Dameon.

Dameon removed his legs from the table, leaning forward as if the new conversation with Percy was the most interesting thing he had spoken of in days. Was this his goal? To expose me now? To make Percy question me? My relationship with Dameon had always been platonic, aside from the one-sided crush I had on him as a child. Surely Percy wouldn't hold that against me–Dameon was two years older than me and always treated me as a person before a princess. He helped to heal the broken girl that I arrived in Greydenn as. What little girl wouldn't have feelings for a boy like that?

"It is abnormal, but not unheard of for people to be nosy around here specifically those that have trouble sleeping." He threw a wink at me so quickly I almost missed it. Judging by the fact Percy looked less full of malice than he had since Dameon arrived, he thankfully missed it too.

"Was anything stolen?" Percy asked.

"Yes, something very dear to me was." He grabbed his chest like he was in pain, longing for what he lost. I was fuming at this point.

I slammed my hands on the table, glaring holes into Dameon when my mouth opened, words falling out before I could stop them. "It was a bag of sweets you left for me!"

"Don't forget the note," Dameon said sweetly.

"A note you left for me! Or do you make a habit of angering more women in Greydenn then just me?"

Dameon laughed, clearly getting what he wanted.

Fuck.

I looked over to Percy. Anger and shock was mixed on his face. Dameon began to laugh and it took every ounce of willpower I had to not dump my drink on his head and bludgeon him with the empty tankard—not enough to kill him, just enough to give him a headache for a few days. Maybe a scar.

"I left it for you to give to the horses, not to pack off for yourself." Dameon spoke to me like you would an indignant child.

"What the fuck is going on, Elora?" Percy said between clenched teeth. I had never heard Percy curse, not even as a young child when we would try on the words in secret with the other children in High Castle.

I was so fucked. How could Dameon unravel all I accomplished so quickly?

"Percy, it's not what you think." I moved to grab his hand. Thankfully, he allowed it. I paused, knowing my next words could make or break things. I talked slowly, thinking before I spoke. "I was so angry with how your first dinner at

Mirador went. I couldn't sleep, so I snuck out to give Dameon a piece of my mind."

"Something she has done regularly through the years, if I might add."

I shot daggers at Dameon, and the smile on his face widened until his dimples appeared.

"I went to the stables, he was not in the loft, but he left me a note apologizing for his actions and a bag of sweets," I said to Percy.

"For you to give to the horses."

"I did! I gave every horse two except the newest foal and took the rest with me! As you intended."

Dameon looked at Percy as he tsked at me. "Was the princess this presumptive as a child, Sir Alderius?" Percy did not respond to Dameon aside from a look that could kill.

Percy turned to me, seeming to ignore Dameon fully in a way that I envied. "Has it been a habit of yours in the past to go to the hayloft with Private Grey?"

I paused, mouth gaping at what he was insinuating. Sure I had had lovers, all of which I never intended to tell Percy about, but *Dameon?*

"It's Captain Grey, actually," Dameon said smugly.

I gritted my teeth. He was being such an ass and relishing in making my life difficult.

"Not like that, Percy. Never like that." My eyes were pleading, begging him to believe me. I looked between the two men as tears began to form in my eyes. To my shock, I saw Dameon's face soften.

Dameon took a breath. "Sorry, I was just having a bit of fun. It has been a very boring few days for me alone in the forest. Since Elora arrived in Greydenn, she would periodically come down on dragon-less nights when she couldn't sleep to see the horses. We became friends, grew up together." Dameon looked at me, the kindness and truth in his eyes melted the anger I just held for him. He turned to Percy again before continuing. "As you can imagine, it was hard for her here at first. We became fast friends and have been ever since." Dameon smiled softly. "I enjoy getting a rise out of her from time to time, to see that fire come out in her. Clearly I overstepped." Dameon moved to get up and Percy spoke.

"No, please stay. I am grateful Elora has had someone looking out for her all these years." He chuckled tensely. "I am not the best with jokes and never have been. Clearly, I read too much into this."

A relieved breath escaped me as I turned to Percy. I gave his hand a squeeze. "Thank you for being understanding." I moved my head to the side, looking at Dameon. "And thank you for apologizing."

Both men gave me a nod of recognition. Relief filled my heart. Could it be this easy? Could I have both of them in my life? Dameon was so ingrained in me–I couldn't imagine a time when I did not speak to him. I took a gulp of my mead, the drink tasting sweeter on my lips than it did mere minutes ago. I was still drinking when Percy began to speak to Dameon, the malice gone from his voice.

"Can I ask you a question, Captain?" Dameon nodded at Percy, welcoming what was to come. "If you care so much for Elora, why did you never try to slay the dragon?"

I nearly choke on my drink. Without missing a beat, Dameon delivered a swift hand to my back, forcing hair back into my lungs and the drink from it.

"And have to marry this beast?" The words rolled off his tongue with a laugh. For a reason I could not place, they seemed to embed in my skin like icy needles.

Percy stiffened. "It would be an honor for anyone to call Elora their bride." He rubbed his thumb across my hand as he narrowed his eyes at Dameon.

"The bastard getting the princess is just a bit too on the nose for me." Dameon took a long drink of his ale.

They both laughed—two entirely different sounds.

"But well wishes for you two. I do hope you live long and happy lives together." The joy from Dameon's eyes had vanished, leaving the deep brown orbs looking hollow, empty.

Percy stuttered, seemingly taken aback by the declaration from Dameon. Did he want to marry me? "Th…thank you. Though I do not want to rush anything, of course." He paused, looking over to me with searching eyes. "And only if the King and Elora approve."

My spine stiffened at the thought of my brother—the beast that controlled my life, and wished for my death from so far away. I did my best to mimic a smile, hoping no one noticed the hollowness of my own eyes. Dameon looked at me and for a second I saw my reflection in his own pained eyes and fake smile.

"Can I ask you a question, Sir Alderius?" Dameon sipped his drink as a calculating look took over his face.

"Please, call me Percy, Dameon." Percy smiled as he looked at me. "If you are so close to Elora, we will be on friendly terms in the future, so might as well start now."

Dameon laughed, a short, joyless sound as he stared into his cup. "You were at High Castle with Elora as children, yes?"

"Yes, I was. I was routinely in the company of both Elora and King Elrick," Percy smiled.

"Very interesting, I bet you have so many stories to tell." Dameon flashed a predatory smile to Percy. "Was your father a knight, Percy?"

"Yes, he was. The right hand of the King, to be exact. Sworn to protect Albaria and late King Rainard." Percy beamed and sat up taller as he spoke of his father.

"Fascinating." Dameon adjusted his seat as he looked at Percy, ever the aurora of complete confidence and control. I did not know what he was doing, but I sensed a trap when I saw one.

"Why ever do you ask, Dameon?" I asked between gritted teeth, hoping my voice was light enough that Percy did not notice.

Dameon ignored me as his eyes focused on Percy, who seemed unaware of whatever Dameon was plotting. "Did you ever notice anything strange in the castle? Anyone with malice in them?"

Oh gods.

"What do you mean?" Percy's face twisted in confusion.

He laughed darkly. "I fear you know exactly what I mean, Percy." Dameon sat forward, mere inches from Percy. "Tell me, Percy, does the person who left those bruises on Elora still have hands? The punishment in Albaria for stealing is to cut off a hand. I imagine hurting the princess carries a much steeper punishment."

"Dameon, please." My voice trembled. I was glued to my seat, unable to do anything to stop this.

Percy stiffened as the color drained from his face. "I do not know what you are talking about."

"You expect me to believe that the knight sworn to protect the royals, nor his son who admitted to being around Elora constantly, ever saw or questioned the marks on her skin?" Dameon's words cut like a knife.

"Dameon, *please*." My plea did not sway him in the least. Tears welled in my eyes as the memories I had pushed down into the pits of my mind clawed their way to the light.

"My father was an honorable man." Percy was red, pure anger on his face but fear in his eyes.

"So tell me, Percy. Do. They. Still. Have. Their. Hands."

Percy leapt up and lunged for Dameon across the table. The table moved with him, almost pinning me to the wall. I stood up, trying to avoid the commotion when a familiar calloused hand gently shoved me out of the way. Dameon stood up in the nick of time, leaning out of the grasp of the shorter man without effort.

"Judging by your response, noble Percy, it appears you not only knew about the abuse, but witnessed it. Do you feel noble? Worthy of your title?" Dameon stood to his full height–he was easily a head taller than Percy, if not more. "Though something tells me you have never felt deserving of your title," Dameon chuckled, "for good reason, I'm sure."

"Leave Elrick out of this!" Percy leapt across the table, a knife appearing in his hand that he lashed out for Dameon. He knocked the table and chairs to the side with a loud commotion. Dameon grabbed me with one hand, removing me from the arc of the knife quickly before dodging Percy. Dameon moved and swept behind Percy with agility I had never before witnessed. The next thing I knew, Dameon had Percy by the back of the neck as he pinned him and his knife against the wall. The tavern was silent, everyone enthralled with what they were seeing.

Dameon leaned forward and spoke into Percy's ear so low I could not hear. His words caused Percy to thrash wildly against the wall, trying to get to freedom.

"Elora?" The words seemed to be yelled in the hushed crowd. Rachel's voice.

Both Dameon and Percy looked to me as I looked at the crowd. My hair was flowing down my back. Dameon looked at me, a soft expression on his face.

"Your hat, Lor."

I picked the discarded hat off the floor and moved to put it back on my head like I could undo what everyone had so clearly seen.

I ran from the tavern, from the hushed voices speaking around me. When I finally reached open air, I gasped. I hoped the cool summer night would still the fire of pain raging in me.

Strong arms enveloped me and pressed me into a chest that smelled of leather. "Lor, I am so sorry. I am so sorry Lor," Dameon whispered into my hair between my sobs.

Fuck. He did this. He caused this. The grief in me turned to rage. How could he think he had the right to comfort me after what he had done? I pushed back from his chest, beating it with my fists.

"How could you? I trusted you!"

"He doesn't deserve you! Don't you see?" Dameon exclaimed, his face pleading.

"What are you talking about?"

"He let your brother hurt you. He knew and he didn't stop it!" Dameon's words were full of anger, but his eyes were full of sadness.

"You don't understand! What could he have done? My brother was the heir and I was the beastly daughter!" My voice broke with sobs.

Dameon moved forward, and grabbed my face in his hands. "You are not a beast, Elora. He is a beast, a monster for what he did to you."

My blood ran cold. I grabbed his hands and pulled them off my cheeks.

"You have no idea what I am capable of."

At this moment, I saw Percy appear in the doorway, my name on his lips. I moved towards him, fully out of Dameon's embrace.

Dameon looked down at me, his eyes full of pain, mirroring my own. "I don't know why I am surprised. Of course the princess chooses the knight." He leaned forward, his lips so close to my ear that they bruised against it. "Even if the knight was sent to kill her."

My blood ran cold as a shiver went down my spine. Dameon backed up, hands in the air like he was giving up, a look of utter resignation on his face. "If you ever need me, you know where to find me." With that he disappeared into the night, leaving me utterly broken.

Before I could process what just happened, what Dameon made so clear that he knew, Percy's hands were grabbing my shoulders.

"Are you okay, Elora? Did he hurt you?"

"I am okay." I lied, my words hollow. "Dameon would never hurt me." I silently begged the long-forgotten gods that my last words were not a lie–that Dameon would keep my secret.

Percy pulled me into his embrace and for a reason I could not explain, it felt cold compared to Dameon's. Clearly Dameon's words had soured what was growing between us. I could not let that happen. I took a deep breath, allowing the air to calm my mind and set my stomach. I had a job to do, lives to save. I refused to give up now when I was so close.

I wrapped my arms around Percy, squeezing him tight into me and I breathed in his scent. "Thank you for protecting me, my honor."

Percy stiffened before melting into the embrace, one hand stroking my hair. "Anything for you, Elora. I am so sorry the night ended like this."

I looked up at him, casting my eyes in the way I knew men loved. "It doesn't have to end this way," I said in the voice of a siren.

Percy blushed, but did not move from our embrace. Sensing this was my time, I stood up to my full height. I quickly pressed my lips to his, intending to pull away. At the last second Percy did something surprising–he pulled me closer and deepened the kiss. I parted my lips, inviting in his exploring tongue. He glided it softly across my lower lip, eliciting a moan from me. His hands started to move, to explore me. They moved from my hair to my backside and back again, one moving up to my breast. I grabbed his bottom lip in my teeth, pulling gently. A moan fell from his mouth into my own, turning me to liquid at my core. We kissed like this for minutes, maybe hours, coming up for air panting and with swollen lips. For the first time tonight, the smile I casted up at Percy was fully genuine.

"Can I escort you to the castle?" he asked breathlessly.

"I would love that–but only to the bridge. I do not want to put you in unnecessary danger, nor call the dragon's attention."

Percy nodded his head and grabbed my hand. We walked hand in hand up the path, taking our time talking about nothing and everything, with frequent breaks when we got lost in the embrace of each other. When the bridge came into view, I pulled Percy to the tree line, hoping to lose myself in him for just a bit longer, in the way his lips moved across mine. I felt drunk, but not on mead.

Percy looked at me, his own eyes glazed over with joy and drunk from touch. "I am so happy I found you again, Elora."

I beamed at him, hoping my smile showed the emotions I felt for him. I wanted him to see how happy I was that he was here, even under the conditions.

"Do you remember the time you brought me flowers?"

He stiffened before placing a hand on my cheek, rubbing his thumb across the high point of my face. "Vividly." The pain in his eyes told me he remembered what precursed the flowers– seeing Elrick flog me. I was left in tears, a broken mess. I would never forget the way he looked, so young but sure of himself when he presented me with the bouquet of yellow flowers, my tears instantly drying at the sight.

"If I am honest with myself," I paused, unsure if my next words were a lie or the truth, of where my own feelings ended and the ones I wanted Percy to have for me began. "I have loved you since then."

My words hit Percy like a cherub's arrow, the smile beaming from his face was so genuine it almost brought tears to my eyes. He leaned down and kissed me in such a way that my toes curled in my boots. I pulled back, taking in the way he looked, how his blond hair shone in the night, glowing like the moon above.

"Can I ask a question?"

Percy's brow crinkled. "Anything."

I bit my bottom lip, afraid of the conversation my words might start, but knowing they needed to be said. "Why now?"

Percy let out a deep breath as he looked up at the star-lit sky then back down at me. He gazed at me like I was the center of his universe.

"There is something I need to tell you." My skin prickled at the seriousness of his tone.

"After you left, things changed in the castle. The joy was gone. It became practice to not speak of you–your mother couldn't handle it. After her death, your father became angry, withdrawn." Percy paused, taking a second to compose himself. The idea of my parents missing me was so foreign–surely Percy was mistaken. They sent me away, after all, and had an entire castle built intended to be my prison.

"When your brother ascended the throne, he was determined to get you back–to stop this creature that haunts you." Percy looked at me in such a way that I knew he believed his words. "The first thing he did as King was make the decree to save you. I offered to go that day, swearing my fealty to the King, to you. But Elrick wouldn't allow it. He said he needed to see how strong the dragon was first. He couldn't risk losing me." A single tear fell down Percy's face.

"What changed?" My voice was barely a whisper.

"Your brother became more angry with word of each failure. One day," Percy's breathe caught, heartbreak written on his face. "One day I angered him. He told me the only way that I will earn his favor again is to show my loyalty by slaying the dragon."

I gasped. Was the only reason Percy was here not his love for me, but his love for Elrick?

Before I could stop myself, words formed on my lips. "Is a life outside of Elrick's favor so bad?"

Percy looked at me like I had three heads. "What cause of life would I have outside of his favor?"

"Me," I said, my voice a whisper.

Percy grabbed my face in his hands. "When I slay the dragon I will have both your favors. You can come *home*, Elora. We can all be together again. It will be just like when we were children."

The thought of being around my brother again made my skin crawl. "Percy, you do not have to kill the dragon to be with me. We can stay here. Learn to live with the dragon as those in Greydenn have."

Percy pondered my words but disbelief was apparent on his face. "Elora, we cannot go against your brother. He misses you, it is so apparent. He hasn't been the same since you left."

A joyless laugh left my lips. "You know as well as anyone that Elrick was never too happy to be in my presence, nor cared for me. You saw the things he did."

Percy took a step toward me. "He has changed, Elora. Grown. That was just him being a kid."

My heart nearly stopped at his words. Beatings, abuse, the things he attempted to do on my final day in High Castle were *not* just a child being a child.

"What if you can't kill the dragon? So many others had tried and failed. Why risk your life when we can be together now?"

Percy moved his hands away from me before looking around as if to confirm we are alone. He reached into his boot and pulled out a small dagger, removing the scabbard to reveal a blade the color of darkness.

"Before I left, Elrick gave me this as a gift, along with a warning. He said that the dragon may not *always* be a dragon, that it can look human when it wants to. Elrick had this blade forged that can prevent the dragon from changing shape."

The world began to spin, the ground no longer solid under my feet at this declaration. I steadied myself, hoping to not elicit suspicion from Percy.

"What do you mean?" My voice wobbled as much as my legs.

Percy grabbed my face and pulled me close for another kiss. "This means that as long as I find out the dragon's other form and use this blade, I can end it. Your siege will be over, Elora. You can come home. It will be us three together again, just like before."

Percy kissed me again, joy pouring from his mouth. I mimicked his movements, cold to the world. I felt more alone than I had in years.

Chapter Eight

THE bath water had long grown cold around me. I rested my chin on my knees as my hair made a dark web around me. Shriveled fingers dug into my legs as I pulled myself smaller and smaller. I stared at the water and saw nothing. The familiar knock of Selena and Katherine entering my chambers pulled me from my wallowing. The fall of their feet reached the bathing chamber door. A hesitant knock came a few moments later, concern evident in Selena's voice as she called my name.

"Just a moment," I responded, hoping my voice carried the levity I knew was expected of me. I took a deep breath before fully submerging myself, letting the cold water leach out the fear, the spite, all the emotions controlling me. I didn't sleep the night before, choosing to spend most of the night like this. Flying felt too difficult, like the dragon was too far gone to be called. I stayed under the icy water until my lungs burned, until I was sure the mask of the princess was on my face so no one, not even those closest to me, could see the cracks and the monster that lies beneath.

I could not afford cracks if my plan was to work. I had come too close to fail now, regardless of Percy's plans or Dameon's knowledge of me, of what I really am. In the wee hours of the morning, every time I remembered Dameon's words I wretched from fear, my stomach emptying its contents completely many times over. The only reason it stopped was because I was able to remind myself of the truth, or what I *hoped* was the truth–if he wanted to reveal me he already would have. My chest ached as I swallowed down the fear building in me.

I took a step from the bath and grabbed the nearest dressing robe without attempting to dry myself off. My dripping hair and slick body were leaving puddles on the floor when I opened the bathing chamber doors, but not before placing a smile on my face. To my shock, the smile was not reciprocated. Katherine and Selena looked as if they had seen a ghost.

"What's wrong?" I asked, my smile fading. "Is Olgara okay?" My breath caught in my throat.

Selena reached for my hand and smiled reassuringly. "Everything is okay, Olgara is fine."

"We just come with news." Katherine's face was neutral as she spoke. Could they have found out about the fight between Dameon and Percy last night? I shook my head–of course they know–there is nothing that happened in Greydenn without Selena knowing.

"What news?"

Selena took a shaky breath as she squeezed my hand. "Gordsby received a royal herald with a letter directly from the King at dawn. There is to be a town hall meeting immediately detailing its contents."

A ragged breath left me. The last time a message like this was given with a herald at dawn, it was to say my father had passed. No good news comes from a moment like this.

"My brother...?" The question trailed off on my lips.

Katherine took a step forward and placed a hand on my shoulder. "I believe he is fine. There were no coverings on the royal insignia indicating mourning this time."

I nodded, the feeling of relief and dread mixed in me. My brother was a monster, and though he wishes for mine, I did not wish for his death. But he would never stop wishing for my own demise. The prophecy made sure of that.

"I am sure it is nothing but the usual boring proclamations that come our way." I smiled, hoping it came across as genuine to my friends.

They both smiled back, but it did not meet their eyes. "Of course, Elora. I am sure all is well." Selena squeezed my hand.

"Let's get you dressed and ready," Katherine said before pausing, taking in the sopping mess that I was. "Actually, let's get you *dry* first."

I moved to grab a towel, only to have my hand swatted away by Selena. "Let us do it, please." Her golden eyes pleaded for me to listen.

"And while we do it," Katherine pulled my hair slightly, making me laugh, "you can tell us all about whatever occurred last night between Dameon and Percy." Katherine winked as she spoke, urging me on.

I moved to protest, only to be popped playfully with the towels by both of my friends. "And you can tell us why you snuck out to the tavern for *boys* and didn't invite us!" Selena radiated as she spoke, unable to convey the fake anger she obviously wished she could.

I squealed with laughter before telling them both all the details I could without revealing too much. By the time I was dry and dressed, there was not a fake smile to be seen. We were all beaming with joy. It felt like old times again, like three friends sharing their love lives without a care in the world.

We carried that levity with us to breakfast before heading down the mountain. For the first time in months, Olgara joined us, cursing the whole way at the indignation she felt in being called down from *her* keep. We all laughed, earning a stare from the old woman that caused us all to hush, hoping her slipper was not the next thing she casted at us.

As soon as we entered town, I felt eyes on me from every corner, searching me for any hint I might have for what was to come. By the time we arrived in the town center, I was picked apart. Every inch of me felt covered in eyes, like there was no detail nor secret I could keep.

A hand slid onto my back as a reassuring weight and warmth coursed through me, reminding me I am not alone. I looked over, expecting to see Selena or Katherine offering me support, but I was shocked by who I saw. Glassy, aged eyes looked up at me. Olgara did not smile. Her firm face was a reminder of what I was capable of, of who I am–of who raised me. I stood a little taller, the realization straightening my spine. Whatever this was, I could handle it. Olgara seemed to read my mind, offering me a tiny nod of the head, barely noticeable before she removed her hand. Without a word, we all went into the town hall.

The room was vast, large enough for all of Greydenn, with rows of wooden seats lining a narrow aisle. The town hall was once a temple long ago, when the gods were not only remembered, but revered. In the corner, one of the statues still stood–a shrouded woman, her face hidden, the Unseen goddess of death. The whole room smelled of the cedar planks that surrounded us, making every surface. Carvings of great animals and beasts were burnt into the walls. Plush purple tapestries lined the wall, carrying the gold seal of Albaria: a mountain peak with a sword across. Behind one of the tapestries was my favorite carving in the entire building–a small dragon breathing fire in flight. The carvings were old, the hands that completed them long turned to dust.

Towards the front, there was a raised dais with a long table and seven chairs facing the crowd, two more than usual or than was needed for the council members. Looking across the crowd, I was able to see who occupied the additions–a stoic looking Percy and a bored looking palace page.

I took a deep breath and walked through the crowd. The people of Greydenn cleared a path for me to the front, many of them offering small nods as I passed. I passed my usual seat at the table to sit next to Percy, offering him a sheepish smile as I sat. Percy nodded at me, the look of confusion on his face evident.

"I take it you do not know what this is about?" I asked in a low voice.

Percy chuckled. "I am not ever sure I know what *this* is." He motioned to the room around him, to the town gathering and mummering, waiting for whatever decree was to come.

"This," I threw my hands out, motioning to the room, to the occupants, their expectant faces riddled with wonder and fear mirrored in my own, "is a town hall. Greydenn is one of the furthest villages from the capital. It takes days for messages to arrive, as you know." I winked at him, eliciting a blush from the knight. "We are so remote that things have to be done a bit differently. We can't rely on decrees and messages directly from the king for every decision, so we have town halls and the town council. This was once a temple to the old gods meant to welcome everyone in Greydenn. When the knowledge of the gods passed, this building remained and we now use it for meetings. It is the only building in town aside from Mirador Castle large enough for everyone to gather at once. Mayor Gordsby presides over it all." I pointed to the short man at the center seat, noting that it was *not* a purple cloak day. "There are four other members of council." I pointed to the tall redhead sitting next to Gordsby in plain clothes, the hems of her breeches still carried the remnants of the rich earth she most likely tended this morning. "That is Angela Baccha, she is the smallfolk representative."

"The man next to her is the head of the guards, Commander Collins, correct?" Collins' large frame seemed to dwarf the chair he was sitting in. Even though he was a head taller than Angela, the angle of her head, the sheer power she exuded, made them seem neck and neck.

"Yes, it is. He represents public safety for the council. Have you spoken to him since you arrived?"

"Not really, but he approved the use of his training materials for you and Selena. He had them delivered to Mirador as well," he said.

I nodded. "He is a good man," I said genuinely.

Percy slyly motioned to the well-dressed man at my right. "And him?"

"That," I whispered, leaning in close, "is Louis Hevante, the head merchant of the town." As if on cue, Louis turned his head and looked down his nose at Percy before throwing me a knowing look. He brushed invisible dirt off his fine top, which was gaudier than even some of my dresses, as if our very presence could soil it. I did my best to stifle a giggle. Louis was the one person I might say is more dramatic than Dameon and Olgara *combined*. He crossed his arms and the feather in his cap swayed with the movement.

"What was that about? How dare he think he can look at us this way?" Percy seemed indignant at the slight, like the look did real physical damage to him. His skin grew ruddy as the vein in his neck throbbed.

"That is because we owe him money." A giggle fell from my lips before I could stop myself at Percy's face. "Louis owns the tavern–you know, the one you made a mess of last night."

"I was simply defending the honor of the king," Percy looked at me quickly adding, "and your honor, of course. It is what is expected of a knight."

I did my best to make sure my smile didn't falter, unsure of *why* Percy's words affected me so. "Yes, of course, Percy. But Louis does not take kindly to people disrupting the peace at his establishment. It makes the girls nervous. Nervous girls hurt his pockets. So anyone that does will have to give him a gold coin as an apology before they are welcomed back."

"I refuse to pay for the fight the stable boy started." Percy's words were louder than necessary. Louis leaned towards us without looking our way.

"Captain Grey has already paid his debt. Did so first thing this morning." Without looking up, I slid two coins from my hip pouch and into Louis' hand under the table.

"For the trouble I caused," I said with a smile. Louis squeezed my hand under the table.

"You're never a trouble, Princess." His words were heartfelt and hit deep. I looked over to Percy, his face contorted at the exchange with too many emotions to place. A silence fell over us for a few moments before Percy tapped me on the shoulder, once again asking for my attention.

"You never told me who the fourth member of the council is," he said.

"Isn't it obvious?" I asked.

Percy's face was a mix of total confusion. He furrowed his eyebrows as he squinted at me, like he was trying to find the clue written on my face.

"I am the fourth member of the council, Percy." His eyes widened, his look of shock quickly replaced by the heat of embarrassment.

"Of course, you are royalty. It makes sense you are part of the council," he said.

Louis leaned in again, shocking Percy and I both. "It is not because she is a princess. It's because she loves this place as much as the rest of us, and loves these people." Louis gently bumped my shoulder with his own before leaning away.

A deep blush set into my features. Before I could address it, Mayor Greydenn slammed a gavel on the table, calling for silence as he stood. The doors to the hall closed in unison as two guards moved to stand next to each door, one much taller than the other. My eyes caught his presence before I realized I was looking for him. The boyish grin on his tan face I was used to was nowhere to be found. No, today Dameon wore the mask of the stoic guard. He had a sword at his hip and an arsenal of daggers strapped tightly to his chest. His tight tunic showed that he was far from the gangly boy I grew up with. I looked up and our eyes met. He had noticed me as I had him. His face did not move, but his soulful brown eyes seemed to be conveying as much as they could. His face softened when he saw me, like he was trying to apologize with his eyes, begging for me to see him. I threw a look to Percy as slyly as possible, making sure he had not noticed which guard was directly across the hall from us. Thankfully, he seemed to be completely unaware. His lack of situational awareness astounded me. By the time I looked back to Dameon, he was focused on the now-speaking Mayor Gordby.

"People of Greydenn…" Gordby looked out to the crowd as he spoke. "A message has come directly from the King's desk to us this morning by way of a palace messenger, who has ridden tirelessly through the night to deliver to us at great haste. May we welcome him into Greydenn and offer him and his horse rest before returning to Vinguarrii, the heart of Albaria, and to our great King Elrick." Gordsby nodded towards the messenger. The young man walked towards Gordby from his seat, a pompous, bored look on his face as he handed a wax-sealed scroll to Gordsby. Gordsby thanked the young man before breaking the seal, opening his mouth to read the letter aloud. The small gasp he took as he scanned the letter before starting set my blood to ice and my spine rigid. This could not be good. Sweat prickled my brow as I prepared myself for whatever was to come. I scanned the crowd, looking for a familiar face, any face to set me at ease. The only eyes that called to me, though, were Dameon's. He offered me a small nod before mouthing one word that I had to squint to make out.

Breathe.

I let out a long exhale before taking a slow breath in. I hadn't been aware I was holding my breath. I slowed my breathing, attempting to calm my racing heart.

Gordsby cleared his throat. "A message directly from the King," he said shakily. "People of Greydenn: for ten years you have suffered under the constant threat of the beast that my parents damned you to." The crowd began to murmur, not used to hearing my parents referred to in such a manner. "You opened your arms and hearts to my beloved sister, Princess Elora Adhelina Galterius, and for that you will always have my gratitude." Gordsby paused and took a shaky breath before continuing. "However, while I have much gratitude and understanding that you did not choose your fates, I cannot help but see the fact the dragon still breathes, that my sister is still a prisoner, as a slight against me, the King himself. I have sent twelve knights, all of which were slaughtered mercilessly by the beast. One week ago, I sent the best knight in the kingdom, Sir Percival Alderius to slay the beast for once and for all, to remove this blight on Greydenn. To my knowledge, Sir Alderius has still not taken up arms against the damned beast." My breath was shaky as I reached for Percy's hand. He held mine back limply as his eyes were cast fully forward unseeing.

"In order to hasten the slaying of this beast, so that both Greydenn and my sister will finally be free, I have issued an order to all of Greydenn: in one week's time, if the damned beast still breathes, the tax owed to me will be doubled for every man, woman, and child found in Greydenn. If the beast is still not slayed, the taxes will be doubled every week until the beast or Greydenn itself is dead."

Gordsby took a breath, tears in his eyes. "Long live the King."

The hall broke into absolute pandemonium–screaming, shouting, sobbing. The people who I had seen as my family for a decade rushed the pulpit as fear and anger contorted their faces. The ground was shaky around me, like it was spinning. I grabbed the sides of my chair until my knuckles were white, attempting to steady myself, to think. The shouts of others were coming in and out of earshot.

"We must kill the beast!"

"How can we do so?"

"Why would the King do this to us!"

"We never chose this!"

I cast my eyes around, seeing all the people looking at me, eyes raging with fear in some, malice in others. In a few I saw pity, the knowledge that I was but a pawn in this game as well.

I stood up, spine stiff as I walked to the podium and gently grabbed the gavel from Gordsby's hand. To my surprise, he handed it over easily, but not before covering my hand with his own. His small eyes peered up into mine, seeming to convey so much emotion, the same fear I know in mine was reflected in his. This tax would be the death of Greydenn, we both knew that. I pounded the gavel thrice. By the third knock, the room was silent as everyone looked at me expectantly. I opened my mouth to speak but was unsure of what to say. I sent a quick prayer up to the gods that my words would do these people, *my people,* justice.

"People of Greydenn…" I paused as I scanned the faces looking up at me. "My friends, I am sorry. I am sorry that my presence has brought this beast on you." A single tear ran down my face, but I refused to let it shake my voice. "You all have been so kind to me for the last decade. You have been my family, and I truly love each and every one of you, which makes this next part even harder." I took a deep breath, steadying myself, the small sound seeming to ricochet in the near-silent hall. Hundreds of expectant eyes looked back at me, wondering where I was going with this. "Which is why I must leave. I cannot continue to harm you in such a way. I refuse to see more people die at the dragon's hand, so I will remove the burden from Greydenn, the thing that draws the beast–me." The crowd muttered, shocked faces seen all around. The scrape of a chair drew my attention from the crowd. I looked to the side and saw Percy still sitting still as a statue, eyes cast straight ahead. The messenger stood up and unfurled another scroll. The bored look on his face stayed, as if this is what he expected to happen.

"From the King's own hand." He ran his thumb under the wax seal. "I, King Elrick, hold that my decree for Greydenn holds if the dragon lives, no matter if my sister tries to exit Greydenn. As long as the dragon is alive, as long as my sister suffers, regardless of location, Greydenn will pay the dragon tax." Before sitting down, he walked towards me and handed me a small piece of paper. My brother's handwriting was on the front, addressed only for me. I slipped it into my pouch and took a seat–stunned by all of this, unsure of what to do. Percy reached over and squeezed my hand as we watched the messenger walk out of the hall altogether, his job here apparently done.   A realization hit me with such force it made my stomach heave. Was my death the only way to free the people I love?

The panicked talks of those in the hall bounced around my ears, but I was no longer able to understand what they were saying. My mind raced as I tried to find a way out of this. I could pay the tax with my own coffers for a short time, but not for long. I had never felt this utterly helpless in my entire life. I was a burden.

A yell came from the crowd. "You did this to us!" I nodded in agreement. This was all my fault. I looked up to lock eyes with the speaker. A young farmer pointed his finger, but to my surprise, I was not the intended target–Percy was. Alfred Willoughby walked forward, anger apparent on his face. "Your inability to kill the dragon got us here! Have you even tried to kill the dragon in the last week?"

Percy started to answer, but seemed at a loss for words. I imagined he had never before been treated like this by a commoner.

"That is what I thought–no! You have been too busy trying to woo Elora to do what you were sent here for!" Alfred threw his hands up in exasperation.

Percy stood up and slammed his hands on the table. "That is enough! I am a *knight!*"

Alfred stood taller. "A damn shitty one at that," he said.

Percy lost whatever control he had left and anger seeped through his every pore, causing his entire body to shake. "And what have you done? Any of you? Elora has been here for ten years and not once to my knowledge has *any* of you taken up arms to save her, not even since the King's decree! You speak of loving the princess but have done nothing to show that devotion."

I stood up and faced Percy. "That is not fair." My words dripped with venom, shocking us both. I took a breath, willing my voice to be more level. "The beast was never the responsibility of these people–I was." I looked out to the crowd, to the faces that raised me when my parents threw me away like trash–like a *beast*.

The crowd murmured, everyone lost in what to do, in how we could fix this. Percy turned to me and raised his finger in my face, as if he was about to shout or scold me like a small child. I stood up to my full height, daring him to do something, to say something to me. Suddenly, something whizzed between our faces and Percy jumped back. A thump came from the wall behind us. As Percy and I both saw the dagger embedded in the wall, a familiar voice yelled through the chamber, calling everyone's attention.

"ENOUGH." Dameon's words carried a finality as his voice pushed through the crowd. Suddenly, all the previously opened mouths began to shut, the murmurs and shouts disappearing altogether as Dameon walked towards the front. The bandolier across his chest had one less knife than it did a few moments ago.

People parted as Dameon prowled towards the front. They were all looking at him in a way that I had never noticed before. While I was still viewing him as a boy these last few years, the rest of Greydenn saw him as something more.

Percy moved his finger from my direction towards Dameon, as if the one digit could stop the storm brewing on Dameon's face. Dameon smiled, almost like he was begging Percy to do something. I grabbed Percy's arm and pulled him down to his seat as I sat. Percy looked at me with indignation as he sat without a word. Dameon stopped for just a moment, seeming to be taken aback by my support of him after last night. I offered him a slight nod–hoping to convey that I was willing to listen, but that did not mean I had forgiven him. Dameon was smart, calculating, and wholly Greydenn. If anyone could convince the people of something, it was him. I offered him a small smile, hoping it would be enough to influence what he had to say.

I hoped it would be enough to convince him to save my life–to prevent me from having to be the beast so many expected me to be. Dameon nodded, a conversation written on his face, words just for me.

Fear gripped me as he approached the dais, the same fear that had kept me up all night. What if Dameon didn't want to save me, but was here to expose me? I took a steadying breath, easing my troubled mind. That fear now felt preposterous. Dameon had always been my protector–my fiercest ally–even if he was a thorn in my side. He would not throw me to the wolves now. I knew he would never desert me. No matter how angry he made me, I would always have hope in him.

Dameon jumped onto the ledge of the dais with ease as he stood behind the podium. "People of Greydenn…" His voice did not shake. Looking out, it seemed everyone in attendance was waiting, listening for what he had to add. I smiled. The child who was once just a bastard working in the stables now had the entire town listening to him. If I wasn't so mad at him, I worried the pride I felt would be too much.

"The King has thrown us away, punished us for something we have no control over. He wants us to believe there are two choices only–kill the dragon and risk being killed, or pay his price." Dameon looked over his shoulder at me. My breath hitched at the look in his eyes before he turned back to the crowd. Any remaining fear I had dissolved. "The King sees Princess Elora as a burden, something that we have been cursed with. I challenge anyone in this town who views her as such to stand." Dameon paused and I held my breath, waiting to see people do as he requested. To my shock, no one did–not a single person.

"That is what I thought. Elora arrived ten years ago. The town I call home now is not the same as it was then." Dameon turned to look at me as he spoke. "Greydenn was not a home for many of us. It was not a warm place. Elora arriving brought us soul. She brought hope to this remote town that so desperately needed it." Dameon turned back around, facing the crowd again, thankfully before he could see the single tear I let fall.

"The arrival of the Princess brought us something we had no idea how to handle–a dragon. I ask you, earnestly, has the dragon ever harmed anyone in Greydenn?"

"The beast killed the knights!" Percy's words dripped with disdain, as if he was shocked he had to remind people of that.

"The dragon has never harmed anyone, to my knowledge, that did not first attack it," Dameon replied. The crowd murmured but Dameon continued. "I see no reason why we should risk ourselves to take arms against a creature which has never harmed us."

Percy stood. His face was red and spittle flew from his mouth as he screamed. "The king demands it! That should be enough, you simpleton!"

Dameon looked unfazed as he slowly turned to face Percy like he had all the time in the world. "Fuck the King." Dameon smiled as the hall fell silent.

After a heartbeat of silence the crowd lost it and things began to happen fast. Dameon was dragged away by other guards, a smile on his face as he made eye contact with me, dimple fully in view. Percy was restrained by other guards after he tried leaping across the table, where they came from I was unsure. Hands grabbed me and I went to remove them when I recognized one set of beautiful brown skin, one set pale and covered in constellation-like freckles.

"Let's go. We have seen enough." Selena pulled me up and we were out the door in record time as we pushed through the crowd behind Olgara who no one in Greydenn would dare cross. I chuckled–people might fear her more than the dragon.

I stumbled out of the building behind my friends, gasping for air, for clarity. The sky had darkened in the distance as a storm crested the mountains. Lightning cracked in the distance. Power flowed through the air, igniting me. I looked around, trying to see the one person I needed to talk to before heading back to Mirador. In a moment I saw him, his head sticking out above the crowd, face as stoic as ever.

I ran towards Captain Collins, only to feel a hand grab me.

"We should head back to Mirador. Now." Katherine's voice had a finality to it, one I wondered if she learned from Olgara in their recent alone time together.

"Not until I talk to him." Katherine nodded and I made a beeline for Commander Collins. When I finally reached him, the heavens opened and water fell from the sky in sheets.

"What are you going to do with Percy and Dameon?" Treason was not something to be taken lightly, especially against the King.

Collins grabbed my shoulders, offering a reassuring squeeze. "Emotions are high right now, Princess. Do not worry for Percy. He will be held until he calms down, a few hours tops." Collins chuckled. "And for Dameon, well, he will be held until he annoys the other guards enough to release him."

"So a few hours at best?" A smile spread across my face. I knew nothing would happen to Percy, but I was grateful Dameon will be okay.

"If the other guards last more than an hour, I will buy everyone the first round at the tavern tonight." Collins chuckled softly before smiling. "Go back to Mirador, Elora. Let this settle down. We will figure something out tomorrow." Collins gave me one more squeeze before summoning two guards to escort us back to Mirador.

As we made our way up the path, the reality of the morning events hit me. I was suddenly grateful for the rain as it hid the tears pouring down my face.

When I got back to my chambers, I sent Selena and Katherine away to tend to themselves while I did the same. As I undressed, I reached into my drenched hip pouch and touched something unexpected–paper. Pulling out the scroll, I suddenly remembered what it was, who it was from. I took a deep breath and unrolled it slowly, as if I could delay the inevitable.

The ink was smeared, but still readable. My brother's handwriting was something I could never forget, the way his letters seem to pierce the paper. The scroll was small, the message just a single line–a line designed to send me into a spiral.

I am counting down the days until I have your head on my wall, Beast.

Chapter Nine

THE thunderous skies called to me, begging me to join them in their misery. The storm blocked out the stars and moon completely, the only light coming from the lightning cracking the sky. I knew I shouldn't fly tonight, it was unsafe for so many reasons, but the itch in my bones was too great for a tea to calm. The misery of the sky mirrored the beast in me, and like calls to like. My feet carried me to the passage without much thought and I descended into utter darkness.

I ran from my cave with tears streaming down my face as I free fell, willing the change to delay until the last possible moment. Mere moments from the rocky ground my wings sprouted, lifting me skyward as I roared, screamed, to release the pain, the guilt that had burned into me. I pumped my wings hard, soaring above the trees by mere feet and used the sail of my tail to bank around the unexpected obstacles.

I flew until my thoughts no longer made me wish for a silent mind, until the muscles of my back were screaming from the effort. The nights lately had been so warm, but the storm had drained any remnants of that warmth and chilled me to my bones. The pain and sadness had been replaced by a chilly nothingness as my teeth chattered. I did not know how long I had been flying, nor where I was exactly, but Mirador was a beacon for me, a home. Like a bird, I always knew where my home was.

By the time I saw the familiar mountain again, I was beyond exhausted, too numb to think, to *feel*. Suddenly, I heard a crack to my left, like the sky was breaking around me. A bright white light blinded me for a moment. Lightning struck a tree mere feet away and a sharp pain in my abdomen sent me roaring as I fell from the sky. I righted myself and blinked rapidly, hoping to clear the lightning burn from my eyes. As my vision focused, I saw something unexpected–a cloaked person kneeling behind a rock with a crossbow still in the raised position.

It was not the lightning that struck me.

The wind roared and tore back my assailant's hood as if the gods themselves wanted to punish me with the identity of my attacker. His golden hair was dark in the rain and plastered to his fair skin. Percy's blue eyes narrowed in a mix of hatred and fear.

The sight of him pierced me deeper than any bolt ever could. No knight had resorted to hiding to try and slay me, yet. He truly caught me off guard. I roared at him, as loud as a lightning crack, and bared my teeth. Percy proved to be smarter than knights in the past. He took my warning for what it was and sprinted deeper into the forest. I used the moment to look down at my abdomen and assess the damage. The bolt was sticking from the side of my stomach, embedded halfway in the groove between two scales. The pain was mild, but the shock was great. The scales on my stomach were near impenetrable; something I only discovered after a knight had tried to slice me open and failed. I never thought the scales on my belly could be pierced.

I felt dizzy–like I was not sure which way was the sky and which way was the ground, completely surrounded by darkness. My eyes were heavy, muscles tired. I could see a light in the distance coming from the side of the mountain, like a match being waved in a great room.

My cave.

I flew in that direction, using the last bits of strength I could to get closer. I suddenly saw *who* was waving the light, as if directing me to find my home–Olgara. The old woman was standing tall, arm extended with a torch in her right hand, waving violently as she guided me.

My wings gave out at the last moment as I slid into the cave on my right side. The scrape of the rocks did not register, either because my scales held up or because I was too shocked to notice.

Olgara ran up to my head and grabbed my face in her hands. My head was almost the size of her full body, my two great horns alone were twice as long as her arms. Her hands were so warm against my scaly cheeks, so comforting. Like I could fall into the most peaceful sleep.

A quick, dull thump on my cheeks had me opening my eyes. I registered what just happened quickly, but had a hard time believing the truth. Olgara slapped me.

The old bitch slapped a dragon.

I bared my teeth as a low growl emanated from my throat. The acrid taste of smoke filled my mouth.

"Oh, hush up, I know you barely felt that. You need to listen. Do not close your eyes and do not change back to human." Olgara's voice was calm, but her eyes were fearful.

I cocked my head to the side, a chortle of confusion coming from me. The muscles in my throat shifted in preparation for speech, but Olgara halted me with a finger.

"You are hurt and exhausted. If you fall asleep, I am not sure if you will wake or change involuntarily. I need to get the bolt out before you change. I worry that if I don't, the damage will be worse." She paused and placed her hands on my cheeks again, urging me to listen carefully. "The bolt compared to a dragon-body might be nothing, it may have missed your organs because of your size. If you change, though, I am unsure if that process will cause you to change around the bolt. You might mortally wound yourself. I need to remove the bolt and clean the wound in dragon form. No matter what happens, you must not change until I say so." Olgara's words were clipped as she stated her order like a general to their army. I nodded my head in understanding.

"Good, dearie. Now I want you to position yourself so your mouth is facing the cave exit." She pointed to the exit with one hand and waved the other, urging me to reposition myself.

"Why?" I gruffed out. Speaking in this form was strange, forceful.

Olgara put a hand on her hip and looked at me like I was the dumbest creature to ever exist. "So I do not end up as a burnt bit on the wall of this cave. This will hurt. It would cause a person to scream–you breathe fire. Think, dearie."

I rolled my eyes but did as she said, positioning myself so my mouth was facing the entrance.

"Are you ready?" Olgara asked.

I did my best head nod while lying fully on the ground. The sky was dark outside, but full of power. The storm did not seem to be letting up anytime soon. I could feel Olgara grab the bolt gently but firmly.

"Okay, dearie. On three." Olgara paused and I took a deep breath. "One…"

At that moment, the sky lit up brighter than before as lightning struck a tree just beside the entrance. As the world lit up around me, blinding me, I felt an intense pain pulling through me. It felt like the bolt was ripping me from the inside as she pulled. I could hear Olgara grunt with the effort.

Olgara did not wait until three.

I roared, but it was masked by the thunder, the two powers together causing the mountain to shake. I started panting and the cave was spinning. I could not feel the cool ground beneath me. Suddenly, there were hands on my stomach and a sense of calm washed over me. My breathing steadied and I was able to hear what I hadn't before–Olgara's lilting voice softly singing, soothing me as she did when I was a babe as she held the wound closed with a hand.

> *The night birds are singing,*
> *And a lone wolf cries.*
> *A loon haunts the ponds*
> *And the air tells the skies.*

> *The cricket are chirping*
> *Yet drowning their mirth,*
> *The roar of my sweet babe,*
> *Shaking the earth.*

The stones now
Do give back the warmth of the day.
A traveler, by remembrance, not sight
Finds his way.

Dark blankets roll over
The crest of the hills,
The cows in their fields
Fast asleep, sweet and still.

You've graced night's old dance,
This new step since your birth,
The roar of my sweet babe,
Shaking the earth.

Olgara's voice trailed off as her hands gently stroked my stomach. She sighed before opening her mouth to speak again. "The bastard shot you with a barbed arrow. Hurts worse coming out." There was a clank in front of me, startling my eyes open. A bloody bolt with barbs down the front quarter stared back at me, taunting me. I blew out a small flume of fire, turning the bloody bolt to ash almost instantaneously. It felt good to remove something from existence that was designed to remove me, like I was able to reclaim a bit of my power in this misery.

The sound of ripping fabric caused me to whip my head around, taking in Olgara as she tore apart her apron with her hands–hands I had thought feeble for so long. Her gnarled fingers made light work of the fabric. Olgara muttered to herself as she reached into her pocket and pulled out a glass jar full of green powder. She uncorked the jar and poured the powder onto the cloth before clamping it to the wound. I shivered at the sting, but did my best to not pull away. If there is one thing Olgara could do, it was this. I learned long ago that whatever scrape or cut I had, Olgara could fix and there was no point in me making a fuss. When the old bat put her mind to something, there was no stopping her.

After a moment of this, Olgara spoke. "Dearie, the bleeding has stopped, but I am not sure if the shift might change that. I need you to change. Slowly." She kept her hand on the wound as she spoke, her voice softening. "It will hurt, but I am here. If anything gets too much we can take a break, see how much I can heal you if necessary."

A gruff was the only answer I could give as I started. The shift was painful no matter what. I usually went as fast as possible to get it over with, but I knew she was right. I could feel it. I took a deep breath as my bones shifted and shortened. The slow ripping of my muscles and shifting left my vision white with pain. Every joint in my body screamed as though I was being slaughtered. I had to grit my teeth to stop the roar, the scream, building in my throat. After a few minutes I was a panting mess and covered in cold sweat. Olgara still held the cloth to my stomach steadfastly. My vision fully returned and I found myself seeing with my human eyes, the world both duller and more vibrant than it was mere moments ago. To my surprise, Olgara grabbed my hand with her free one before bringing it to her lips, planting a kiss on the top before patting my shoulder. I pretended to not notice that her eyes were glossy with tears.

"You did amazing, dearie. I am so proud of you." Her voice cracked, so faintly that I almost missed it. She removed the makeshift bandage from my stomach. We both gasped at the sight–the wound was small, no more than a red mark the size of a coin on my abdomen, blood fully stopped.

"Thank heavens," she breathed. She removed the cloak from her shoulders and placed it gently over my naked body.

I breathed deeply, not sure if I should yell my thanks or curses at the gods for the events of tonight.

"How did you know to come down here?" I asked.

"I feared someone would try something tonight," Olgara scoffed. "Hoped I was wrong."

"Hope is a dangerous thing." My eyes strung with tears. I set my jaw, determined to keep them back. I was done showing weakness.

Olgara took a deep breath and weariness crept back into her voice. "That it is, dearie." She sat down beside me and pulled my head into her lap. I lost the battle with the tears and began to weep. Olgara stroked my hair, offering no soothing words or harsh tone. We sat like this until the tears ran dry and a hollowness remained that only sleep could erase.

*   *   *

SLEEP did not erase the hollowness, only dampened it for a few dreamless hours.

I got out of bed only for the routine and drew my bath, foregoing warming it entirely. I slipped in, the icy water drawing a gasp from my chapped lips. The pain soothed me and brought me back to my body as my thoughts were blown away by the piercing cold. I slipped under the icy water and opened my eyes. The pain blocked away all thoughts and I felt free, like I was back in my lake. The lights in the room distorted and the sounds were muted by the water. Morning sun beamed in from the painted glass window, throwing a rainbow of color around me. From under water, I could pretend all was okay–that nothing had changed–that I hadn't changed. I was living in a painting–a perfect world, imagining what my life could have been when a faint knock pulled me from my dreaming. Muffled speaking reached my ears, but I could not make out the words. I sat up and swallowed air soundlessly into my burning lungs.

"One moment! I slept a bit late this morning!" I hoped they could not pick up the lie in the carefree voice I slipped on like a mask.

"Are you okay? Did you hear what I said?" Katherine sounded concerned. Clearly my lie was not convincing.

"Yes! I will meet you down for breakfast in a few moments!" The footsteps I heard leaving my room proved me to be at least somewhat convincing. I exhaled a breath I was unaware I held, grateful to be alone again. I removed myself from the bath, wringing out my hair before setting on drying myself. I dressed myself in my simplest dress before tying my still damp hair in a single braid down my back. The cold, damp hair soaked through the spine of my dress.

The mirror was not my friend today. My skin was paler than usual, eyes puffy and red, but not as severe as they were before my plunge. It would be obvious to anyone who saw me, let alone my closest friends, that I spent the night crying. I ran to my armoire and reached into the drawer for a little jar. Opening the top, I was hit with the scent of herbs and citrus. Breathing it in, a faint smile built on my face. This salve was made by Olgara for me to help cover the evidence on my face after extreme nights. She had been dutifully making it for me since I was first sent away, back when nights I didn't spend with Dameon or flying meant I would most definitely have use of it in the morning.

I dabbed the concoction under my eyes gently. Within moments, I looked more like myself. Adding stain to my cheeks and lips was the final touch. I felt good enough to meet my friends now, like they wouldn't immediately see right through me. As I made my way to the dining room, I planted a faint smile on my face. I opened the door, ready to greet them.

"Good morning, ladies! That was quite the storm last ni…" I was shocked silent–it was not just Olgara, Selena, and Katherine sitting down for breakfast. "Percy?" His name fell off my lips, a question and a statement of shock all at once.

He looked haggard. His skin was pallid and dark circles were under his sullen eyes. A faint smile appeared when he saw me, before dropping once again. "Elora." His voice croaked out, like my name was the first word he had spoken in hours, in days. His blue eyes pierced into my own, glossy with tears. "I failed you, Elora."

I rushed to him and kneeled in front of his seat, grasping his face in my hands. I swept a thumb across his cheek and wiped away the tear that fell. He turned, kissing my wrist.

"Take your food and leave us," I commanded the others without moving my eyes from Percy. The clanking of dishes and patter of feet told me they listened. Once we were fully alone, Percy wrapped his arms around me and pulled me up and into his lap as he buried his face in my chest. Without hesitation, I ran my hands through his hair, kissing his forehead while offering hushed soothing words.

"I failed you, Elora," he croaked.

"You acted in anger and desperation, Percy. I understand why you did it," I said softly.

Percy sat back and looked at me with a quizzical expression. "What are you talking about? How could you know?"

Fuck. I shouldn't know about his attempt with the dragon last night. I grabbed his face and planted a kiss on his lips to buy me time. His lips did not move with mine.

I pulled back and furrowed my eyebrows, feigning confusion. "Yesterday, at the meeting. I assume that is what we speak of?"

"I have nothing to apologize for how I treated the stable boy," Percy's voice was harsh, like a knife across skin.

I sat back, distancing myself. "Of course not, Percy. I meant…I meant how you spoke to me." My voice was smaller than I aimed it to be. I suddenly felt as though I was a child once again sitting in my father's lap apologizing for something I did not understand, begging him to love me.

"I stand by my words, Elora. Words, *honor*, are all a knight has." Percy grabbed my face in his hands. I fought my every instinct and let him, doing my best to swallow the anger that built in me. "Though I do apologize for my tone. Your words paired with your brothers, with the talk from the townfolk riled me up." He kissed me on my forehead softly, gently. When he retreated, I leaned forward, pressing our foreheads together. "I promise to be more mindful in how I speak to you, even in times of anger."

"Thank you, Percy. I am sorry I pushed you to that point." The words felt wrong falling from my lips in a way I could not place. Percy wiped away the tear I was unaware of from my cheek with his thumb, the sensation sending a shiver down my spine. "What is it you wish to apologize for if not the town hall? Why were you in tears?"

Percy stiffened under me, a shaky breath escaping him. "I attempted to kill the dragon last night."

"Percy…" My voice was a hushed whisper.

"The beast nearly killed me–it roared in my face and I ran. After that, I shot it with an arrow from my crossbow. I hit it, but not enough to kill it." His eyes stared blankly into mine as he spoke.

The lie rolled effortlessly off his lips. If it wasn't for the fact I was there, I would almost believe him–believe that the dragon was the aggressor, that the dragon asked to be hurt, that *I* asked to be hurt.

"Why are you crying, Elora?" Percy's words were hushed and full of concern for me. The concern caused me to break down. Tears flowed as freely as they did in the cave last night and an ache opened in my stomach where the bolt hit. Percy pulled me to his chest, resting his chin on my head as I lost myself in the grief, the grief that was actually pain or anger, I could not be sure.

"I do not wish for you to be hurt on my account, Percy. I could not bear it." For once, I was telling him the truth, or at least the fullest truth I was able to tell him. Sobs broke me apart, but his arms held me together.

"Elora, I would do anything for you. It is my duty to protect you," he said as he pressed his lips to my forehead.

"Dying for me is not what I want! Why can't you see that you do not need to risk yourself for my love? You already have that!"

My words stunned me–the honesty in them was unexpected. I loved him. The time I spent trying to make him fall in love with me was futile, for I always loved him. I sat up and looked at Percy as he looked at me, blue eyes unreadable. I moved to get up, to distance myself. To run, maybe? I could not believe I just said that, admitted to Percy what I had been too afraid to admit to even myself. I loved him. I had loved him since we were children. I felt exposed, completely open in a way I had always tried to not be, to never show such weakness with anyone.

"Percy… I." I stood up and turned to run when his hand grabbed mine, pulling me back to his lap. Within seconds, his lips were on mine. The hunger in them, the desperation, surprised me. His lips had never felt like that before. I kissed him back, losing myself in the wildness, in the hunger. His lips parted and I opened mine in invitation as he grabbed my face with one hand, the other pulled me closer to him. Want washed over me with such force that the flick of his tongue caused me to moan. I felt a hardness pressing against my backside–clearly I was not the only one full of want.

We parted, panting, holding each other. Before I could talk myself out of it, I stood and grabbed Percy's hands. I pulled him from his seat and led him from the dining hall to the stairs without a word. He followed me, not once protesting as we silently ascended the stairs. When we arrived outside my chambers, I pulled him in. Percy seemed to not even notice, like he was lost in looking at me. I moved forward and kissed him. This kiss was lighter than before–an invitation. He grabbed my waist and pulled me closer as he deepened the kiss. His lips danced across mine as I took his lower lip between my teeth.

His moan was my undoing. I stepped back, wanting him to see me as I did this, to see my love for him. I slid the straps of my dress off my shoulders, leting the silken fabric pool around my feet. He averted his eyes for just a moment before gazing on me again, heat in his cheeks. Percy drank me in, his throat bobbing as he eyed me up and down slowly. The hunger on his face caused my core to warm in anticipation. An odd look came across his face that I couldn't place before he quickly moved his eyes back to my own.

"You're so fucking beautiful, Elora." With his words, he pushed off the door and moved with speed and grace until his hands were around me, feeling what his eyes had just taken in as his lips met my neck. The graze of his teeth was electric and another moan fell from my lips as my head rolled back, giving him more access. I reached down to his shirt hem and pulled the fabric up so I could slide my hands under. His chest was taut and warm as my hands roamed the lithe muscles and slopes of his body.

He pulled back and I whimpered as coldness hit my neck. Percy grabbed the hem of his shirt and pulled it swiftly over his head before untying the laces of his trousers. It was now my turn to drink him in. Percy's body was lithe and strong. I casted my eyes downward to the considerable length I had felt pressed against me. My feet carried me forward instinctively and I kissed him, wrapping my hand around his shaft as I did so. The moan that fell from his lips onto my own made my core throb, eager for what was to come.

"Elora," he croaked as I moved my hand slowly up and down his shaft before running my thumb across the head. The bead of moisture I found there sent me further wild. "Are you sure?"

The question stopped me for a moment. He most likely thought this was my first time. Our eyes met and I nodded. "Yes, Percy." My next stroke sent him shivering around me. "I need you."

With that he was undone. Percy picked me up and I laced my legs around his back. The kisses turned more fervent, more demanding as we made the way to my bed. He laid me down on my back and placed himself over the top of me. His cock was at my entrance when he kissed me, whispering in my ear, "This might hurt for a brief moment." He slid in easily to the hilt and I arched my back at the fullness, wanting more. His name was a breathless moan on my lips.

"You feel so good, Elora." Another thrust sent my head spinning as we lost ourselves to the bliss.

*   *   *

WE lay there afterwards, limbs tangled in my bed. Words felt unnecessary, like what we did was enough to prove our devotion for each other. My head was on his chest as he stroked my lower back, fingers moving absentmindedly.

"When did you know?" My voice was little more than a breathless whisper as the afternoon light drifted in through the windows, illuminating him in hues of gold.

He looked down at me, a faint smile on his lips. "Know what?"

"Know you loved me," I said.

Percy laughed awkwardly. "What a strange thing to ask."

"Well?" A smile danced across my lips at his coyness, like the admission of when was somehow more sacred than the act we just did.

"For me, it was when we were children, when you gave me the flowers. You took my pain and made it into something beautiful." I moved my hand up to cup his cheek. "But this morning, seeing you the way you were, the pain you felt, it made me realize I would do anything for you, Percy."

Percy smiled softly before grabbing my hand in his own, planting a kiss on the inside of my wrist. "And I would do anything for you, Elora."

I sat up onto my legs, hands on the bed to steady myself. "Then please stop the rubbish with the dragon."

"Elora." His voice was full of exasperation.

I grabbed his hand and pulled it to my heart. "Percy, we don't have to wait until you kill the dragon to marry just for my brother's permission. We can run away, figure something out. There must be a way out of this."

"Elrick's proclamation was very clear." His voice was soft like one used to console a child.

"Percy, I am serious. We can figure something out." I kissed his hand. "All that matters in the end is that we have each other."

Percy looked down, taking in my still naked body. His eyes widened for a second as he looked at my stomach like he was thinking of something. Could he be thinking of our future, of a way out of this like me?

Suddenly, the toll of the clock rang and before I could stop him, Percy was up, puting back on his clothes. "Where are you going?" I asked.

Percy kissed my head before stepping back. "I must be going, Elora. I will see you tomorrow."

"Shall we meet in the training hall at midday?"

"Yes, that would be perfect, my love." Percy moved to the door, turning back as he opened it. "Come alone, we should make our plans away from prying ears."

I beamed–Percy was agreeing to run away with me. I ran from my bed and threw my arms around him. He was stiff in my arms, like he wasn't expecting this at all.

"Tomorrow will be our new beginning, Elora." Percy kissed me and left. For the first time in days, months even, a joy so warm spread through me that I felt as though I was floating.

Chapter Ten

MY skin was still stained with the smell of Percy and what we had done. I lay in my rustled bed and basked in the glow of love in the afternoon light. I knew I needed to go talk to Selena and Katherine about this, to prepare them for my departure, but the thought scared me. Being without them for the first time in a decade felt as though there was a knife in my gut. I couldn't go to them now with no plan–I needed a clear idea before they questioned me. If anyone deserved the truth, it was my two friends.

I drew my second bath of the day, this one warm and scented with lavender oil as Olgara always did for me. I ran my hands through the water as I thought of the old woman who saved me last night and so many countless times before. Telling Katherine and Selena of my departure would be hard, but Olgara? There had not been a day in my whole life where we had been apart. Being without Olgara was as foreign to me as being without a hand. She was part of me and I was part of her.

I sank into the bath, letting the heat and oils relax my tired muscles and dissipate the heady smell of sex. I had fully leaned back in the tub when a sudden realization sent me upright. Water sloshed out of the tub onto the floor. I couldn't tell *anyone* of our plan until it was fulfilled. It was too dangerous for me to disappear and anyone left behind have any idea beyond the knowledge that I was gone and would be coming back. If my brother found out of my absence, he would sink his talons into anyone left behind to track me down. The mere thought of my loved ones being at the mercy of Elrick caused bile to rise in my throat. I knew what he could get away with as a prince, the evils he bestowed on me. The things he could do now as king were best left out of the mind.

No, no one could know where I was or what I was doing. It is not like we wouldn't return in a few days, a fortnight at worst. Perhaps we could go to a neighboring kingdom, the border with Venhalia was a few days North of here past the forbidden forest. Or maybe we could go to a neighboring town and wed there?

I let the water envelop me as I sank down. It was no use letting my mind wander, not until I talked to Percy tomorrow. I was sure he had a plan and was busy readying himself for the trek. He left with such haste that there was no way he was not already plotting our next move. No, today I should focus on my loved ones. As Olgara said a few nights ago, I needed good memories to power me through the dark times. No time could be truly dark, though, with Percy at my side. The way the sun glowed through his hair and sent his blue eyes dancing would make anyone think he was blessed by some ancient god of light. He was mine–and I was his. Whatever hardships came, I knew it would be worth it to be at his side forevermore. I swallowed down the uneasy feeling in my stomach. *It would be worth it*, I told myself.

I left the bath to search out my friends–my *sisters*. I wanted to spend as much time with them as possible today in the few hours I had left before sunset, with Olgara too. I found all three of them in the sitting room on the second floor of the castle. Selena was reading in a sunny alcove while Katherine watched distant Greydenn from a window. Olgara was lounging on the chaise, legs up and hands resting on her stomach, the picture of total comfort. I paused, taking the moment in, committing how all three of them looked to memory. I wanted to keep this image tucked away in my mind. This moment was something to be treasured and revisited time and time again.

"Doorways are for entering or exiting, dearie. Not for ogling." Olgara's eyes were still closed as she spoke. I chuckled as Katherine and Selena looked up to take me in. Concern and questions were written plainly on Selena's face while Katherine's devilish grin communicated she had *no* questions about what transpired between Percy and me.

She was as nosy as Olgara.

I breezed into the room and took a seat on the chaise next to Olgara. The old woman huffed at the shift of weight. She took me in with one eye open, like a cat awoken from its nap by an insolent child. I leaned back, relishing in the sunray hitting the chaise so perfectly. No wonder Olgara picked this spot.

"Someone is awfully chipper after her visitor left." Olgara's voice displayed that she knew all. Heat crept up my neck and face. It was not like Olgara was unaware of my bedmates in the past. This just felt different. Percy felt more final. He was not a tryst–I was in love with him.

"We had an eye opening conversation." The smugness in my voice startled me. Katherine breathed out a gruff laugh from her windowsill.

"From what I heard, there wasn't much speaking." Katherine whispered this without looking up. Selena laughed in an exhale, like she had been suppressing the urge for quite some time and finally lost the battle. I picked up a small pillow and chucked it at Katherine. She laughed at the impact and Selena snorted at the spectacle.

Olgara sat up, irritation written plainly on her face. "Can an old woman not get a moment of peace? You three are worse than children!"

At Olgara's indignation, I too began to laugh. The joy of the moment seemed to fill me up. I was positively glowing with love for these women–for my life. Dampness hit my eyes and I did not know if it was because of the pure happiness that I felt in this moment or the grief in knowing a moment like this was not sure to happen for some time after tomorrow.

Olgara looked over as the tear fell and wrapped her wrinkled hand around my own. She squeezed it before turning to Katherine.

"Katherine, would you mind being a dear and going to grab something from my chambers for me?"

Katherine rolled her eyes as she slid from her seat. "What do you need, Olgara?"

"I need you to mix up some more of my salve for my achy bones. The one I taught you last week." Olgara rang her gnarled fingers together as she winked at me.

"Okay, but that shall take some time for me to do. It is a lot of work," Katherine said with indignation.

Olgara motioned to Selena. "Take Selena with you. It's about time she learned some of my old tricks as well."

Selena and Katherine nodded before heading out, sure to be gone for some time. I had seen Olgara make her concoctions in the past–each one was chock full of different ingredients and herbs, each with their own need for preparation. I sighed, thankful I was not sent to assist in this task. I had neither desire nor talent when it came to helping Olgara with her concoctions. Olgara had long ago tried to teach me the names and uses of herbs, but I was completely useless.

Olgara reached for the teapot at the table end and wordlessly poured me a cup with a spoonful of honey.

"Here, dearie," she said as she handed me the cup.

"Thank you." I smiled as I brought the tea to my mouth. As soon as it touched my mouth, the bitter taste made my nose crinkle. Not even a full jar of honey could hide the flavors of this concoction, one I was all too familiar with.

"Can't have any proof of your morning with Percy, as you know."

I swallowed the tea, knowing it was a good call on Olgara's part to have it ready. "Thank you." The bitter taste lingered well after I drained the cup. It had been weeks–nay, months–since I last needed the liquid. No matter how much I took it, I would never get used to the taste.

Olgara took my cup, glancing in and studying the dregs for a moment. Why she always did this, I did not know. When she looked up, her face was unreadable.

"So, it appears you have forgiven him for trying to kill you." Her eyes bore into me as she pursed her wrinkled lips.

"That is unfair, Olgara. He had no way of knowing it was me. He thought he was doing the right thing."

Olgara moved to get up, shocking me. "No, I guess he could not have. Just be careful, dearie. A snake that has proven to bite does not usually strike only once."

I shook my head as my irritation grew. "He loves me, Olgara. This morning proves this. I will be okay. Percy only tried to kill the dragon because he wanted to save me."

Olgara patted my hand, a solemn smile on her lips. "How I hope you are right."

She moved out of the room quickly, leaving me alone. The sun had seemed to lose its warmth as the cool embrace of loneliness enveloped me. I knew how Olgara felt about hope after last night. Hope may be a dangerous thing, but I no longer hoped Percy would love me–*I knew it*.   A knock at the door startled me, but I did not bother turning around as the door opened. "Back so soon, Olgara?"

"That is the first time I have been confused for an old woman." I whipped around at Dameon's voice, shocked at what I was seeing. Dameon was standing in the door with his hands in his pockets. He had a sheepish smile as he crept in, making sure to keep his distance. The guard from yesterday was gone, replaced by the ghost of the boy I once knew. He wore a loose black tunic, untied at his chest and simple black breeches. His shoulders were hunched, like he was cowering from my gaze, trying to make himself look smaller.

I turned around, arms crossed firmly across my chest as I stared at the wall. I never noticed the small discoloration in the stain of the windowsill before, but at this moment, it was the most interesting thing I had ever seen.

"What do you want, Dameon?" My voice was cold, my words clipped.

I heard his footsteps as he walked from the other side of the room until he was across from me. He motioned to the seat next to me. I nodded my head in invitation, still refusing to look at him. A fingertip away from the discoloration on the windowsill, there was a small crack in the mortar. I should tell someone about that before I leave–the cold air in the winter swept through the castle enough as it was. The chaise shifted as Dameon gently sat on the other end, less than an arm's length away. From the corner of my eye I could see him looking at me. His full lips opened and closed several times, like he was trying to speak but at a loss for words.

"Well?" I hated the way my voice sounded, like an impatient child. Spoiled.

Dameon breathed out, suddenly as interested in the floor as I was the wall. He took a deep breath before looking at me again.

"I want to apologize, Lor."

His words surprised me and I whirled around, fully facing him. He looked much younger than he was, like the boy I met all those years ago. He was wearing the same face he did anytime his antics got me hurt or us in trouble. To be fair, it was usually me in the past who pushed us to do such unsafe things. Not that I would ever admit that to him, though.

"You must be more specific than that." I learned my lesson this morning about assuming why a man deems to apologize.

Dameon breathed out as he shifted to fully face me. "For my actions. I am sorry for throwing the knife and riling Percy up." He took a breath, steadying himself. It looked as though he was pushing anger back. His brown eyes met my own and I couldn't help but notice how the light made them shine like pools of honey. "I saw him put his finger in your face and I felt so much indignation that he would dare do that."

"Why? Because I am the princess?" I scoffed.

Dameon looked appalled. "No, because no one deserves to be talked to that way. And I know what you think, I wasn't trying to save you. I know you do not need my saving," Dameon chuckled. "If anything, you are the most capable person I have ever met. I just hated seeing him speak down to you about your home, about you."

"Did you really mean those words you said?" My voice was soft. I needed the truth from him.

Dameon reached forward and grabbed my hand. I let him. "Every word."

"Do…do you see me differently? Think I am a beast?" The sting of tears surprised me, but my lack of shame at Dameon seeing me this way was more shocking.

He ran his thumb across my hand. "Elora, I did not *just* figure it out. I have known the truth for years." His lip twitched up in a half smile.

My jaw dropped. "How? How could you have known? How long?" Had I not been as thorough in preventing others from figuring it out? Did others know? Questions and concerns raced through my head, thundering through so quickly I could barely keep track.

"Don't worry, I have kept your secret. It will follow me into the grave if that is what you wish." He squeezed my hand before releasing it, setting back against the couch and distancing himself from me once again. "Which is what brings me here right now."

"I thought you were here to apologize?"

"I am, but that is not all. I am worried, Elora," he said.

"About?" I asked, daring him to say it.

He looked at me through his eyelashes, long and dark in the light. "Your safety."

I laughed. "I thought we established I am a beast. Why worry for me?"

"Because I do not trust Percy or his intentions." His voice rose slightly as he spoke.

"You have no right to speak ill of Percy." My voice reeked of indignation as I stood.

Dameon fell to his knees in front of me, all but begging me to stay, to listen. I was too shocked to move. He grabbed my hands gently and my stomach flipped.

"I do not care what rights I have in the matter. As your friend, as someone who cares for you, I beg you to listen." His voice cracked as he spoke. I nodded for him to continue as I sat back down. A ball formed in my throat at the thought of this possibly being the last time we spoke. After the last decade together, I owed him this much.

"I do not believe Percy will ever stop his hunt for the dragon. I fear for your safety if he ever puts together what I have on my own, Elora."

"You do not know him like I do, Dameon."

Dameon gritted his teeth and let out a long exhale before continuing. "I know I do not know him personally, but I know men like him. He is looking for validation. His actions yesterday at the hall show he is not searching for that validation from you–but from your brother. He sat by and witnessed the things Elrick did to you and did nothing. That is not a good man, nor a safe one."

Tears stung my eyes once again. "You do not understand, there is nothing he could have done." I repeated the words I had told myself over and over again for years.

Dameon stood to his full height. He was well over a head taller than me standing and towered over me sitting, but he was not domineering over me, even though indignation was written plainly on his face. "Tell me," he said, "did he wear the same bruises as you? Feel the same sting that marked your skin? Did he ever speak against it? Comfort you after?"

"No, but it's different. Percy loves me!" I did not mean for my voice to rise to a shout–the loudness startled me. I did not sound like myself. I sounded desperate, like a woman shaken to her core.

"Elora, please. If he speaks to you like that in public, I worry what he will do in private. If he finds out your truth, are you sure he won't immediately do as your brother commands?"

"I am sure. He loves me!"

"More than he loves your brother?" Dameon's face was colored with a mix of sadness and rage.

"How dare you," I bit out as I stood to my full height.

Dameon stepped forward until, closing the distance between us. "I saw the rage in his eyes when I denounced Elrick in the meeting. Percy is desperate for his approval."

I scoffed. "Elrick is the King, of course Percy said an oath to him." I pointed at Dameon. "The same oath you said, might I remind you."

"He will never go against Elrick, Elora. He will always come first. That puts you in danger," he said.

I laughed, Dameon was so wrong. "He is already going against Elrick," I said. "He is taking me away to wed without

Elrick's knowledge." My indignation led me to say the truth, but my words felt hollow as soon as they fell from my lips.

Dameon took a step back, pain written across his face. I covered my mouth.

"So he knows the truth?" Dameon's eyes were glassy as he set his strong jaw.

"No, but I will tell him!" The lie was plain on my lips, as not even I believed it.

"Elora, please. Don't do this." Tears streamed down his face. The sight was too much. His tears watered the seed of doubt building in me–the fear that I was wrong. I swallowed it down, cutting the fear at the root. Neither Percy nor I could afford for me to second guess us. This was how we both survived.

"Get out," I said between gritted teeth.

"Elora," Dameon pleaded.

"GET OUT!" My voice was shrill and tears burned my eyes. I tried to swallow them down, but the gates opened and they rushed down my face like a river. There was no hope in stopping them now.

A defeated-looking Dameon stared at me, his face a mix of pain and sorrow as he made for the door. He paused before opening it, but did not turn around. "If you change your mind, or ever need help, you know where to find me. I will…I will always be here for you." His voice cracked and he exited. The door clicked behind him and I waited until I could no longer hear his footfalls before falling to my knees. My grief consumed me and I lost myself completely as Dameon's words repeated in my head.

*   *   *

I tried to not let Dameon ruin my last day with the others. I took time to piece together my broken heart before seeking out my friends. We laughed, enjoyed dinner, and by the time the sun fell behind the mountains, I felt light. Exhaustion weighed heavy on my bones, but there was one more thing I had to do before I could say goodbye to this life. Even if Percy and I did not leave tomorrow, I was unsure when I would get the chance again. The sky was clear and stars bright when I leapt from my cave in dragon form, not wanting to risk someone seeing me change. If last night taught me anything, it was that I must be more on guard when able to take this form.

I found joy while flying that I hadn't felt in months. I climbed to the highest heights I could manage before free falling through the clouds, blowing fire and diving through it when I got too cold. By the time I reached my lake, I was elated with glee. I dove in head first in the deepest portion, letting the water completely cover me before initiating the change. When my head popped out of the water I was not a dragon, nor a princess. I was just a woman embracing in the simple joys while I could. I would never be able to fully give up my dragon form. The sky would always call to me, but I hoped I could manage to keep that part of me subdued for the next few weeks or months until I could tell Percy, or I find the opportunity to sneak away. He deserved to know the truth. I told myself he would be okay, accepting in time if not at first. A growing knot of doubt formed in my stomach, but I pushed it down. Percy loved me and I loved him.

What is love if not sacrifice?

*   *   *

I woke in my quarters the next morning sore but well rested. My sheets still smelled of Percy and I breathed him in, letting the scent wrap around me. There was a pep in my step as I got ready for the day, dressing myself in my most beautiful gown. If Percy and I did leave today I could change, but the dress was valuable and we might need the money on our journey. It did not hurt that I looked beautiful in the gown. The lilac silk hugged my curves in an effortless way. The bodice of the dress was covered in incandescent beads. The lighting in the ballroom would shine through the beading, making me look otherworldly. I wanted Percy to gaze upon me and know he was making the right decision. I braided half of my hair into a halo that collected at the back of my head before cascading in loose curls down my back.

Breakfast was a quick affair and my eagerness for my meeting with Percy showed. I sent Katherine and Selena to town for errands and I was pacing the chamber long before Percy showed, simply waiting. After an hour, I forced myself to sit and calm myself.

Ten minutes before he was to show, the sound of the door opening sent me to my feet. Percy was wearing the same clothes as yesterday and his face was unshaven. I squinted my eyes, unsure of what I was seeing.

"Elora, you are here early." His words were clipped and his voice had a hint of indignation to it. Clearly he wanted to arrive before me.

I smiled, trying to hide my confusion at his tone as I walked towards him, practically skipping as I did so. When I reached him, I kissed him, the smile on my lips spreading so wide that my cheeks began to hurt as our lips touched. I parted my lips, but Percy's movements did not mirror my own. We parted moments later and as I looked at him, I had never been so sure of my decision.

The wine I tasted on his lips didn't even sway me. Nothing could take away my elation.

Percy smiled at me, but it did not reach his eyes. His blue eyes were a storm of pain and something I could not place. "Percy." My voice was barely above a whisper as I reached for his hand. "What is wrong, my love?"

He reached up and placed a hand on my cheek. I leaned into the warmth–into the rightness of it. "Nothing, Elora. I just did not sleep much last night."

His face looked tired, haggard, like he was up all night thinking about something. I wondered if he was beating himself up for defiling me before we wed.

"Percy, I hope what we shared yesterday is not what kept you up all night, for I do not regret anything." We made love, that much was apparent to me. My heart broke thinking about how he must have thought of himself afterwards, like someone who stole something from me. A thief of my virtue. There was no way he could know that he was not my first.

Percy smiled, his eyes dead. "No, Elora. I do not regret anything that transpired yesterday. It illuminated so much for me."

I beamed. "Yesterday illuminated so much for me as well. I am so grateful to be in love with a knight as true as you." I wrapped my arms around him and buried my face in his neck. He stroked my hair before gently pulling us apart.

"So what is your plan, Percy," I asked.

He chuckled, the sound devoid of joy. "I have been thinking of one all night." He paused. "First though, we must address the dragon."

"I promise you it will not be a bother on our journey," I said.

Percy tilted his head as he smiled, eyes still cold. "How do you know?"

I stopped, unsure of how to continue. I laughed awkwardly. "It did not bother us on the journey to Mirador all those years ago." I stopped, picking my lip before continuing. "It is only an issue at night. As long as we are somewhere safe by nightfall, we will be fine," I said.

Percy smiled, patting my arm reassuringly. "Of course we will be. You will always be safe with me." He leaned forward and kissed me on my brow. I closed my eyes and breathed in the touch.

"Just to be sure, though, to make sure I am prepared, can you tell me about the night the dragon first appeared?" Percy still had a light hold on my arms as I looked up, his face serene.

"What is there to say that I'm sure you have not heard?" I smiled as my scalp prickled. Something was off.

"Oh no, actually. People were banned from talking about whatever incident occurred." Percy's dark chuckle had my skin prickling more. "I only know what everyone knows: that the dragon appeared, Elrick tried protecting you, and he lost an eye for it." Percy paused, taking me in. I did my best to keep my face neutral, even though this was the first time I had heard about my brother's eye.

Even after all these years, even though it was the day my parents lost all love for me, I still held no regrets for what I did to my brother. If I had any regrets, it was that I wished my talons went deeper. If that made me a beast, I would wear the title with honor.

"You look shocked, Elora?"

"I...I did not know Elrick lost his eye. The last thing I remembered seeing was him bloody and the beast attacking as I hid under the bed. I was not permitted to see him before I was sent away for everyone's safety." The lie blended with the truth effortlessly. Though I had not spoken of this night with anyone else, I had been rehearsing for this moment for years. There was no dragon that night. It was merely the first time I successfully shifted just parts of me, exchanging the fingers and nails of a princess for the talons of a beast.

Blood flowed down my arm as I slashed my talons into his eyes.

"Did the dragon appear from thin air? How did it get into the castle? A beast the size I have seen would not be able to do so."

"It was smaller then. The best the court mages could make of it is that the beast seems to grow with me. It was attached to me by the witch who cursed me at birth. Elrick was spared. When it appeared, Elrick tried to protect me by throwing me under the bed."

He straddled me as he pulled a dagger from his boot and held it to my neck.

Percy laughed, a dark sound. "Now that is the part I do not understand! Forgive my candor, you know I love your brother more than anything," he paused for what felt like a century but could be only a moment. "The same love I hold for you, of course, my dearest Princess. But in all the days of our youth, I cannot think of one moment where Elrick showed you any favor, let alone gave an inclination he would stand in the way of danger to protect *you.*"

The truth of his words stung, and I made a move to step back, but Percy's grip on my arms tightened.

Elrick's long fingers wrapped around my arms and flung me to the floor.

"Percy, you are hurting me." My voice was small, empty. He stepped forward and I was forced to take a step back to maintain what little space I could. Before I knew it, my back was pressed against the wall, any hope of exit removed.

"So the idea that your brother moved to protect you is a bit laughable." Percy's eyes were wild.

You do not deserve to live, beast.

"Maybe he had a moment of bravery." I squirmed, trying to get free. When I realized there was no exit, I looked Percy directly in his icy blue eyes. I turned my head to the side, taking him in–the unshaven face, unkempt clothes, wine on his breath. His undereyes were dark from lack of sleep. Maybe there was another way out of this trap. "You speak so highly of Elrick, surely you think our king brave, no?"

A pillow pressed against my face woke me from my slumber. I shifted my hips under his weight, sending him off of me.

Percy laughed, a dark and soulless sound. "No wonder your parents banned others from speaking about the incident. They didn't want the secret to get out."

Guards rushed in as Elrick screamed, clutching his bloody face. My father came in, sword drawn. Any love for me drained from his face as my brother's blood dripped down my scaled hand. The wild smile on my face at what I had done cemented me as a beast in his eyes.

"What secret?" I whispered, hoping, screaming to the gods that *this wasn't happening.* Percy moved one hand down to my waist, sticking his thumb onto my wound, pressing deeply. I gritted my teeth to silence the scream building in my throat.

Percy leaned in, a predatory smile on his lips. He presses his mouth to my ear. "That you were the true beast all along."

Chapter Eleven

MY head was screaming from the weight of Percy's realization and the memories I repressed so long clawing to the light. The pain of the unhealed wound on my abdomen paled in comparison to the anguish I felt at the memories. I steadied my breathing—I refused to let my fear show on my face. I could still recover from this. I had to.

"Where would you get such a ludicrous idea as that, Percy? How could I be the dragon? You think me a beast?" The tears welling in my eyes were genuine, the pain genuine even if my words weren't. "I…I thought you loved me." Percy softened and removed his hand from my wound as a single tear streamed down my face. Red stained his thumb—my blood. The sight of it made my skin itch as the dragon begged—*demanded*—to be released.

I swallowed the feeling down. If I did anything, I would just confirm his suspicions, damning us both to violence. I steadied my breathing, five words repeating in my head over and over: *I can still stop this.*

Percy backed up, releasing me from my confines. I let out a breath as I relished in the distance, in his retreat. He still had doubts, and I could work with doubts. If I made the correct moves, I could save us both.

As I took a step forward, I planted a look of confusion on my face. I hoped that is how it came across as I widened my eyes and softened my jaw. Percy's eyes were unseeing as he walked backwards, staring at his feet. His mouth moved but words did not form.

"I…I was so sure," he stammered. "Elrick warned me that it would be someone in the castle, that the dragon would have a human form." He looked up finally, making eye contact. His eyes narrowed at the small bloody spot on my dress. Any trace of doubt in him was wiped away in an instant. There was no more denying. I wore the proof on me of what I am.

Of what he tried to do to me.

"Elora, maybe you are not aware of what happens to you at night. If that is the case, none of this is your fault. I am sure Elrick can be reasoned with." Fear had crept into his voice.

I laughed without humor or joy, a dark sound as the reality of my situation hit me like a wave, pulling me deeper into the monster I was always destined to be. "My brother? Understanding? Of me? You just do not want to admit that your beloved King sent you to kill his sister."

The words slipped out before I could stop them, damning me. He had tried to give me an out and I blew it. Percy tensed. His steps stopped as he brought his right hand to rest on the hilt of his sword.

"Which is your true form?" He avoided eye contact like I was Death herself.

"What do you mean, Percy? Do you think I am a beast? Have you ever known me to be a beast?" I asked.

He set his jaw before looking at me, anger clear in his beautiful face. "I know that I shot the dragon in the stomach–a non-fatal wound. And I know that you have a wound in the same spot currently leaking blood." His voice raised to a shout, and I winced. "So I ask you again, Elora, what is your true form?"

My spine went rigid at his tone. Anger filled me, but not a hot anger that had the danger of spilling over like Percy's, or like my brother so often showed me. No, my anger was cold, calculating. If I was to be the beast in his story, I would not settle for hot anger. If this was my role, I refused to be anything but the stuff of nightmares. "Have you never considered," my voice was light but held the edge of a knife, "that they are both true to me? Both come to me naturally and have for as long as I can remember." I prowled towards Percy, careful to always keep my distance from his sword arm. "There is not one I dread or feel cursed to assume, I can go between them as smoothly as you change a shirt, but neither is a costume."

Percy watched my steps closely, making sure his back was never to me. His steps were slow, calculated, like he did not want to startle me into action. He gritted his teeth, his voice more level than it was as he spoke. "But what shape were you born in, Elora?" I smile coldly. It is about fucking time he learned how to speak to me.

I laughed, a cold and carnal sound, devoid of joy. "What do you think of me Percy, that I was hatched from an egg? That poor Elrick had to share a womb with a dragon all those months?" I pursed my lips, clucking at Percy. "Surely you are smarter than that."

"Tell me, Elora," he ground out.

"Tell you what, Percy?" I flinched at the volume of my own voice. Percy's eyes narrowed. I took a deep breath before continuing. "Which truth is it you would like to hear? And quite frankly, I do not see the importance of this question when I am both now." I paused, sending Percy a knowing look as a joyous smile crept across my lips. "But I think I know why it matters to you." I pointed and Percy squirmed under my gaze. Did he think me a witch, too? Foolish man. I continued to move around him in a circle, slowly leading us to what I needed.

"If I say human then I am just a damsel trapped in a beastly form in your story, someone you need to save. Granted, you will see me as a full person and I am sure it will fill you with less regret about what we shared yesterday." He winced at the memory, horror in his face at the thought that he fucked such a monster as me. His turmoil drove me on, sending me into a spiral. "If I say dragon…" I paused, watching the color drain from his face, "then I am just a trickster beast, yes? A temptress who lured the innocent knight to her bed. A cruel creature meant to torment you, something for you to overcome."

"You have not answered my question."

"Why are you so afraid of me containing multitudes? Of having complete and utter control of my body? Of me having the ability to don whatever traits I choose at that exact moment?" Percy's eyes widened in fear as wings emerged from my back. Color completely drained from his face as his throat bobbed as the sound of bones snapping into place as my wings took shape. Weak man.

"Aren't they beautiful?" I said with a smile. The afternoon light streamed through the stained glass and onto my wings. The almost black scales shone purple in the light. The membrane of the wings started dark blue and faded to sky blue at the tips. Percy was aghast as I reveled in my beauty. Men never did like a confident woman.

"It's not possible." His mutter was barely audible over the rustle of my wings as I stretched them to their full size. I had never done this before, never fit my wings to my human body. I was suddenly struck by the rightness, by how well they fit. Granted, they were much smaller than usual, but more than adequate to get me aloft if I saw fit.

"Haven't you learned yet that anything is possible?" Percy was too stunned to speak, so I kept going, too stunned by the events to stop. The dragon in me was done being contained. There was a freedom in being known, even if I was reviled.

"To answer your question, dear Percy, I never had to learn to control either of my forms just like I never had to learn to breathe. I am not cursed to be a dragon only at night. No, I can be whatever I want, whenever I want."

"You are a beast.," Spittle fell from his mouth as he hurled his insult. It had little effect as I had called myself much worse. The title might as well have been a pet name for me by my cursed brother and parents.

"I fear you are just jealous, envious of my power, of something you could never understand. Reminds me of my dear brother who has sent so many like you to kill me, the evil creature ruining his kingdom." Percy flinched at the mention of my brother. "But a weak man can only command weak men. The previous dozen were honestly no challenge at all." Percy's feet had assumed the attack position. I squared my body, ready for whatever was to come. "I know what weak men do to people like me in your stories. But this is my story, my castle, and my home." All at once my fingernails were replaced by sharp talons. My vision became much sharper, clearer as I moved to my dragon eyes. This room was too small to accommodate me in dragon form, but tall enough that I could fly with my smaller wings. If this fight happened, I needed to be prepared.

Percy gritted his teeth as he removed his sword from the scabbard. The glinting lights made it appear as if it was made of holy fire, like the glowing weapon of a blessed knight. But there was no blessed knight in front of me, only a scared man who did not seem to have the honor befitting of his title.

I took a breath. Percy may not be honorable, but *I was*, regardless of what a prophecy said. I put my hands up, retracting my talons, as I softened my face. "Percy, we do not have to fight. I do not wish to hurt you." I placed my hands on my heart, hoping he could see the genuineness of my statement. To be honest, I did not believe I had it in me to hurt Percy. The mere thought of his blood on my hands made my stomach uneasy and the floor equally unsteady. "If you leave now, I will not follow. You can go anywhere you wish. Your hands will be washed of me, of this." My voice quivered but I did not let it halt me. "I genuinely do love you and will always have love for you. I will not fight you, so please leave."

He paused, seeming to consider my words. His sword arm dropped to his side as he pondered. "Your brother is a beast for setting us up like this."

Tears filled my eyes. Could it be this easy? My heart swelled at the idea that Percy had finally seen the truth. "Yes, he is."

"And that beast is king." Percy's words stunned me, but I did not say anything as he looked out the window, seemingly lost in thought. He turned around, locking his blue eyes with mine. "If I leave here, I can never return to Vinguarrii, to Elrick's side."

"I can give you gold. More than enough to set you up for a good life somewhere else, anywhere else."

Percy laughed, a dry and joyless sound. "Do you know what the main thing I have learned from your brother?"

"Please tell me."

Percy's smile turned lethal, "A beast can never truly love." His words hit me like a dagger to the heart, stunning me. I was shaken and before I knew it he raised his sword and attacked. He arced his sword high, the tip barely grazing my neck as I used my wings to shoot myself backwards and out of range. I touched my neck, my fingers coming back with a small smattering of crimson liquid.

Two things happened simultaneously. First, I realized Percy was trying to kill me, second, he was once again coming at me, his sword drawn and mouth agape. A warrior's cry flew from his lips. I pumped my wings hard as I pushed up with my legs, sending myself skyborn and out of reach. My talons emerged again as I tasted blood in my mouth. I touched my lips, only to find them tattered by my sharpened teeth. I bared them at Percy, hoping to scare sense into him as he lunged for me. He looked down at his sword, anger on his face.

"Wishing you had your crossbow?" Blood trickled to the floor from my tattered mouth.

He smiled. "No, actually I was just thinking how monstrous you look. Truly a beast–like you are at your core."

I smiled. My lips ripped further with the movement across my teeth, but I no longer cared. "What can I say, I am the King's twin."

Percy's face contorted. "Do not dare utter his name, filthy beast. You are unworthy of him!"

Percy hurled his sword like a javelin directly at my chest. I banked, but the ceiling was not high enough for me to get out of range. A white-hot, searing pain caused me to scream as the sword tore through my right wing, ripping the delicate blue skin from middle to bottom before clanking to the floor. I fell to the ground, and by the grace of the gods, landed with my feet underneath me. Percy looked to my side and I saw another blessing, my saving grace covered in my blood: Percy's sword was at my feet. Percy's eyes widened with horror at the crunching sound of my wings retreating back into my body.

I grabbed the sword and held it aloft and parallel to the floor. I moved my feet slowly as I walked backwards towards the corner of the room where supplies were kept. Percy's eyes were full of venom and fear as he watched.

"Are you going to kill me now, beast? Or run away?" His voice broke as he spoke. He was nothing more than a boy playing knight.

I smiled, a joyless movement that made him jump at the sight. I imagined I was quite the image right now in my tattered dress as blood stained my chin and neck. I felt savage, unwound, as I reached my free hand covertly behind me, silently feeling around for what I sought. "I was just going to ask you again to revisit my earlier offer. It still stands."

"Fuck you, beast." The warmth in his tone and eyes that I had always known before this day was gone. The man before me was but a shell of the one I fell in love with.

"I may be a beast, but I believe in a fair fight." Without blinking, I threw his sword on the ground with enough force that it slid to his feet. Percy's eyes widened in surprise as I pulled a shortsword from behind my back. He quickly reached down and grabbed the sword, charging me. I raised my sword to meet his as I moved to the side, hoping he would fall into my carefully laid trap. I had been studying his fighting techniques for days, comparing it to my previous opponents. I knew his foot placement was the base of all his strength and speed.

I also knew that he was too angry to be careful, to watch where he planted himself. Percy was much too angry, too unhinged, to notice that his left foot landed in a pile of my blood on the tile floors. His eyes widened as he arced his sword, aiming for my head. I fought every instinct as I stood in place, so sure of my plan. As he twisted, he began to fall backwards. He dropped his sword in a futile attempt to right himself and fell to the ground. The move meant to be my death, my beheading, was the one that brought him down to his knees before me. Within seconds, I was on him, my blade pointed at his neck as I kicked his dropped sword out of reach.

"Get to your feet." Percy eyed me suspiciously as he did as I commanded. His moves were slow, methodical as he stared down my blade into my eyes.

Percy took a breath, his whole body rattling with the effort. Tears formed in his eyes.

"I offer you the same deal. Go, be free of me, of all of this. Live a life to be proud of. Find happiness, Percy." Tears stung my eyes. "Please."

Tears streamed down his face as he nodded. "I am so sorry, Elora."

With that, I lowered my weapon. The broken man in front of me was no longer a threat. "Bless the go…." The words died on my tongue as Percy lunged. A pain like I had never known before–somehow both icy and searing–hit me in my abdomen. Percy retreated, tears streaming down his face. I looked down, and my eyes widened at the black dagger buried to its hilt in my stomach. To my horror, the blood oozing from the wound was not red, but the same color as the blade–black as night.

The Dragon Blade.

I drove my blade into his stomach reflexively, skewering him on the sword. I dropped the sword from my hands in horror as I watched Percy fall, blood trickling from his lips. He landed with a wet thud at my feet, eyes glued to his wound, his hands stained with our blood. I sank to my knees, seeing what I had done, realizing what he had done to me. My teeth returned to normal as my talons disappeared. But it all felt wrong, like something was being seeped from me, my power becoming unreachable no matter how much it yearned to be free.

I looked up only to see that Percy was now looking at me, his eyes glassy. "Why…I trusted you. Why?" I exclaimed.

Percy took a small breath as he looked at me. Blood trickled from the corner of his mouth. "A knight is nothing without his King."

The words died on Percy's lips as his eyes faded. He fell forward, further driving the sword to the hilt with a wet, tearing noise. He won.

Sir Percival Alderius defeated the Great Dragon of Mirador.

Chapter Twelve

PERCY'S broken body was crumpled at my feet, his brow pressed to the floor. If I ignored the bloody sword protruding from his back, I could almost pretend he was just bowing at my feet–a deep bow, one reserved for the ruler of a kingdom, usually only when the person is begging for forgiveness.

But I was no ruler, and Percy was not bowing. He never felt the need to beg for my forgiveness, for I was never the most important person in his life. He was dead. I killed him. A shuddering sob built in my throat as numbness spread through my body. I didn't even notice the pain from the poisoned blade sticking from my abdomen. I could feel the blade poisoning me, killing me. My only thought was that I wished it would work faster. I knew what happened to beasts in a story like this.

I threw my head back as I fell to my knees, trying to escape the carnage before me. No matter how hard I tried though, I could not forget the image before me–the one of the man I loved, dead at my feet, from my hands. My heartbeat echoed in my ears. I was going to be sick. I closed my eyes, begging the gods to wake me up from this nightmare.

I killed him.

I killed the boy who brought me flowers.

I killed him.

My throat felt raw as I heard a shattering noise. Someone was yelling, the room seemed to shake. Even the realization that *I* was the one making that noise was not enough to make it stop. It was like the dragon in me was begging to be heard one final time before the fire was snuffed out. Maybe the poison was finally working–first the beast would die, then the princess.

Suddenly there were hands on me, but I did not open my eyes. Not until the smell of leather and peppermint overpowered the metallic scent of blood. I opened my eyes to see tanned skin and dark hair. Dameon's dimple was nowhere to be seen as concern was written on his face. His lips were moving, but I couldn't hear him. Was it the poison that prevented me from hearing? I did not know. If so, I was glad the last face I saw was his. There were no other arms I would rather die in. I smiled, and the room was quiet. I reached my hand up and placed it on his cheek. The gore on my hands stood out stark on his skin but he did not waver as he picked me up like I weighed nothing. My eyes felt heavy and sleep called to me with a ferocity I had never before known. Dameon had always had that effect on me, even on my most sleepless nights.

"Oh shit oh fuck Elora do not close your eyes!" His voice was raw. Desperate.

I tried to open them, only because he told me to, but sleep had its hold on me, like claws dragging me into nothingness. Nothingness felt like a warm blanket just out of reach. Surely a bit of sleep would not be an issue. Maybe I would wake up and this would all be a dream, I thought. Yes, that seemed right. It had to be a dream–I hoped it was a dream. I buried my face into his neck and inhaled his scent as I wrapped my arms around his neck. I was so cozy. His steps were even and quick as we moved through the halls.

All at once, the searing pain came back like someone jarred the knife still embedded in my stomach. Opening my eyes, I saw Dameon had done just that, using the hand wrapped around me to jostle the blade. My vision went white with pain. I was fully consumed by it.

"Elora, I am so sorry but you have to stay with me. Focus on the pain, please." His voice was strained as he begged. My face felt wet and I tasted salt. I looked at Dameon's face, only to see tears falling down as his eyes looked forward. I reached up and wiped one from his cheek.

"Why are you crying?" My voice was barely more than a whisper. My throat was raw and the taste of blood filled my tattered mouth.

He looked down for a brief moment as his face softened. "Don't worry about that, Princess. We are almost there. You will be okay."

"Maybe I shouldn't be. Maybe the beast should die. It would save everyone a lot of trouble," I croaked.

Dameon's face drained of color. "You are no beast."

"I killed Percy."

I waited for Dameon to respond, but he didn't. Unease filled me. Did he not know? Was he regretting saving me? Holding a beast so close? I did not get to ponder this long before I felt Dameon kick a door open.

"Olgara! Selena! Katherine! Someone, help!" He turned to me, looking me in the eyes. His eyes reminded me of fresh tilled soil mixed with honey. They held an entire universe. "You have to stay with me, Elora," he said as he placed me on the table, laying me gently down. He had one hand under my cheek as he stroked my hair with the other. His tears were flowing, leaving tracks on his skin. I reached up, touching his cheek again. He planted his lips softly on the inside of my wrist as his eyes begged something of me.

"Am I going to die?"

"Not on my watch, Princess."

Suddenly, the door opened again and Olgara hustled in with Selena and Katherine quick at her feet.

"Oh my god, dearie. What has he done to you?" Olgara's blue eyes were worry stricken as she came to my side and eyed the hilt of the dagger embedded in me.

"I killed him," my voice was lost in a sob. Olgara looked in my eyes, but did not shy away.

"The blade is poisoned," Dameon said.

"I gathered that by the black blood, boy." Olgara turned to Katherine and rattled off a list of supplies to grab from her chambers before instructing Selena to clear the castle of everyone but them.

"You," Olgara spoke to Dameon with the authority of a general addressing her men. Dameon stood up as much as he could while keeping his hands on me, waiting for his orders. "Fetch clean cloth and boil all the water you can find." Dameon looked down at me, hesitating to leave. "Go, boy. Now!" The urgency in Olgara's voice set him in motion as he gently removed his hands from me and planted a brief kiss on my brow. I closed my eyes, inhaling the smell of him as he turned around and ran from the kitchen.

Suddenly, it was just me and my nurse—the person who raised me, stayed by me no matter what I would become. Staring into her cool blue eyes elicited a shudder from me, at what I had become.

"I'm so sorry, Olgie." A sob broke my words. "I became the beast." Olgara softened. She should know more than anyone about what I was capable of. She was the one whose mouth was cursed by the witch to speak my curse into existence. She was just a midwife aiming to help the Queen when my fate stole her life from her.

"You are no beast, dearie." She stroked my hair, easing the tension from me. I felt as though I was floating, unable to feel anything around me but her hands. "You are a brave girl, who loves wholeheartedly, and hopes even more." Her eyes shone with tears as she continued. "Unfortunately you put your trust in the wrong person today. That does not make you the beast, but him." She stood up and lifted her hand from my head. "Now, I am going to look at the wound. I need you to be as still as possible. Stare at the ceiling and do not look down."

I nodded my agreement as Olgara looked over my abdomen. She pulled scissors from her pocket and began cutting the dress, removing fabric gently from around the wound. "Shame, this was my favorite dress I made you," Olgara muttered as she worked. I stared dutifully at the ceiling, focusing on the large wooden beams that held it together. The only sound was the clanking of hundreds of crystal beads hitting the floor around us. When my midriff was completely bare, I couldn't help but glance down. Bile filled my mouth at the sight of my stomach. The blade protruded from my left side, just above my hip bone. Black blood oozed from the wound as the poison spread through the surrounding area. Trails of black extended under my skin several inches, as if the poison was leaching itself into me slowly.

"I told you not to look, dearie." Olgara sighed as she eyed the wound. "Can you access the dragon?"

"No," I said through gritted teeth. "It is like there is a wall blocking me from shifting." I could feel the dragon lashing to get out, to protect me, but nothing changed. "I had my talons out when he stabbed me and my teeth were sharpened, but they all disappeared the second the blade entered me." I looked at Olgara, concern written on her weathered face. Fear caused my stomach to drop as I realized there might be a fate worse than death waiting for me.

"Olgara…" I paused, my hoarse voice barely a whisper as tears burned my eyes. "What if I lose my magic?"

"Not on my watch," she said as Katherine and Selena both returned. Katherine had filled her skirts with supplies from Olgara's room and Selena helped her set them all on the table next to the old woman. Olgara directed Katherine on grinding herbs in the mortar and pestle as Dameon returned with a large bin of water and clean cloth. The scared looks on everyone's faces sent tears to my eyes again.

I did this. I killed Percy and now the ones I love are scared of me.

Suddenly, Dameon was at my side, "Not scared of you, just of losing you." His thumb stroked my forehead as he looked me in the eyes.

Olgara stood up, taking in everyone before her. "Elora, are you sure you cannot access the dragon?"

I hastily looked around, knowing that Selena and Katherine did not know my secret. I expected to see shock on their faces, or horror, maybe confusion. Instead, they looked as shocked as one does when remarking on the color of the sky.

"You two knew?" The shock in my voice was not lost, even with the hoarse whisper.

Selena walked towards me and grabbed my hand. "I put it together when we were sent here."

"As did I," Katherine echoed, a queer look in her eyes as she glanced at Selena. "I did not know that Selena knew, or Dameon." She paused, anger causing her pale skin to redden. "I am honestly just disappointed you never trusted us, but told him."

"She didn't tell me, I figured it out about a year after you all arrived here," Dameon said.

Shame reddened my face at the idea that my friends thought I did not trust them. That shame quickly turned to anger. "You knew all this time, all of you, and never said anything? Do you know how much pain and fear you could have assuaged in me?" The contortion of my lips sent then tattered flesh to burning as blood filled my mouth.

Selena's face contorted as she looked at me. "You are the one who never trusted *us* with the information, Elora."

"Stop bickering! We have more important things to worry about at this moment!" Olgara's yell quietened us all, as it did when we were children. "Now, we have to get the blade out and the wound closed." She looked at me before continuing. "This will be a thousand times more painful than going in. Prepare yourself, dearie." She looked at Dameon. "Grab her arms and pin them to the table. Selena, grab her legs." Katherine looked at me before darting out the kitchen and returning a moment later with a tin and a leather strap. She gently slathered the cream on my tattered lips before placing the strap in front of my mouth. I eyed her, unsure of what she was trying to do.

"Bite down on this. It will help." Her voice had lost all the edge from before. I opened my mouth, allowing her to place the leather between my teeth. When I sat my head back against the table and looked up, I saw Dameon looking down at me, his face unreadable.

"Princess," he said with a voice barely above a whisper, "no matter what happens I want you to keep your eyes on me." His voice was smooth and low, a smokiness I was not used to hearing from him. I nodded my agreement and accepted the challenge in his words. No maĖer what happened in the next few moments, no matter the pain I felt, I would keep my eyes on him, just to prove I could. I could withstand anything.

"On three," Olgara said. "One…" I braced for the pain, knowing that last time her counting was merely an illusion of timing, but it never came. I relaxed, hoping she would actually wait until three. "Two…" I took a deep breath in, preparing for the pain to come with her next words, only to feel the worst pain in my life as she removed the blade. I arched my back, thrashing against my holds as my vision became spotted. It felt like she was ripping my innards from my body.

"Look at me, Elora, look at me," Dameon's voice pleaded as he adjusted himself, sitting beside me on the table and moving my arms so he could hold both my wrists above my head with one of his hands. He used the other to stroke my cheek, wiping the tears that fell freely from my eyes. I could feel hands and pressure on the wounds, hear Olgara shouting orders at Katherine and the clanking of bottles, but I could only see Dameon's face, his brown eyes staring directly into mine.

The pain in my abdomen doubled, sending another shockwave through me as I felt something being added to the wound. My ears rang as the pain became unbearable. Dameon's full lips moved, but I couldn't hear his words. I could no longer feel the table underneath me, or the thrashing of my body. My vision went black and I sank into a void of nothingness.

* * *

THE sky stretched endlessly around me as I pumped my wings under the beaming sun. I could feel the warmth in my scales, feel the way I was *meant* to be doing this. Flying made me feel as though I could do anything, and nothing, *nothing*, felt as good as this. Soaring under the cover of darkness was amazing, but could never come close to the feeling of flying under a full sun on a spring day like this. The forest stretched endlessly underneath me, with colorful dots of the first flowers of the season poking through the sea of green. I inhaled, hoping the scent of the life spread underneath me would reach me as I soared.

But it was not life I smelled, but death.

Blood. My blood.

I looked down, only to see a massive black wound open in my abdomen, liquid ichor leaked from my body. My wings shriveled as my muscles and bones contorted painfully back to my human form as I fell from the sky. A scream built in my throat, but seemed to be stuck there, like I had lost the ability to control even my own body.

I jolted awake in my chambers, pain ripping up my side as I tried to sit up. The afternoon sun beamed through the window and onto my face and my vision turned to spots. I blinked, hoping to clear my vision. Instead, all I saw was Percy's crumpled body at my feet, like the image was imprinted into my very mind, something I would *never* be able to escape from. My body felt muted, like something was missing, or blocked.

The dragon.

Suddenly, there were hands around my shoulders, pushing me back down onto my pillows.

"Elora, you must be careful. Your stitches might pop." Selena's even tone soothed me. My eyes cleared and I could see her smooth, cool skin shining in the sun. The light hit her from the back, adding an ethereal glow to the halo of curls surrounding her face.

"You fret so much." The rawness of my throat caused my voice to crack. Selena wore a tired expression on her face as she reached to the side table next to my bed and grabbed a cup, handing it to me.

"Here, drink this. It will help." Knowing better than to go against a command from Selena, I brought the cup to my tattered lips and tried to not wince at the pain. Cool water rushed into my mouth and I drank deeply, hoping to drown the pain in my soul, but settling for the relief of the stinging in my throat. I drained the cup in fervent gulps before handing the vessel back to her.

"How long have I been out?" I asked.

"Less than an hour." The familiar lilt of Olgara's voice caused me to turn my head as the old woman walked towards the bed from the sitting area. She sat on the corner of the bed, taking care to not jostle me, as she placed a hand over my own.

I thought back to the last thing I remembered, to Dameon's worried eyes and lips pleading with me to hang on, to stay awake. I looked around the room, expecting to see him and Katherine, to no avail.

"You're a tough girl, dearie. Better you passed out when you did. The stitches would have been worse than the stabbing." Olgara's voice was low, but distant. I removed my hand from under hers and lifted the clean shirt I was wearing, wondering when and *who* got me into this. The wound was covered in wrappings, but I could still see the trail of ichor extending under my skin–spreading throughout my body. I met Olgara's eyes, noting the shame in them.

I wasn't healed.

"The blade wasn't regular poison, dearie. It was magic, some of the strongest I have ever seen. I did as much as I could, but I could not remove the taint it left on you."

My heart rate increased, panic rose in me. "What…what does this mean? Am I going to die?" I paused, my voice falling to a whisper. "Have I lost the dragon forever?" My skin prickled at the idea of being stuck in this form with no reprieve for the rest of my life.

Olgara and Selena shared a knowing look, seeming to have a silent conversation right in front of me.

"What are you two not telling me?" I asked.

Olgara sighed, her small shoulders sunk down with the effort, making her look utterly defeated. The sight sent fear tingling down my spine. I had never seen Olgara defeated before.

"The poison is spreading. The further it spreads, the more damage it causes–permanent damage. If the poison spreads to your heart, it will become lethal," Olgara said. Her eyes were glassy.

"For the dragon?"

"For you. You and the dragon are not two separate entities, Elora. You must stop thinking of it as so. Your ability to shift is as integral to who you are as your mind is. You are the dragon and the dragon is the princess. If that poison makes it to your heart, then there is nothing more that can be done."

"How long?" My voice was hollow as I fixed my eye on the wall, refusing to look at Selena or Olgara in the moment.

"Three days? Maybe four. I cannot be sure." Olgara's voice cracked, as if the words alone nearly brought her to tears. In my twenty-one years of life, I had never seen Olgara cry. I could not even fathom the possibility until this moment.

"What can be done?" My voice was low, but the desperation was present. How strange that I begged for death a mere hour ago only to now be shocked that the Unseen, the god of death answered my call. I chuckled dryly. Clearly I was not as brave as I once thought.

"I have done all I can for you. There is only one person in the entire kingdom who I know is strong enough to remove this blight on you." Olgara paused, placing a wrinkled finger under my chin and pulled my face towards hers until our eyes met. The steely blue was extra bright, as tears shone through. Her jaw was set with determination. "You must seek out the witch who cursed you."

Chapter Thirteen

OLGARA'S words hit me like a thrown stone. I could feel my mouth moving, but no words were coming out. I was left there gaping like a fish plucked from water as Olgara and Selena exchanged a worried look. The thought of seeking the person who cursed me, who made me a beast, made my blood turn to ice.

Suddenly, the chamber door swung open and Dameon and Katherine came in. As soon as I locked eyes with Katherine, she ran towards me, throwing her arms around me. "Thank the gods you are finally awake," she whispered. Her care and candor shocked me, she was never the one to drop niceties, usually biting comments. I hugged her back, squeezing her willowy frame as much as I dared in my condition. Looking over her shoulder, I saw that Dameon had stopped a few feet back, a sheepish look on his face, like he was concerned he should not be here. I locked eyes with him and offered a soft smile. To my relief, it seemed to calm him.

"Good gods, stop squeezing her before you pop a stitch I worked so hard on." Olgara's rough voice caused Katherine to finally break our embrace. Katherine locked eyes with me before looking over her shoulders at Olgara.

"Have you told her?" Her voice was soft to the old woman, like what she was saying was a most guarded secret.

"You do realize I can hear you. The poison has not reached my ears." My attempt at a joke earned a cold look from the women in the room, but I couldn't help but notice Dameon's smirk, his dimple fully on display.

"I will take that as a yes." Katherine's retort was drowned in her usual sarcasm. I smiled at the small amount of normalcy in the moment.

"Your plan won't work." I looked Olgara in the eyes and set my jaw.

Olgara rolled her eyes at me, the action making her look younger than I have ever known her to be. "And why do you say that, dearie? Please, enlighten me." The level of sarcasm in her tone rivaled even Katherine.

"Well for one, no one knows where she is. Remind me, but didn't my parents send knights scouring the *entire* kingdom after the curse? How am I supposed to do what they couldn't in only three days?" I asked.

Olgara sighed and looked to the ceiling before turning back to me. "You're right, Elora. Most of the knights did not return and those that did had no information on how to find the witch." Olgara paused. "Except for one." Her face fell. "Though he did not return whole."

My jaw fell open at her words. I had never known any of the knights returned from their journey. "What happened to him?"

"He committed a grave transgression, one almost unforgivable and he paid dearly for it." She paused, looking me in the eyes. Gone were the tears that shone in them a few moments ago. Now they were back to the steely blue I was used to. "He tried to find those who wished to never be found again."

"What did he see?" My voice was low, fear creeping in.

"He went into the forest north of here. He passed a great lake rimmed with cliffs on three sides about a day's journey away. Two days north of there, he found a stone with strange markings on it. Said he could feel the magic in the air before the witch attacked. He barely made it back to Vinguarri with his life to tell the King and Queen."

I was stunned. "Where is he? Perhaps he can lead me to her?"

Olgara laughed darkly. "The man did not survive the night. He died from his wounds and the magic coursing through his veins."

"The forest is a lawless place. How do you expect Elora to get there?" Dameon's voice was rimmed with annoyance. My blood boiled. How could he have such little faith in me?

"Do you think I cannot do it? That I am not strong enough? How do you even know anything about the deep forest?"

Dameon scoffed as he walked towards the bed and looked down at me. Long gone was the lanky boy I met a decade ago. From this angle, he looked unnaturally tall as he stood well above the women in the room, broad shoulders taking up more space than I ever realized. "Because I am the one who patrols these woods. Why do you think I leave so often?" Heat creeped across my face at this. Dameon softened minutely as he looked down at me. "Also may I remind you that you were stabbed less than two hours ago and can no longer shift? You won't be able to defend yourself."

"She has no other choice." Selena bit out her words, shocking us all. "It is either she tries to find the witch or she dies. Are you forgetting that?" She extended her finger in Dameon's face. I chuckled–she barely reached his chest.

I turned back to Olgara. "Even if I were to find the stone and make it there, why do you think the witch won't attack me as she did the knight? Why am I any different?"

Olgara took a deep breath before speaking, her tone much softer than before, almost wistful. "I think the witch will be willing to speak with you. She has been in hiding for so many years. Maybe she will see you coming to her to be saved as an olive branch, a way for her to regain her freedom."

I let out a laugh devoid of joy. "And what if she doesn't? What if she just ends what she started all those years ago? You could be sending me to my death." A pig to slaughter, just as my brother sent Percy to me.

Olgara patted my shoulder. "You will die whether she chooses to end you or this poison does. I see no shame in hoping."

"Hope is what nearly killed me. It is what killed Percy," I called out.

"No, that was the result of putting your hope in the wrong person." Dameon's voice was edged with a sadness I could not place.

I lay back on the pillows, staring at the ceiling of my chamber. I felt robbed of choice in this scenario. Lying here and waiting to die was not an option, even if it was what I begged for just hours ago. No, I could not let Elrick win like that. Be it for spite alone, I knew what I had to do. I sat up as quickly as I could, setting my jaw before meeting Olgara's gaze. "Fine. I will go."

Dameon spoke up. "Not alone, you will not. If you are doing this, I am going with you."

"That isn't necessary, Dameon. I can take care of myself!"

Dameon threw his hands in the air, anger shone on his face. "We get it, Princess. You are so strong and think you should do everything on your own. Need I remind you that you were stabbed! There is a magic poison running through your veins. You cannot do this alone and whether you like it or not, I am going with you."

"As am I." We all turned to look at Selena, everyone's jaw hanging open at her words. She looked at me sheepishly. "You will not be doing this without me."

"It is decided then. Katherine will stay with me and we will cover for you while you are gone. Two hours should be enough time to prepare. You will leave then." Olgara's words had a sense of finality to them, one that none of us would be brave enough to question.

"I will go down to town and say you are too ill for anyone to come to the castle. That should buy you the time you need for the journey and explain the supplies I will be gathering for you." Katherine dusted off her dress before moving towards the door, walking out without another word.

Suddenly, everyone left the chamber, leaving me alone as they prepped. I did my best to get out of bed and walk over to the window overlooking my beloved Greydenn. As I gazed at the rolling green hills and cottages, I hoped that I would see them again.

But after today's events, I knew hope was a dangerous thing.

* * *

I was not able to ponder my fate for long. Selena returned quickly with an arm full of supplies, followed by Katherine with her own load. I was precariously trying to put on my breeches without causing excruciating pain to rip up my side when they found me.

I was failing miserably.

"Stop moving so much and just ask for help," Katherine said as she rushed over, grabbing the breeches and helping me pull them up. Shame reddened my face to be rendered so incompetent.

"I am so sorry you have to do this," I said.

Katherine pulled the breeches the rest of the way up before moving on to my undershirt, carefully placing it over my arms and pulling it down before lacing the breeches. "Don't be. I am sure if the roles were reversed, you would be doing the same." A soft smile softened her usually sharp features. Her freckles seemed more prominent than ever under the light, like a constellation spread across her face.

I was lost in Katherine's face when Selena handed me a brown piece of leather and I took it quizzically. I unrolled it, revealing a leather corset. I examined the garment closely–I had only seen guards wear them. Leather laces went down the front and the back. The leather panels were overlapping and supple. Minor scuffs dotted the leather. Clearly someone had gotten their use of this.

"Olgara said we might need these for protection. It will also help to keep pressure on your wound. Should stop any bleeding,"she said.

"Thank you. I hope I look half as good as you in it." I sent her a wink, trying to relieve the tension in the room. She looked every bit the warrior princess in her leathers. Her curly black hair was braided down to her scalp and collected in a bun at the base of her neck, adding to her regality. My own hair was still free flowing, the tresses falling down my back unbound. I had tried to braid it earlier while I waited, but raising my left arm caused the stitches to feel as though they would burst.

"I suppose we should do something about my hair," I said sheepishly. "I tried to do it on my own earlier, but I couldn't raise my hand to get the back."

Selena smiled. "Good thing I have always been better at this than you." Selena guided me to a seat as her nimble hands began to work. Within minutes, my hair was neatly braided back and around my head in a crown.

"There, perfect for a princess." Her words stung, but her smile was so light that I could not help but reflect it back to her.

The bells of the clock tower ended our moment, making all in the room more aware of what was to come. With each stroke, I inched closer to an uncertain future.

"Olgara should be here any moment with the rest of the supplies," Katherine said as she handed Selena and I both a rucksack. I opened my bag to examine the contents. There was some food, a jar of tea leaves, and a small container of a balm.

"For the pain at night. It will help you sleep," Katherine said as she gestured to the leaves. "The balm is for your lips."

"Did Olgara make it?"

"No," Katherine blushed. "I did."

I reached forward, grabbing her hand in my own. "Then I know it will be excellent." I paused before grabbing Selena's hand as well. The realization that this might be the last moment I spend with both of my friends sent the room spinning. I did not want the last words any of us speak to each other to be anger, not when my days may well be numbered. "I'm sorry I never told you. It wasn't because I did not trust either of you." I took a deep breath, my voice shaky. "I was…I was just afraid to lose you."

Selena squeezed my hand, her soft smile reassuring me. "I understand, Elora. I am sorry for not letting you know there was no secret to keep." She turned to Katherine, "And I am sorry that I did not tell you. I should have trusted you more."

"Yes, you should have." Katherine's words earned a look from me that quickly had her backtracking. "And I guess I could have told you I knew. I should have trusted you as well."

"Friends?" I said sheepishly.

Katherine laughed, a joyous sound. "For–"

Suddenly, the door to my chamber opened and Olgara walked in, a large bag on her shoulder. Her entrance halted Katherine's words as we all turned to her, awaiting her orders as Olgara, bent under the weight, looked up at us.

"Is no one going to help an old woman?"

I moved forward, rushing to her aid. When I reached her side, she moved her bag out of my reach. I looked down, questioning why she didn't want my help, my thoughts going to dark places when she gave me a look that could melt the iciest lake. "Preferably someone without a stab wound."

Heat crept up my skin, followed closely by shame. Olgara would never turn on me when she was the one person who knew me for all I was, all I was prophesied to be, and never shied away. Katherine and Selena quickly took my place and took the burden from the old woman. The weight of the bag was almost too much for them both to bear together. They slumped under the weight, their faces clearly strained.

"Much better." Olgara squared her shoulders and stretched her back, her bones creaking under the effort as she let out a sigh. "Okay, off we go." Olgara opened up the secret passage behind the painting of Greydenn, revealing a narrow staircase built into the fake wall.

"Now that is a surprise," Selena said with a shocked face.

"Why are we going to the cave?" I asked Olgara.

"Cave?" exclaimed Katherine.

"Well you can't exactly waltz out of the castle onto a secret mission, now can you dearie." Olgara threw a wink at me. "Okay girls, follow me." She stepped into the passage, quickly disappearing down the narrow stairs.

I followed behind her as Selena and Katherine, impeded by whatever was in the bag, followed behind me.

"Now architecture has never been my passion, but isn't there a wall here?" Katherine eyed the corridor as she spoke, questions written on her face. I turned back around before she could see me laugh. Strange as it might be, it felt good to have something still be a secret, something I knew to shock them.

"The passage is built into a false wall of the castle that leads straight into the rock of the mountain." As I spoke we entered the winding corridor, the temperature instantly cooling as the air became damp. "Watch your step, it can get a bit slippery down here. We will arrive at the cave shortly."

"Why was this built? When?" Selena sounded wonderstruck.

"My father had it carved out sometime after I first changed before he sent me here. It is supposed to be a way to conceal my secret and act as a way for me to sneak back into the castle." Suddenly, the dark, musty smell was blown away as light shone through dimly. The smell of summer drifted in on the breeze as we walked out to the caldera.

"It is beautiful." Selena's voice was strained, but I could tell she meant her words. Pride beamed in me. This is one place that always felt like home, even if it was designed to be my prison.

"Okay, dearies. Drop the bag there." Olgara vaguely pointed to an area near the front of the cave. I walked towards the edge, the several hundred feet fall looking completely different to me now. To think I usually ran and jumped from this edge and free fell before I shifted. I longed for who I used to be. I was unsure if I would ever be that carefree, feel that safe again.

Katherine joined me at the edge, carefully looking down before taking a massive step back. "How do you expect them to get down from here? Elora can't exactly fly right now." Katherine grunted as Selena elbowed her.

Her words stung, but I made sure to not grimace where she could see. I know she did not mean to be callous.

Olgara sighed, giving Katherine a withering look. "No, she cannot. But luckily, I think of everything. Open the bag." Selena moved forward, revealing the contents of the bag—an ancient looking rope ladder.

I turned to Olgara. "Can you please explain to me why you have a rope ladder?"

Olgara beamed with pride as she looked up at me. "You can never be too prepared, dearie. I wove loops in the end just in case we ever needed to make a quick get away from the cave."

I threw her an incredulous look, making Olgara laugh. "A dragon was my ward. I wanted to have a backup plan for escape."

"From me?"

Olgara softened. "No, dearie. From the town or anyone who aimed to hurt you."

I smiled, looking down at my former nanny. She really did think of everything.

"Ladies, secure the end of the rope to those hooks," Olgara said as she motioned to the curved metal hooks embedded deep in the metal that faced inward. "There are loops in the rope at the end. Fasten them here." Selena and Katherine hustled to do the work as I looked on, wishing I could have helped them. Within moments, they were done and after coaxing to the edge, Katherine threw the other end down. The wooden rungs of the ladder hit the rock wall one by one on the way down and seemed to go on forever. When the noise stopped, Olgara turned to Selena.

"Dameon will meet you with the horses on the path just past the thicket blocking the cliff from view. You will go first, Selena." Olgara reached into her pocket and pulled out a pouch of white powder. "For your hands on the way down. It will keep them from dampening." She handed the pouch to Selena before wrapping her arms around her. Selena hugged her back, thanking her before saying her goodbyes to Katherine as well.

Within moments, she was at the edge. She rubbed the powder on her hands as she looked at me.

"See you at the bottom," she said with a nod. With a bravery I had never before seen, Selena took the rope in her hands and descended down.

"We will give her a few minutes to get to the boĖom before you go down, Elora. That way the rope does not have an unnecessary sway for either of you."

I nodded my agreement and waited for what felt like hours and mere moments all at once. Before I was ready, Olgara nodded to me before handing me my own pouch of powder. Olgara hugged me and I rested my cheek on her head. "Be careful, dearie."

I squeezed, causing the old woman to huff and pain to rip up my side. I did not care though, for if this was the last time I was able to hold the woman who raised me, I was going to make it count. "I will do my best," I said as I let go.

I moved to Katherine to say my goodbyes. We hugged deeply, her long arms feeling like home.

"Take care of Selena. And yourself," she said as we parted.

"Thank you, for everything, Katherine. We will see you soon."

I parted ways and walked to the edge, rubbing the powder on my hands. I grabbed the rope, easing my way over the edge until my foot hit one of the wooden rungs. The ladder swayed slightly and my stomach dropped. I refused to show weakness, setting my teeth as I began my descent down.

By the time I was halfway down, my muscles burned and my hands had been rubbed raw from my grip. Each time I extended my left arm, the stitches dug into my skin. I felt as though I was slowly being torn apart. Looking down, I still had several more minutes of this and as the wind whipped around me, the ladder swayed under my weight. Long gone was the girl who would free fall nearly the entire height. As I slowly worked my way down, I promised myself to be a careful woman for all of my days, be that for years or until the poison took my life.

Looking down, I was able to make out Selena in the distance watching me intently. After a few more minutes of scaling, I looked up to see my blood was now on each rung I touched. Thankfully, though, this blood was bright crimson and untainted. I still had about thirty feet left to the bottom of the cliff, and my heart sank.

There was only fifteen more feet of ladder. I would have to jump the last several feet.

"It will be okay, Elora! I am here to help!" Selena called out to me.

Before I was ready, my feet hit the bottom rung. Looking down, the few feet I had to fall seemed much further than I knew it was. How could someone who loved flying now be afraid of falling? How could someone who begged for death mere hours ago now be running full force away from it? My mind reeled, but I had an idea. If I was able to get my hands around the bottom rung and dangle, the fall might not be as bad. To do so, though, I would have to fully extend both arms, my weight fully held by my tattered hands. I weighed the options in my head and felt that if my wound opened, I could be restitched, a painful process I am sure, but breaking an ankle or a leg would make my mission impossible.

I reached down, making sure my hands were fully around the rungs before taking one foot off, then the next, bracing them on the rock wall until I was fully extended. The pain in my hands was unrecognizable compared to the wound in my side. I could feel it tearing, knowing there would be hell to pay. When I could bear it no longer I closed my eyes and let go, sending a silent prayer to the gods as I fell. After what felt like a lifetime, I landed on my feet, knees bent to lessen the impact. I felt a shock wave go through my ankles and up my spine as my feet landed in what sounded like broken pottery. I opened my eyes and stepped towards Selena as my foot hit something that crunched under my weight. I looked down, expecting to see long discarded vases of some kind based on the sound. What I saw stopped me in my tracks–sun-bleached bones. Human.

Selena grabbed my hand, pulling me from the de facto graveyard as I noticed dozens of skulls, rib cages, some with tattered clothing still on them, scattered about. "What happened here?" Her voice was soft, like she did not want to disturb their peace.

"When my father built the place, he had the masons and architects killed so as to not dispel the secret." I paused, tears shining in my eyes. "I thought it was merely a rumor. It looks like he did have them pushed over the edge after all." These people died for me–because I was an insolent child who refused to not embrace the dragon. Anger and pain crept into my heart. I had never felt more like a beast than I did at that moment.

"Come on, Elora. We do not have time to waste." Selena's voice was distant, coaxing. I sent a silent prayer up to the gods and promised myself that if I made it back alive, I would bury these men and thank them for their sacrifice. Though in my heart, I knew it would never be enough. My choices ended the lives of these men, just as I had ended Percy. Their blood stained my soul.

Chapter Fourteen

THE sunlight danced through the treetops. Selena moved through the thick brush ahead of me. Brambles grabbed at our clothing, ripping tiny scratches into our skin. After a few minutes, the thicket cleared and we arrived at a path in the woods. Dameon stood there with three horses, saddled and ready to go. I faltered at the sight of him. He was standing in a beam of sunlight, back to the horses with his eyes closed, face towards the sky. His brown skin glowed in the afternoon light. A smile crept across his full lips as the solid black horse behind him nuzzled his shoulder. I recognized it as his favorite horse, one we both played with as a foal. Poppy stood taller than any other horse in the barn, her long and lean frame perfect for speed. This was the horse Dameon was able to race the dragon on. As we walked forward, the horses looked towards us, nickering softly at our approach. A red gelding with a white star on his head reached towards my hand before nipping at me gently, angry to find it without a treat.

"I see you survived your descent," Dameon said without moving. His eyes were still closed as he drank in the light.

"Mostly," I said as I looked down at my tattered hands. Selena had checked my wound moments before to find it mostly intact, only a small amount of the tainted blood had leaked out.

"Now the real fun begins." Dameon opened his eyes and turned to fully face us. He was wearing a cloak over his light leathers. He stood up straight to his full height and his face neutralized. He looked every bit the soldier. "We will have a hard journey. The woods here are not forgiving." Dameon grabbed cloaks from his saddle, giving one to Selena and me. "Put these on. It will be warm, but wear the hood."

"Why must we wear the hoods? It is summer." Selena said with disdain.

"Because I do not want the vermin in these woods to see that there are two women in the group. Which reminds me, Percy taught you both to fight, yes?" Dameon spit out his name like it was rancid meat, but even hearing him speak of the man I loved made my blood run cold.

"Some. Mainly long swords," I said.

"Perfect," Dameon handed us both sheathed daggers on leather straps. "There are long swords sheathed on your saddles. Strap these daggers to your thighs just in case." He motioned to his own leg, which wore the same contraption. Across his chest there were six daggers strapped to leather. He looked every bit the trained killer. Dameon passed us the dagger straps and we hastily attached them. I fumbled with the straps, my tattered hands unable to get a grip on the leather.

"Now, Elora, I know you are comfortable on a horse, but Selena? Is there anything you do not know?"

"Besides how you know that Elora is confident when riding?" she said with a knowing look.

Dameon laughed, softening his features. "Why do you think I was caught with two horses all those times and not one?"

I smiled as I remembered all those midnight rides with Dameon. I was able to feel a freedom with him that I had only ever felt when I was the dragon. He made me feel safe to be myself, like nothing could hold me back.

"I have only ridden sparingly, but I am a quick learner," Selena said with confidence.

"Perfect. We will ride hard today to get as many miles as we can before sundown, which will be in about 4 hours. If we ride hard, we can reach the lake. Selena, you will take Squid, he will be the easiest on you," Dameon said as he pointed to the grey gelding on the other side of Poppy. I recognized him as a steady animal that I knew would take care of Selena while still being able to keep up with Poppy, even if he was much shorter than the other two horses. Selena nodded and headed to him.

"Elora, I wanted you to ride a smoother horse, but I knew you would be cross if I did not bring Oak." I smiled as the red gelding nudged my back, softly nipping at my clothes. Oak had always been my favorite with his long legs and abrasive personality. He was an ugly young thing when I first arrived, all awkward limbs, but now he had grown into himself. I turned around and placed a hand under Oak's chin while using the other to stroke over his dark eyes slowly.

"You would be right." Oak softly nickered and a smile spread across my lips.

"Let's get going then." Dameon walked over to Selena, and offered her assistance to mount her horse. Her bewildered face as she adjusted herself in the saddle while gathering the reins in her hands made me giggle. Within moments though, she looked as if she was born in a saddle and Dameon made his way over to me. I looked up at him, his face neutral as he bent down, offering me a hand as well.

I put my foot in his hands as I grabbed the mane and reins in one hand, jumping onto Oak's back. I reached down and stroked Oak's neck, sending a silent thanks to him that he stood still, when I heard Dameon's low chuckle. The sound sent shivers down my spine as I looked over, seeing him beaming up at me. I felt his large hand on my thigh as he adjusted the dagger strap. When our eyes met, his face changed, falling back into the mask of neutrality.

Dameon cleared his throat as he walked back to Poppy, quickly mounting her, before he turned to face Selena and me.

"We need to warm the horses up. We will trot them for a bit before we canter. I want as much distance between us and Greydenn by nightfall as possible."

"Do you really think we can make it to the lake by nightfall? Olgara said it is a day's journey," Selena asked.

"Only one way to find out." Dameon kicked Poppy, and she trotted off. Selena looked at me before squeezing her legs, signaling to her mount that it was time to go. Oak shook his head as I signaled him to follow the horses ahead.

*　　*　　*

THE sun was barely visible by the end of the third hour. The path we started on had long since narrowed to barely noticeable in the dense brush. Dameon rode ahead, his back straight as he scanned the surrounding forest. The forest looked so different on the ground than it looked from the sky–I had long lost my bearings on where we were. Oak was damp with sweat and my thighs burned from exhaustion. Every step he took sent a ripple of pain up my left side as we trotted along. I was grateful for the physical pain–it offered me a reprieve from the mental anguish of what I had done. I moved forward to stroke Oak's neck, biting through the pain as the salty sweat burned my tattered hands. I was covered in dust from head to foot from the trek. Selena had fallen behind me a short while before. As I turned around to check on her, I saw an equal look of misery on her face. I nodded to her before turning around as Oak had begun to slow.

Looking forward, I saw why–the sun was completely obscured now by the forest behind us. Ahead, the crystal blue waters of my lake shimmered with the dying light as the alabaster cliffs glowed like the moon. Dameon stopped at the edge of the clearing, seeming to take in the image before him. Oak closed the distance between us quickly, leaving me beside Dameon. As we came to their side, Dameon's horse turned around and nipped at Oak causing him to sidestep from the mare's reach. Dameon laughed as he stroked Poppy's black neck, locking eyes with me as he did so. His brown eyes were piercing and held me in their gaze. I sucked in a breath. So much happened today between us. The vulnerability of it was striking. His mouth began to open when Selena's voice jarred us apart.

"It is beautiful," she said in a wispy voice from my side. I turned around, slightly startled as I did not hear her approach.

"It is my favorite place in the world," I said looking forward. Peace filled me and for the first time in hours, I felt like

I could take a breath. The cool mountain air soothed me, calming my heart.

"You've been here before?" Selena said, raising her eyebrows.

"I would come here almost every night as the dragon. Flying is much faster than horses," I said with a sad smile.

Dameon cleared his throat, ushering Poppy forward into the clearing as he did so. "Let's set up camp before the sun goes down."

We walked to the edge of the lake. Dameon dismounted gracefully and moved like he felt as good as he did when we left, seemingly completely unaffected by the journey. He was covered in significantly less dirt than should be possible as his skin glistened with sweat. He walked up to Selena and her mount, briefly speaking to her in such a low tone I couldn't hear before placing his hands on her hips and helping her off. The stiffness to her movements and the grimace as she hit the ground made me feel better, as clearly I was not the only one who found the journey difficult. Dameon quickly removed his hands before handing her the reins of both horses and walking towards me, petting Oak and allowing him to nuzzle on the way.

"Do you need help off?" he asked.

I reddened, suddenly embarrassed by the fact I knew I would need his help. I jutted my chin out and set my jaw. "What makes you think I do? We both know I am an accomplished rider," I said with a sense of pride, hoping it was enough to throw him off.

Dameon smiled, before throwing his hands in the air in defeat. "Oh I am fully aware. I just thought maybe you were stiff from the ride. That plus the stab wound would make anyone need assistance, but not you, Elora. Of course you are better than us all, Princess." He laughed as he spoke, softening his words, but they still hit. Dameon turned around, leaving me on my own.

"Wait," I whispered. Dameon turned around and looked at me again. "I need help," I said.

"What was that, Princess? I couldn't hear you." Dameon cupped his hand to his ear as he spoke.

I gritted my teeth, knowing I had been caught. "I said I needed help, Dameon." I felt uÈerly weak. I despised needing his help.

Dameon smiled as he strutted back to my side, placing his hands on my hips. He stroked his thumb over my hip as he looked into my eyes. "My pleasure," he said. I placed my hands on his shoulders, bracing myself as he lifted me from the saddle and placed me on the ground, the whole time never taking his eyes from my own. We stood there for a second, my hands still on his shoulders and his hands on my hips, only inches between us. He was so much taller than me–the effort of lifting my arms to this height stretched my wound, but for once today I did not mind.

"We should get camp setup," he whispered. I nodded, removing my hands from his shoulders and placing them back at my side. A heartbeat later he removed his hands from my hip. He walked over towards Poppy and I breathed out the breath I didn't know I was holding when I grabbed Oak's reins. He was happily munching on the green grass, but followed me easily to the edge of the lake. We all stood there for a moment as our horses drank greedily from the crystal clear waters.

After a few minutes, Dameon and Selena had set up camp while I held the horses. Selena walked back over to me as Dameon continued his work methodically. He untacked the horses and placed the damp blankets on the rocks to dry in the waning light before leading them to a rope he had strung up between two trees. The horses followed him calmly without a lead or a hand.

After the horses were tended, he finally returned to us, bow in hand. "I am going to go and see if I can find us some meat in the forest. I will be back within the hour," he said as he looked at us both before he headed into the woods without another word.

I crawled onto my favorite rock and closed my eyes. It was still warm from the waning light and if I tried hard enough, I could pretend it was any other visit to the lake, and that I flew there and would soon return to Mirador and the life I had known. And that Percy's blood did not stain my soul. A small hand grabbing my own was the gentle reminder that I needed that my life would never be the same. Selena lay beside me, our shoulders just barely touching.

"This was my favorite place to fly to," I said.

"It is a beautiful place," Selena said as she squeezed my hand. "Is this what you did when you came here all those times? Lay on the rocks?"

I laughed. "Somewhat. But usually I swam in the water first," I said wistfully while sitting up to look at her. The dying light shone on her dark features. She opened her eyes like she could sense my gaze, her golden brown eyes staring into my soul.

"I can't imagine a dragon swimming," Selena said with a melodic laugh.

"I wasn't always a dragon. I would turn back and forth. Usually if I was in the water though I was Elora," I said while motioning to myself. "The water is always cool no matter how hot it is. It would clear my head when I needed it." I looked over the expanse of the lake, the small ripples seeming to dance with fire as they caught the light of the dying sun. As I looked out, I wondered if I would ever feel the water's icy grip again–feel cleansed by it. The idea of this being the last time I saw my lake set my eyes to stinging.

Suddenly, Selena stood up and jumped off the rock, untying her corset as she made it to the edge of the water. She took off her boots and walked in, the cold water causing a yelp to escape her full lips. She reached up and unwound her bun, releasing the small braids gathered at the nape of her neck.

"What are you doing?" I asked with a laugh as I watched my friend undress. Selena threw a smile back at me before beckoning me to join her. She expertly tossed her discarded clothing on the bank and away from the reach of the water.

"I don't know about you, Elora, but I am disgusting and feel a quick dip would raise my spirits." As she spoke, I made my way off the rock, inching closer to the water like some unnamed force was drawing me towards it, towards Selena. By the time I made it to the edge of the lake Selena was left only in her undergarments as she walked into the water.

"What about my wound?" I said as I began to undress, knowing already that no matter the answer, I was swimming in this lake again. If the plan did not work and I died, not taking this moment to be happy would be one of my greatest regrets.

"It would be good for it to have a moment of breathing and to clean it after our journey today," Selena said before she ducked her head under water, coming back up with a yell. She shook her head and water droplets flew from the loose braids at her neck.

Her words unleashed me. Before I knew it, I was left only in my undergarments as well as I ran into the lake. The icy slap of the water made me flinch, but not in a painful way. I felt alive, free, like I only ever had before when flying. I dove in the water, letting the dust and debris wash off of me. The water did more than cleanse my body, it cleansed my very soul. The tension in my muscles and the agony I had felt seemed to wash away, like the events of today, nay the last several months–were all a distant memory. Nothing could hurt me in my lake.

The lake seemed to bring out the long-lost girlhood in Selena and me. One moment we were seeing who could hold their breath the longest, the next we were racing to see who swam the fastest. Splashing each other caused an explosion of giggles and the only way I could have been more filled with more joy was if Katherine were with us. There was freedom in the water, the words left unspoken between us did not ring in my ears. I could pretend I wasn't a beast, but just a girl. We existed as we always had–together.

We were floating on our backs, hand in hand when Dameon's deep laugh shocked us back upright. I looked over to see him standing on the bank of the lake, two rabbits in his hand as a boyish grin lit up his face. The sun had long since set, leaving only the light of the moon.

"You two will freeze," he yelled at us.

I rolled my eyes. Dameon was always a baby about cold water, even as a child. "It is not that cold, Dameon."

"Oh I am not talking about the water," he said. "Stay in until I build a fire." He walked over to camp and placed wood in an intricate design. I watched him as he struck stone and flint until small flames ignited the kindling. The fire lit a pain in my heart. He walked over moments later and grabbed our discarded clothes.

"Hey, don't take those!" I yelled. I looked over to see Selena equally as shocked and confused as me. Dameon began to shake out our tops and I swam to the shallow section I could stand in, ready to run and get them back. The water hit my hips before I looked down and saw how exposed I was. The undergarments were thin and left little to the imagination when wet. I shrunk down until the water hit my collarbone while scowling at Dameon.

"Don't worry princess, nothing nefarious planned here," he said with a grin. "I am just shaking out the dust and hanging them over the fire so you both have something warm to wear." He proceeded to do just as he said he would and did his best to clean our clothes before prepping the rabbits to cook. Once everything was set, he walked to the other end of the fire, facing the forest.

"You both should get out now. Take off your undergarments and put on the dry clothes and your cloaks. If you hang them over the fire they should dry by morning. Yell when you are decent."

"I will have to inspect Elora's wound," Selena warned.

"And I will just pretend this tree is the most interesting thing I have ever seen." Dameon's voice dripped with sarcasm. I nodded to Selena, knowing we could trust Dameon's word.

There wasn't enough time to explain to her how I knew he would be honorable, but she nodded back in understanding.

Selena and I sulked out of the water, the cold night air sending shivers down my spine. It was strange to be completely naked in the company of others, but I knew Dameon would be true to his word. As we shed our soaking garments, Selena inspected the wound and seemed satisfied with the way it looked. Neither of us mentioned, thankfully, the obvious spread of the poison under my skin. Within moments we were both dressed and our garments were left to dry.

"We are decent now," I said.

"Perfect," Dameon said as he turned around with a roguish look. Before I had time to process, Dameon had his shirt off, revealing tan muscles and a broad chest as he moved to take off his trousers.

"What are you doing?" I asked. I tried to avert my eyes, but I couldn't.

"It's my turn, of course." Dameon grinned as he ran to the water. Even in the dim light, the muscles of his back were visible. I blushed as I realized the lankish boy I grew up with had long gone. He turned around to face us as he reached for the waistband of his undergarments.

"You best turn around now ladies," he said. Even in the dim light I could hear the wink in his voice and feel his eyes on me, daring me to look away.

"Not like we would see much," I said.

"Whatever helps you sleep at night, Princess." Dameon pulled his undergarment down and I averted my eyes before I could see anything. I heard splashing as he ran into the water, and a shout of glee came from his lips. When I looked back over, I saw only ripples from where he had gone under the surface. He surfaced moments later, standing so the water hit him just at his hips as he shook out his dark hair. Water droplets flung from his black hair as water dripped down his muscular frame. He looked like some ancient god as the water beaded off his tan skin.

Selena elbowed my good side softly while she motioned to her mouth. "Careful, the drool," she whispered. I blushed as I threw her an indecent gesture, causing her to howl with laughter.

"I'm not drooling," I said.

"No, just staring." Selena's words dripped with laughter. Her skin glowed in the firelight as she eyed me like a predator, like she could see all my innermost secrets. "Not my type, but I understand."

My feelings for Dameon had always been complicated. As a child, I was hopelessly in love with him at moments, and then couldn't stand him at others. But any time I couldn't sleep, or I just wanted to forget all of who I was and be free, it was always him I sought out. As we grew, the feelings shifted. He was my best friend at times, even when he knew how to push all my buttons. After all, he was the first person in my life who wasn't mandated to care about me.

"He's insufferable," I said.

"Whatever helps you sleep at night, Princess," Selena said mockingly. A wicked smile spread across her lips in the firelight.

*   *   *

SELENA'S rhythmic snoring made me envious. Each breath was a punch to the gut–a reminder of what I longed for. Why, after all that happened, did sleep escape me still? I was exhausted, both mentally and physically, but the sweet release of sleep seemed a distant memory. No matter how hard I tried, my mind seemed to focus on one image, like the gods were punishing me for my transgressions: the sight of Percy kneeling at my feet with my blade sticking through him. The few moments of sleep I had gotten tonight were fleeting and ended with nightmares somehow even worse than the truth.

My body felt jittery, even in exhaustion. Looking over, I saw that Dameon was nowhere to be found. Deciding he had most likely gone to relieve himself, I got up, aching for a distraction. My feet carried me to the horses seemingly on their own volition. I found the three of them munching on the lush grass. As I approached, Oak lifted his head, knickering softly. I went straight to him, stroking his head as he nipped at my palm, once again angered to find me coming to him without a treat.

"Spoiled boy," I whispered.

"Well, you are the one who spoiled him." I jumped at the unexpected response and squinted my eyes in the low light to pinpoint his location. Dameon laughed and I was able to figure out where he was. I saw him sitting under the tree, legs sprawled before him in the middle of the horses. His white undershirt was unbound, exposing much of his chest.

"You scared me shitless," I said breathlessly. Dameon laughed again. He patted the ground next to him and I walked over to sit, our shoulders touching as we both had our back to the tree. His bedroll was neatly at his side, like he had no intention to sleep at all tonight.

"Couldn't sleep, Princess?" he said.

"No," I let out a sigh before I continued. "It appears the gods will not grant me that peace after what I have done today." I couldn't blame them. After what I did, I did not deserve another moment of peace in my life.

Dameon turned to me, his face soft. "The only thing you did wrong, Elora, was trusting someone who didn't deserve it." He spoke softly but earnestly.

"You can't know that, Dameon. You weren't there."

"Then tell me. Tell me it all, every detail and I will listen objectively," he pleaded.

My eyes stung at the thought. "Shouldn't we both try for sleep instead?" I laid my head on his shoulder like I would do as a kid. The smell of leather and peppermint grounded me–Dameon grounded me.

I felt Dameon turn his head towards me. "We both know that isn't happening for either of us. But it might help, Lor. To get the thoughts out of your head."

I looked forward, letting his words hit me. Would speaking all the awful truth help me? Would Dameon see me as the beast after this? I hesitated. Dameon grabbed my hand, and whispered, "You can trust me, Lor. Please talk to me."

And so I did–I told him everything. I did not know why, maybe because he said please, or maybe it was because I knew Dameon was always my safe space. Even as children, I would go to him when I needed to be seen as more than a princess. Speaking to him had always felt natural. If I couldn't sleep, talking to Dameon always helped. I started at the beginning, when I first turned. Every insidious detail of my brother's abuse, of me fighting back and being sent to Greydenn. I told him about killing the other knights. I told him of my time with Percy and the details of our battle, how I begged him to stop and he refused; how he stabbed me when I least expected it. How I really did think he loved me, only to realize he never could love me as much as he loved Elrick.

How I drove a sword through his stomach.

Dameon sat there the whole time not speaking, taking it all in. When I finished, I held my breath, waiting for him to tell me I was the beast all along, to cast me out as my family did. I felt him let out a long shaky breath before he let go of my hand. My heart felt like it was being ripped into a thousand pieces. I waited with baited breath for him to tell me what I already knew. Bile built in my throat as I accepted my fate.

Before I could react, his hands were on my face, guiding me to look into his eyes. There was no anger written on the face, only sadness as tears stained his tan cheeks.

"I am so sorry I was not there to protect you, Elora." His voice was raw with emotion.

I reached up, cupping his cheeks in my hand and wiping his tears with my thumb. He leaned into the touch but did not close his eyes.

"You tried to be, I wouldn't listen."

"If I had been just a few moments earlier I could have saved you. I could have prevented all this pain." His voice cracked with emotion.

My eyes welled with tears and I put my hands back to my side. Clearly he saw I was wrong to kill Percy now. For some reason this shattered me. "I am a murderer," I sobbed out.

"No, my darling…" He pulled me to his chest as he spoke. "You gave him so many opportunities for it to end. But there was no way he was leaving that chamber alive." He held me gently against his heart. The rhythmic beat calmed me for a moment–to hear the life in him–but soon it just turned to another reminder of whose heart I had stopped.

"How can you say that?"

Dameon set his jaw as he spoke. "Because I would have killed him no matter what." His voice had a finality in it that shocked me and I knew he meant it. His heart rate remained steady, his words not changing him in the least. I glanced up at his face, shocked by the coldness carved into his features. I had never seen this darkness in him before–this predatory side. He looked different from the boy that would tell me stories, different from the man I had always known.

Dameon removed his hands from my face and placed them in his lap. He looked over at the horses as I sat up. This seemed to ease the tension in him. As quick as it had appeared, the predator in him receded.

"How did you know?" The question fell from my lips as soon as the thought formed in my brain. I had always been so careful in hiding my secret. Dameon chuckled as he looked at me.

"Here," he said as he grabbed his bedroll and placed it in his lap. "Lay down and I will tell you a bedtime story like when we were kids." His voice was light with an air of laughter. I did as he said, situating myself so I was facing the horses. Within moments of me lying down, his hands were in my hair, lightly twirling the ends between his fingers.

"Where should I start, Princess?"

"The beginning," I said. I truly wanted to know everything. Where did I go wrong?

"When I was a child, my mother died. I spent the next few years wandering from town to town, trying to find a place for myself."

I tensed at his words and moved to sit up. "Dameon, I am so sorry, I didn't know." He gently held me in place, keeping me in his lap. I settled back in. Clearly telling his story like this, without seeing my face was easier. I forced myself to relax because I wanted to give him the safe ear he had given me.

"Those years were hard. I mainly ate scraps, occasionally a warm meal from a kind person, or when someone wasn't paying attention. Eventually, the towns would run me off. When I was ten, I made my way into Greydenn."

"Where people took care of you," I said.

Dameon laughed. "Hardly. It was harder to find food there. I was very skinny and I thought about leaving numerous times, but knew I wasn't strong enough for any journey. Plus I had nowhere to go. I stole scraps from the inn and the tavern, occasionally an egg from coops when I could, but it wasn't enough. I slept outside mostly, but one night, it was so cold and I was desperate." His voice cracked with emotion at the memory. "I saw no lights in the stables, so I snuck in, thinking I would sleep in the hay and leave before anyone arrived." He chuckled darkly before continuing, "That night I even ate a handful of dry oats that I found. It was horrid, but it stopped the hunger pains." Dameon's fingers continued moving through my hair as he spoke.

"I crawled into the hayloft and buried myself in the straw. For the first time in months, I was warm and full. I slept like a baby. Apparently too good. I woke up to someone tapping my legs with their boot. The stable master found me, gave me an earful for being a thief."

I seethed, wishing I could go back to town right now and make the stable master beg for forgiveness. "What did you do?"

"Oh I cried like a baby. Had a complete meltdown, yelling at the man. Asked him if he had ever been so hungry he ate horse food. If he knew what it was like to be a child with no one to care for you. I was waiting for him to wallop me, or to throw me out, but he just pointed down and said to go muck the stalls. So I did what I was told, even though I was barefoot. I mucked all of the stalls, filled the water, and did everything he asked of me that day, hoping he would just let me stay the night again. When I was done, he brought me a hot plate of food and some shoes."

I could hear the tears in his eyes as he recounted his story. I started to gently stroke his leg, knowing it would not be enough to console him.

"They made me the stable boy. Told me the job came with board in the stables, hot food, and a few coins each week. The animals made me no longer feel completely alone, but Greyden still wasn't a welcoming place. One day a few years later, I overheard that the Princess was being sent here, a princess who was cursed by a dragon." Dameon laughed again, as he spoke. "And for some reason, I decided at that very moment I hated her. She most definitely never struggled nearly like me and I didn't want anything to change. I worried about the safety of the horses with the dragon. I remember watching your carriage pull up and taking care of the horses. I saw you step out in your pretty gown and the town covered in flowers and ribbons to welcome you. I thought about throwing manure at you, but decided not to."

I chuckled. "Why not?"

Dameon let out a sigh before continuing. "Because I saw the same sadness in your face that I felt my whole life." He twirled a lock of hair around his fingers.

"A few nights later, I saw some scoundrel trying to break into the barn–a kid. I was worried that another boy would take my spot and I would be on the streets. I watched for a while, ready to stop him but the kid seemed content to just pet the horses. I realized a few moments later that the kid was you. I went down there to talk to you, to tell you to leave the horses alone and you extended your hand to introduce yourself. Your sleeve pulled up and I saw the bruises and knew we had more in common than I wanted. At that very moment, I decided nothing would ever hurt you again."

Tears stung my eyes as I remembered that night. How he surprised me by being there, or speaking to me. How he made me feel like a person, and not just a princess or a monster.

"A few weeks later, I decided that I needed to protect you from the dragon. I snuck up the mountain and was hiding in the tree in the courtyard with a dagger in between my teeth one night. I watched the dragon fly closer and closer, circling Mirador. I stayed still and hidden, waiting until it got closer. Eventually, it flew feet away from me and it looked right into the tree. We were face to face and I knew instantly."

"How could you have known?" I asked. No one else I knew of had ever seen the resemblance I so thoroughly looked for between my two forms.

Dameon grabbed my shoulder, softly turning me so I was facing him. His thumb lightly grazed my cheek. "I'd recognize those green eyes anywhere." His voice was soft, a smile on his lips.

"You have known for ten years? Why did you never say anything?" I asked

Dameon's response was low, barely above a whisper. "Because I was afraid to lose you."

Several moments passed in silence, like the weight of his revelation was something we both needed time to process. "I saw you shift at the lake, after our race," he said, finally breaking the silence. "That was the first time I'd ever seen it." Dameon paused like he was reflecting on the moment. "It was mesmerizing to see how effortless it is for you to walk between forms."

"I knew you knew that night. It terrified me," I said with a shaky breath. Dameon grabbed his cloak and draped it over me.

"You should never fear me, Elora."

Chapter Fifteen

THE orange and pink tinged sky stretched endlessly around me. I pumped my wings and soared through the colors of the sunset. The summer sun was waning, but still able to warm my dark scales. I felt infinite–completely safe and whole. Looking down, I saw a hooded figure atop a large black horse keeping pace with me. Dameon threw back his hood and shot a smile full of warmth up my way. The sight warmed me in a way even the sun could not, I thought, as butterflies filled my stomach. The smell of leather and peppermint mixed with a summer breeze permeated around me.

A light touch on my cheek roused me from my slumber. I stretched, remembering where I was as I opened my eyes and saw Dameon smiling down at me softly in the twilight of sunrise.

"Good morning, Princess." His voice was a husky whisper. Dameon's face looked relaxed, all the hard emotions of the last few days completely gone. He looked younger than he had, more boylike and rested. How many times had I awoken through the years in this exact position? More importantly, why did this time feel so different? "Sleep well?" he asked.

I sat up, suddenly embarrassed at the closeness. The sudden motion set my vision spinning as pain ripped up my left side.

"Careful, Princess." Dameon grabbed my shoulders as he spoke, gently steadying me.

I took a deep breath and my mind steadied as the smell of summer sunrise mixed with leather and peppermints soothed me. "Better than expected," I said as I looked up at him. "Did you sleep? I hope you weren't uncomfortable."

Dameon chuckled softly, as he looked down at his empty lap. "I slept better than I have in a long time. We should get going, though. I am sure Selena will wake soon and we need to pack up and move out."

Dameon stood up slowly, throwing his arms above his head and stretching. The movement caused his tunic to ride up slightly, revealing a small line of tan, muscled abdomen. I looked away quickly, hoping he didn't see me staring. His small chuckle told me I was caught.

"There you both are," Selena said, saving me from my embarrassment. "I woke to an empty camp…" Her voice trailed off. She stood in front of us, hands on her hips as she looked to me, then Dameon, and back again. Her face remained cool, but I could tell she was thinking–calculating which reason *why* she found Dameon and I here, lines of sleep still blatantly on both our faces as I still laid upon the ground, seemed most plausible. I moved to my feet quickly, Selena's keen brown eyes holding mine the whole time.

"Elora woke early and came to chat. We were both about to come and rouse you," Dameon said, the lie falling effortlessly from his tongue.

"Right, of course," Selena said, her eyes never leaving mine.

An awkward length of time passed with us all standing there, staring at each other. Finally, when I could take it no longer, I moved forward, walking past Selena and towards camp.

"We should get going," I said with the cheeriest voice I could muster as I marched past Selena. I made it to camp and instantly started rolling up my bedding, only for Dameon to quickly materialize beside me, doing the same. He knelt over as his hands brushed my own, causing my neck to heat.

"Smooth, Princess," he whispered. "But why so nervous?"

"I just...it is embarrassing to be caught like that with Selena. I know what she thinks happened, and honestly, that would be less embarrassing for her to see than to know the truth." My blush deepened for an inexplicable reason. Why was I so nervous? It is not like Dameon and I did anything to be embarrassed of. But the night felt intimate, the secrets we shared too vulnerable to share with anyone else. I looked over, my eyes narrowing when I saw Dameon's jaw had set, the soft boy I was reminded of this morning now completely lost in his features.

"Right, nothing more embarrassing than a Princess choosing to spend time with a bastard stable boy."

I moved to speak, but Dameon's words left me utterly shocked. He got up and walked away, his stuff neatly tucked under his arm.

Within moments, Selena appeared beside me as she gathered her things in camp. I looked out at the trees as I worked, hoping to figure out why his words took the air from my lungs.

*   *   *

THE day had grown unbearably warm as we trekked through the forest. Long gone was the trail and fast riding. Oak lumbered beneath me slow and steady as he sure-footedly moved through the rough terrain. The trees around us were massive, but wide apart, leaving patches of grass and wildflowers to overtake the forest floor. Dameon rode ahead, marking a path for us to follow on his war horse. I could see his head subtly moving from side to side as he scanned the surrounding area, still wearing his hood, with Selena stationed behind me.

Sweat trickled down my hooded face. I had never in my life had such contempt for a fucking piece of fabric. I reached for the waterskin on my pack, my side wincing at the sudden movement. I tried not to think about the way the poison had spread to the boĖoms of my ribcage as I greedily drank the warm water.

Suddenly, Dameon stopped ahead and dismounted Poppy. I froze, waiting for something to happen only to see Dameon begin to stretch as Poppy happily munched on grass. I trotted up on Oak as I glanced around. There was a small spring before us and the sun shone down in the open spaces making the green grass glow. A soft breeze tugged at the cloak, bringing much needed cool air to my face. In any other situation, I would be entranced by the beauty around me. Not today, though. Only one thought occupied my mind, a nagging realization I could not banish. The spread of the toxins told me all I needed to know.

Olgara was wrong about how long I had.

Dameon looked up at me and the cool smile on his face somehow pulled me from my spiral. He reached over, stroking Oak's neck before turning to me again. "Horses need to rest before we trek further. This seemed like the best place." I nodded to him and before I could process, he had already grabbed my waist and lifted me off the horse. He did not linger like before though. As soon as my feet hit the ground, his hands were off me and there was no lingering stare. Before I could even process, he had turned away from me and walked towards Selena. For a reason I could not understand, a dull ache hit my chest.

We rested there for an hour as the horses ate their fill and drank from the spring. Dameon passed out a lunch of cheese, stale bread, and apples. As I lay in the soft grass in the sunlight, I felt true peace. Like I could pretend I was just on a trek with friends and I could fly back home whenever I wished. I found much needed peace in this lie, like a key had been left to free me of the mental prison.

The dragon seemed to be moving further and further away from the surface. I could feel my power aching to be released, like it was stretching against the chains that bound it. But as more time passed, the feeling became more and more faint. Now it was barely a whisper in my bones. The quietness gutted me and made me think of things I wished not to. I wondered if death would be better than to live without part of my soul.

"Get up," Dameon's voice was low, the command in it sending shivers down my spine.

"What?"

"Get up *now*, Elora," he growled. I did as he commanded instinctively, my feet moving before my head could even process. Dameon did not look at us as he spoke. "I want you both to slowly walk to your horses on the side of your sword. Do not grab them until I tell you." I looked over to Selena as we did what was commanded of us. Even under her cloak I could tell her jaw was set and her eyes quizzical as she prowled to her mount. I thought I saw her skin twitching slightly, but shook it from my mind. Maybe the poison was making me see things.

Oak's ears were pinned back as he stomped the ground beneath him. Clearly the horses and Dameon sensed something I did not. I stroked his neck as I covertly scanned the woods. I tried to call forth my dragon eyes, but it was like my senses were too far away. No matter what happened in the next few moments, the dragon would not come to save me. I would have to save myself.

Suddenly, from behind one of the trees halfway up the hill, a man with stringy straw-colored hair in tattered clothes appeared. He prowled down the hill towards a relaxed looking Dameon. Behind him, two more men—one bald and one barely more than a boy– did the same. All three men had rusted swords at their sides.

"Aye travelers," the first man said. "We have become lost in the woods. Can you spare any supplies for some weary poor folk?" All three men grinned as the first one spoke. The dark brown stains on their tunics were not from dirt, I thought, but dried blood.

Dameon smiled warmly, like the threat before him was nothing more than a child's game. "Sorry men, we do not have anything to spare for you. We are simply travelers ourselves. My men and I are just passing through on a quest for our lord."

The first man laughed, a joyless sound. "I am afraid I might have misspoke. For this is not a request, but a demand, boys. We will be taking your supplies, and anything else we like from you." As he spoke, three more men appeared from behind the tree.

Dameon laughed darkly, the sound sending a shiver down my spine. "Six to three doesn't seem like a fair fight, my friends."

"Never said it was fair," the man shrugged as he spoke.

"Now you misunderstand me. I will give you one chance. Leave and I will not kill you." Dameon grinned as he spoke, his features suddenly predatory. I had the sneaking suspicion that he *wanted* them to try us, that he thirsted for blood on his hands at this moment. Like it would allow him to not think about whatever had made him so unpleasant today.

Suddenly, the men drew their swords and began prowling towards us. Dameon turned to us, a wild unhinged smile on his face. "Fuck them up, ladies."

Selena and I drew our swords as we turned to face the men head on. I walked forward, bracing myself as one of the men walked towards me. He was short and stout and eyed me like I was a meal. Dameon met the first man blade to blade. The clanging metal distracted me as the short man charged me. Before I could realize, I threw my blade forward, impaling the man. An all-too familiar squelching sound ripped through my ears. His face was stunned as blood trickled out his mouth, like he did not think I was capable of doing what I just had. He slumped to the ground at my feet as I released the blade from my hands. My vision went black. I did not see this stranger at my feet in his dying throws, but a familiar face with cool blue eyes and golden hair. My breathing became rapid as I felt something hit me hard to the ground. My vision came back and I saw the world around me again as one of the greasy men pinned me to the ground.

"You little bitch," he said as he grabbed my throat. I thrashed underneath him, trying to get to the blade at my thigh but could not reach it. "Keep trying, girl, I like the fight." He grinned as he spoke, revealing several missing teeth. I felt the truth of his words against my thighs as he bent down to whisper in my ear. I fought harder trying to remove him from me. I reached further down, my fingers grasping for the hilt. A ripping sensation hit my side as excruciating pain caused me to scream. The man laughed as he removed one hand from my neck and moved it lower. "I'm going to have fun with your body for da..." The words died from his lips as a blade lodged itself in his throat. I gagged as his blood trickled onto my face. He went slack on top of me and I struggled to wiggle out from his weight as he choked on his own blood.

"Elora!" Dameon yelled, his voice all raw emotion. I looked over to see his arm still extended from throwing the blade. Unadulterated fear marred his features. I finally was able to get to my feet, only for the sensation to send me to my knees. My vision spotted as I gritted my teeth to prevent the scream from leaving my lips. I looked up and saw Selena deliver a beheading blow to one of the men. She looked like a warrior goddess as the blood splattered onto her dark features. Her face was serene, ever the level headed beauty. Three men lay at

Dameon's feet, the boy kneeling before him with a terrified expression. Dameon looked otherworldly, like a god the boy was begging for forgiveness. Dameon bent down and picked the boy up by his throat until his feet barely touched the ground. Dameon snarled in his face. "Do not let me ever find you again," before throwing the boy to the ground. He scrambled to his feet, his breeches suddenly dark with wetness. The boy ran away for the hills before Dameon turned to me again, terror written on his face as he beheld me. He was covered in blood as he ran towards me, sliding in the dirt until he was on his knees before me. He wrapped his blood stained hands around my hips, guiding me to stand.

"I need to look at the wound," he said gently. His fingers began unraveling the leather corset, moving quickly and gently up.

"You're pretty good at this. Lots of practice?" I cringed, as the words from my lips were breathier than I intended them to be.

Dameon looked up at me, a sly smile on his lips. "Wouldn't you like to know." He reached the top and a shiver went down my back as his fingers lightly brushed my collarbone. He guided the straps from my shoulders and gasped. "Fuck."

I looked down to see blood the color of ink staining the bottom half of my tunic. "This is going to hurt, Elora, and I am so sorry for that." As he spoke, he lifted my shirt up. I gasped in pain as the fabric ripped away from the wound. I put my hands down on his shoulders to steady myself as he placed one hand on my bare hipbone, the other hand holding my tunic just below my breasts.

"Selena, bring me the pack from Katherine for the wound. It is in Poppy's right saddlebag," Dameon shouted over his shoulder. I moved to look down, only for Dameon's words to halt me. "Don't look, Princess."

I considered listening for a moment, but curiosity got the better of me. My stomach was a tattered mess, the puckered wound now open and freely flowing tainted blood where the stitches burst. The broken strings stuck out, reminding me of when the hem of a dress tore.

"Shit, Elora." Dameon's fingers lightly traced the black trail moving up under my ribcage. Mere inches from my heart. "You should have told me," he whispered.

"Apparently guessing the time frame for poison is not one of Olgara's specialties." My voice was devoid of humor, hope a distant thing of the past.

Suddenly, Selena appeared behind Dameon as she handed him a small pouch with a gold buckle. Dameon removed his hands from my skin, the sudden loss of warmth hit me in ways I could not explain. He undid the buckle, revealing the contents of the pack–a needle, thread, and a jar of green powder.

Dameon looked up at me, his brown eyes shining with worry and another emotion I could not place. "Princess, I need you to be a good girl and take steps back until your back hits the tree behind you."

The familiar nickname and banter soothed me. "When have I ever been good?" I said.

Dameon chuckled, a deep, breathy sound that made my toes curl in my boots. "Give it a try for me, Princess." Dameon stood up and looked towards Selena.

"Can you please grab all the moss you can and rinse the dirt from it in the spring?" he said.

"On it." I couldn't help but notice the worry on Selena's face as she turned around.

My back hit the tree and Dameon crouched down before me again. His finger trailed the small mark from the bolt, now almost completely healed. "What is this from?" he asked.

A humorless chuckle left me. "That was my undoing. Percy shot me with a bolt a few nights ago. The mark is how he realized."

Dameon's features darkened as he gently brushed the mark with his thumb. He looked up at me and a rage I had never known before clouded his brown eyes. "I fear I am not a good man, Elora." His voice was breathier than I had ever heard before.

"Why?"

Dameon looked up at me. My stomach dropped at the sight of him on his knees before me, his eyes dark. "I wish he was alive so I could kill him. Slowly."

The honesty in his words made my breath hitch like there was not enough air to fill my lungs. As soon as it overtook him, the rage was gone, the boy I knew now apparent again in the features of the man who knelt before me. Dameon broke our eye contact as he threaded the needle and opened up the jar. He grabbed the hem of his shirt, ripping a clean section off.

"I need you to put your hands back on my shoulders, Princess." Dameon paused, his movement as he looked up at me again. "This is going to hurt but you cannot scream and you cannot fall unconscious. We do not have time for either."

"How will putting my hands on your shoulders prevent either of these things?" My tone was acidic as I spoke back.

Dameon chuckled. "This way you can just dig your nails into me. Get all that anger out in a healthy way." I hesitated to respond and in that time, Dameon grabbed my hands and placed them on his shoulders.

"I do not wish to hurt you," I said.

"Nails in my back have never hurt me before," he said with a wry grin.

I suddenly no longer felt bad for hurting him. The look of pure annoyance on my face caused Dameon to laugh.

"Okay, I am going to dry and wipe the wound off, then I will pack it with yarrow powder and sew it up. It will be a bitch and I am sorry."

"How sweet," I said between gritted teeth. "You've never apologized for being a bitch before."

"Rude, Princess," he said as he winked at me. He reached for the waterskin at his side and poured some on the cloth. He began to gently wipe the skin around the wound. My fingers tensed around his shoulders as my nails dug in in an attempt to silence the scream that built in my throat.

"What a good girl you are."

"I swear to the gods, Dameon. I will kill you one day," I said between clenched teeth. I looked down to see a smile on his face as he opened the jar and placed a large pile of the powder in his hands. He quickly held the powder to my wound, shoving the mixture into the wound.

"Fuck you," I growled.

"Is that a threat or a 'to do' list?" he whispered so low I could barely hear it. Before I could respond, I felt the sharp sting of the needle passing through my flayed flesh followed by the sensation of the thread moving through the skin. It made me want to vomit.

"Oh gods I hate that," I breathed out.

Dameon laughed. "The feel of the string is worse than the pain of the needle. My first set of stitches made me want to vomit."

For some reason, his admission of that made me feel better. Like I wasn't so weak.

"Your seams are not very straight," Selena said behind him as she eyed his handiwork. The wet moss was in her hands. I wondered how long she had been standing there. I blushed at the idea of the things she might have heard.

Dameon did not turn from his task as he moved down the wound. "Well good thing I am not making a dress, Selena."

Selena tilted her head to the side and pursed her lips, like she was considering his words before responding. "Fair point," she said. "Elora, would you like me to hold your hand?"

"No," I began to say before Dameon cut me off.

"Judging by the digging sensation in my shoulders, she would break your hand." Dameon turned to look at Selena before continuing. "And we can't afford for that to happen considering how well you did with the sword."

Selena smiled softly, glowing at the approval. I was stunned to see her so nonchalant about her first kill.

"How did I do?" I asked, trying to distract myself. I waited for the compliment, sure that he would tell me I did well even if he did need to save me.

Dameon looked up at me, his face neutral. "You fought like shit, Elora. Like you had never held a weapon in your hands before. I would think to blame it on Percy, but Selena was able to hold her own."

"That is not fair," Selena said. I grinned, waiting for her to come to my defense. "It is Percy's fault she fought so poorly for two reasons. The first one being he fought horribly, like he had never been in combat before. I only learned to hold my own by watching the guards." My mouth was agape as I listened, stunned by the turn of events. "Secondly, Elora never truly needed to learn to fight until he took the dragon from her." Selena turned from Dameon towards me, her gold-brown eyes shining with pride as she spoke. "I have seen Elora fight in her other form. It is awe inspiring."

My blush turned into a wince as Dameon tied off the last stitch. "Well, we can all agree on that." Dameon grabbed the moss from Selena, thanking her as he did so. He pressed the cool moss to my wound. It hurt for only a moment before the plush, cooling feeling abated the pain. He wrapped a piece of cloth around my abdomen and tied it gently over the wound before he helped me back into my corset. His fingers worked swiftly with the laces. Each time they grazed my skin it sent shivers down my spine.

"You can let go of my shoulders now, Princess. I'm not going anywhere." Dameon smiled as he looked up at me, looking every bit the rogue. I rolled my eyes before I pushed him off me. Dameon rolled onto his back as he grinned up at me. He got to his feet quickly. Once standing, he made a show of brushing the dirt from him before looking down at me. "So cruel, Princess," he tsked at me. "We should get going now, I want to cover as much land as possible today." I waited for him to tell Selena why we needed to move faster than before, but thankfully he did not. He nodded at me, like he understood what I was feeling, my desire to not worry her.

We walked towards the horses. Selena mounted on her own—she was always a fast learner. It did not surprise me to see how quickly she took to riding. Dameon walked me towards Oak. He stood in front of me as I put my foot in the stirrup, so close that our bodies were almost pressed together. As I looked up at his face, I saw so many hidden emotions. He reached down and tucked my hair behind my ear before gently placing the hood back on my head.

"What is it?" I said. His eyes seemed so sad, so worried.

"Nothing," he smiled weakly. He laced his hands together and gave me a boost to mount. Thankfully, the red gelding stood still, barely twitching a muscle. Dameon patted my thigh before walking towards Oak's head. He stroked his forehead, as Oak nipped at his clothing. "Take care of my girl," he whispered to the horse, so low I could barely hear. Before I could respond, he walked towards Poppy. He mounted her gracefully and with that, we were off.

The forest gave way to more steep terrain quickly, but we moved with haste through the rocky ground. Trees still grew all around us, but gone were the smells of summer. Instead, we were surrounded by pine and spruce as far as the eye could see. The mountain before us told me that the hardest part of our journey had only just begun. A sinking feeling hit my stomach as we began our trek again. As the poison inched closer and closer to my heart, I wondered when my journey would end.

Chapter Sixteen

WE passed the rest of the day with little of note. The terrain grew much harsher than before and we had ridden further than even I had ever dared to fly. Pine trees dotted the rugged landscape. The ground was almost all rock as we traversed up and down steep mountain passes. For the first time on our journey, I was grateful for the protection my cloak offered.

We set up camp in a small pine grove with a stream in a gulley well before sunset. After the attack and the spread of the poison was discovered, conversation was sparse as we moved through camp. Selena dismounted on her own today, proving once again how fast of a learner she was. I looked at her movements enviously. She was much shorter than me but still moved with a grace and sureness I couldn't help but be jealous of. Dameon helped me off Oak. The necessity made me feel helpless. His hands did not linger on me like in the past–it was just business. As soon as the horses were taken care of, Dameon disappeared into the forest, his face unreadable as he went to find game for dinner.

I found Selena sitting on a log near the horses, watching as they grazed on the long line tied between trees. Her gaze was long, like she was seeing nothing and everything around her all at once.

"Mind if I join you?" I asked as I motioned to the space next to her. Selena smiled softly as she looked up at me.

"Please," she said. I sat down, unsure of what to say. Whether it was the exhaustion from the trip or the rapid progression of the poison that made words seem so hard to come by, I did not know. We sat there like that for several minutes as we looked out before us, eyes unseeing.

"You did really well out there, Selena. But I am not surprised, you are good at everything," I said. Selena's skin deepened as a soft smile spread across her lips.

"It is a strange feeling, to be told I am good at killing," she retorted. There was no anger in her voice. She sounded like she was just stating a fact. My jaw dropped and heat crept up my neck. How could I be so foolish?

"I'm so sorry, Selena. That is not what I meant." I wanted to crawl into my own skin in retreat as she looked upon me. "I should have been more mindful. Do you need anything? Is there anything I can do?"

Selena smiled softly. "No, Elora, it is alright. I feel oddly fine. It was him or me and I knew it would not be me. I have too much ahead of me to let a monster steal it away." She turned to look at me, her honey-brown eyes shining in the dying light as she reached for my hand. "I think you of all people understand that feeling."

Her words hit me like a thrown stone. I pushed back the bile in my throat as the image of Percy kneeling bore into my mind. I instead thought of the men before him, the dozen knights I ended. Selena was right, it was them or me, but did that make it just? I gave each of them a choice, but was that choice an illusion? I did not know what I would have done if they chose to leave. I liked to think that I would have let them go peacefully, but did their transgressions demand the violent deaths I dealt them?

"Can I be honest with you, Selena?" I asked with a shaky breath.

"Of course, Elora. Always."

"I did not mourn any of those men I killed. It didn't seem to affect me. But since Percy, it is all I can think about." My voice cracked with emotion. "I fear I am not a good person, that everything that has happened to me is deserved." *I feared I was becoming the beast I was cursed to be.*

"I do not think you are evil, Elora," Selena said. I scoffed at the idea. She was so wrong about me. "I think you and I did the same thing–we killed strangers. These men were not people to us. Our minds would not let us think of them as whole because it would be too hard to come to terms with what we did. I took a life today–my first life. I will carry his face for the rest of my days, but his choices lead to it. I will not squander my happiness away because a weak man tried taking mine." Selena turned to me, squeezing my hand before continuing, "and you should not either. We do not relish in the lives we have taken, nor did we set out to kill others. That is why we are not evil. But sometimes, unfortunately, it is a necessity. The fact you feel so strongly for Percy's death tells me you are not evil. I know you never let the previous knights suffer. You delivered clean deaths and that is the most honorable thing you could do."

"Not to all of them," I retorted. "The one who tried to hurt Katherine suffered." I did not even give that monster a choice. After what he tried, he deserved no choice. That is one death I would never feel any remorse for. If that made me evil, then so be it.

"That creature did not deserve an honorable death. I hope he suffered every second." The acid in Selena's tone shocked me. She had never been violent, but I knew she meant her words. I fear she would have given the man an even worse death than the dragon had if she had him in her hands.

"I am so sorry I dragged you into this, Selena. You do not deserve this." My voice was barely above a whisper.

"I am only sorry you did not drag me in sooner, Elora. This is too much for one person to bear."

Her words struck me as I wrapped my fingers around hers. We sat there in silence, her head leaning against my shoulder and our fingers intertwined until the raw feeling in both our hearts subsided. We were girls together, but now we were becoming something different—only time would tell if it was heroes or monsters.

In some stories, there is no difference.

*   *   *

BY the time we walked back to camp, Dameon was preparing two ducks to roast. His face was unreadable as he placed them on the fire. Dameon had dragged some logs around the fire to act as seats for us as he sat on the ground, his back propped against one. We all sat there in silence, at times uncomfortable, until dinner was ready. The duck was delicious and lifted my spirits, helping to distract me from the mental and physical pain that had weighed me down all day. I rubbed the fat from the meat on my healing lips. Cracks had formed because of the dry air, but the fat soothed any pain.

"The duck is delicious, Dameon. You should give Chef the recipe," Selena said between mouthfuls.

Dameon chuckled, a small smile on his face as his tan skin flushed at the compliment. "I am sure Chef would not take too kindly to a ranger telling him how to roast a duck. You are just hungry, Selena."

"It is actually quite good," I said.

Dameon turned to me, his hand over his heart. "A compliment from my dear princess? Alert the town–I can now die happy."

I rolled my eyes, which only caused Dameon's smile to widen. "With how dramatic you are, I am always surprised you did not become a minstrel."

"I tried once, they told me I was too good looking," Dameon said as he made a sad face. "It is my burden to bear." I was contemplating throwing the cleaned duck bone in my hand at him when Selena's laugh brought me back to reality. It was a deep, belly laugh that filled my spirit with joy.

"What?" I said to her, a smile appearing on my face before I could stop it.

"Oh nothing, you two just amuse me," she said like there was more to say, but she knew to keep it to herself. She picked at the bones in her hand absentmindedly.

Dameon threw his bones in the fire before stretching out to his full height on the ground and placing his arms behind his head. I tried not to notice the way the movement caused his arms to strain against his tunic, or the way it caused a sliver of muscle of his stomach to become visible.

I failed miserably, and that failure was noted when I looked up at Selena to see her eyes trained on me, a knowing smile on her face.

"Dameon, why don't you tell us a story? I have heard from Elora that you tell splendid stories," Selena said.

Dameon did not open his eyes or move before responding. "That has to be a lie, Selena. We both know the Princess would refrain from saying such kind words about me."

"That is true. I believe I said they were okay at best. Definitely the type to put you to sleep." The lie flowed effortlessly through my lips. Dameon's soft smile at my words set my stomach upside down.

"That is more like it. Selena, I am tired and I would like to hear a story tonight. I would ask Elora, but she is not good at it. Why don't you tell us a story?"

Selena smiled, setting her scraps to the side. "That sounds like a challenge and I aim to win. So I will tell the story." She turned her eyes to the star-studded sky and gazed. I could see the wheels turning in her head as she prepared herself. Selena was a wonder to watch, she always seemed all-knowing. I adjusted myself, giving her all my attention. She turned her gaze to the fire, her face unreadable as she began. The howl of a distant wolf echoed through the mountains around us. Selena smiled and set up straight, like the sound reminded her of something.

"I have thought of a story. It was one I heard many moons ago. Are you ready?"

"At the edge of my seat," Dameon said from his spot, eyes still closed.

"Never more ready in my life," I responded.

"Many moons ago, in a distant land, there was a wolf pup. She was young, too young to be on her own. She did not remember what happened to her parents or littermates, or if she had ever had any. As far as she could remember her world had looked the same. She longed for love as she moved from place to place finding food in the forest when she could. She was lonely, but had no word for it because the feeling is all she had ever known, just like she had no word for hunger. It was a constant."

"One day, the wolf pup made it to the edge of a stream. She could see fish moving under the water and thought that if she was quick enough, she could have an easy meal. But it was too long since she had eaten and she could feel herself fading. The wolf pup knew she was dying and was content with the knowledge. When you only know pain, the absence of it seems like heaven. She held her eyes open as long as she could as she took in the beautiful views of the mountains around her. Flowers bloomed around her little body and she felt safe and ready for the next world, for it could not be as cruel as this one." Selena's voice broke as a tear fell down her cheek. Tears stung the back of my eyes at her story.

"Suddenly, the wolf was shaken awake by something cold slapping her nose. She opened her eyes to see a small fish still flopping in the dirt. As if on instinct, she caught it and ate it in one gulp. As soon as she finished that one, another fish appeared, as if dropped from the sky. And then another. By the time she ate the fourth fish, she was able to stand and see that the fish were not falling from the sky–the gods had not finally taken pity on her. Instead, she saw a hooded figure with a fishing pole facing away from her. Each time the figure caught a fish, they threw it to the pup. The pup creeped slowly up to the figure, hoping to see who or what it was. Her hackles rose, but she kept inching closer and closer until she was seated beside the person. A hand suddenly appeared from the figure and reached for the pup. She thought about biting the hand, but it felt wrong."

"Never bite the hand that feeds you," Dameon said.

Selena smiled. "Something like that. The hand softly stroked the back of the pup and for the first time in its life, the pup felt safe. She slept right there beside the person. By the time she woke, the person, a woman with long silver hair, had stood, gathering her supplies to go. The pup whined, worried to be alone again. It is so much harder to be alone once you know what it is like to no longer feel lonely. The woman looked down at the pup, her face neutral before speaking." Selena lowered her voice, preparing to don a character. "I am the Witch of the Wood,' the woman said. 'Would you like to come with me?' The pup considered these words before barking her answer."

"Well okay, pup. But you will have to help me with a very important mission. Can you do that?' the Witch asked."

"The pup once again thought about this before once again barking her answer as she pawed at the woman. She would do anything if it meant no longer starving or being alone. She could not bear to be either ever again."

"The witch smiled, 'Okay, pup. But to do this, you will need to shed this skin. This is not fully who you are.' The witch waved her fingers and where there once was a small wolf pup, there was now a small girl. The girl's memories suddenly came back to her—she remembered being a girl and then suddenly being a pup. She was unsure how long ago that was, but she knew both forms fit her. The witch promised the girl she would never be lonely or hungry ever again and the girl pup followed the witch into a new life."

"What happened to the girl?" I asked. "Did the witch harm her?"

Selena smiled. "That is all of the story I know. It was told to me many years ago, well before I met you, so it is a bit hazy."

Dameon set up and looked at Selena. "That was a great story," he said. "Thank you for sharing."

"I am glad you enjoyed it," Selena said. Her voice cracked as she spoke. I sat back, wondering where Selena had heard this. I had never heard a story where anyone could shift like me.

*   *   *

THE night was cold, much colder than the previous night. Dameon set our bedrolls in a row with mine in the middle. When I protested, he would not hear it.

"You lost blood today. We need to keep you warm," he retorted.

"I agree," Selena said. I gave her an incredulous look, her betrayal not surprising me in the least. Dameon took his spot the furthest from the fire. I lay in the middle, hoping to keep as much distance between us as possible, even though this was not the first time he and I slept in such close proximity. I could not understand why it felt so different with Selena here to witness it all.

Dameon scooted himself as close to me as possible, flipping me on my side and nestling in behind me. "Stop squirming," he said. "The closer we all are the warmer we will be." My teeth were clattering too much to protest as Selena slid in front of me, huddling close for warmth. Though I never would admit it, the closeness of the two comforted me, and not just because of the blood loss and cold. I slept deeply that night, surrounded by the smell of leather and peppermint.

I awoke as the sun rose to find we had shifted in the night. My head was on Dameon's chest with my leg draped over his hip as his arms wrapped around my waist. Selena had flipped, scooting herself as close to me as possible. Thankfully, they both still slumbered around me. I tried to move my head slowly from Dameon, trying to not rouse him. The gods know he would never let me hear the end of it if he woke to see us so entwined. Or worse, if Selena realized and gave me a look that told me she knew me better than even I knew myself.

As I slowly lifted my head, Dameon's arms tightened around me, like he was protesting the loss of warmth. I froze, hoping he would stay asleep.

"Where are you going, Princess?" he whispered in a dreamy voice. I looked up at his face to see his thick, dark lashes had barely parted. His brown eyes seemed almost black in the low light.

"I…I…" I tried forming a coherent sentence, to explain myself, but could not. What would I say? Why did I feel the need to run? To lie. More importantly, why did I feel an even bigger need to stay?

Must be the blood loss, I told myself.

I lay my head back on his chest, hoping if he fell back asleep he wouldn't remember this. Dameon nuzzled his face into my hair and tightened his arms around me. "Much better," he whispered. Within a moment, his soft snoring told me he was asleep once again.

*   *   *

WE unraveled ourselves some time later, when the sun had finally made its way into the sky. Despite the cold and my protests, Selena and Dameon insisted on checking the wound before we set back on our journey. The bleeding had stopped and Dameon's stitching had held. The pain was much more bearable today, thankfully. It should have made us all feel better.

But the spread of the poison was ever-closer to my heart. Now mere inches away. Dameon nor Selena mentioned what I already knew, but judging by the speed at which we traveled, they were aware that I would be lucky to survive until the night.

We did not stop all day as we moved through the terrain. The mountainous terrain and sparse trees soon gave way to forest once again. As we moved, I munched on the snacks Dameon had handed out. I tried to make them last, knowing that the rations would be needed for the trek back.

But it wasn't me I was saving the rations for. I could feel the poison inching closer and the dragon in me further and further away. With a steady breath, I came to understand the inevitable–I would not be making the return journey. If Dameon and Selena would allow it, I would ask us to stop this pointless search, but I knew asking that of my friends would be too painful. They still had hope, even if the concept to me was just a distant memory.

The sun was nearly setting when I felt the life draining from me. Dameon turned around ahead, his tan skin paling. My mouth moved, trying to find the words to tell him it was time. I knew how I wanted to go–laying with them both how I had found myself this morning.

"Elora," Dameon said before he turned around and pointed. Before him, a few hundred paces ahead was a large, flat rock with strange carvings on it. As I got closer, I felt an energy tugging me towards it. Oak pinned his ears back and stomped his foot. Something was clearly off with this place. Dameon dismounted from Poppy before he ran towards me. Surprisingly, I found the strength to dismount myself. If this was my final act, I did not want my last memory to be of needing assistance. I wanted to go out like a dragon.

"Do not give up on me yet, Princess." Dameon whispered as he reached for me. My feet were unsteady as the poison worked its way through me. The horses stomped their feet, like they could sense there was something off about this place, some unseen power surrounded us. I walked towards the stone, in a dreamless haze. I laid my hands on it to find it warm, despite the chill to the air. Dameon and Selena were back at the horses, several paces behind me.

The stone needed something. It demanded something to be given to find what I needed. Without a thought, and maybe with a little hope, I unsheathed the dagger at my thigh before dragging it across my palm. Thankfully, the blood that welled was still red.

"Elora," Dameon yelled.

"Stop, give her a moment," I heard Selena say.

I placed my bloody palm to the stone. The air around us changed at that moment and where there was just forest before, a small cottage with a heavy wooden door appeared a few paces ahead. Smoke wafted from the chimney and light emanated from the windows. I sent a silent prayer to the gods before walking the distance. My legs felt like they were made of stone, but still carried me until I reached the door. I gently knocked after sending a prayer to the gods to protect me.

The door creaked open slowly and I heard two words that sent me to my knees and the world crashing around me.

"Hello, dearie."

Chapter Seventeen

"HELLO, dearie."

Two innocuous words spoken by a voice that brought me comfort my whole life. Any other time and I would have been grateful to hear them, to run to the arms of the person stating them. But the comfort in these words was a distant memory. Hearing them now only served to throw my entire world further upside down.

I mouthed to speak but was unable to form words. The cobblestones dug into my knees as I looked up at the woman in the doorway. She was what I would imagine Olgara would look like several decades younger. She stood straight and proud as she peered down at me from her nose. Her eyes were the same color, her skin the same hue just with less wrinkles. Her long, grey hair was unbound and danced lightly in the wind. Youth was still a distant memory in this face, but the power radiating from the woman, from Olgara, made her seem as ageless as the ground itself. She was immovable, a force to be reckoned with.

My vision went black. I was unsure if it was from the poison or the shock, but my breathing became even more labored.

"Selena, Dameon! Come and help me carry Elora!" The crone screamed. I felt hands scoop me up as I nestled into a chest that smelled of leather and peppermint.

"Olgara, if that is your name, you have so much fucking explaining to do," Dameon growled. I opened my eyes slightly and was able to see his face contorted in anger. He looked powerful, like the rage he felt would drive him to do anything. The rest of the world was a blur, all I could see was him.

"How could you?" Selena spat.

"Oh, hush up you two. I owe neither of you an explanation, but I prefer to give it all in one go," the crone said. "Place Elora on the table. I have work to do."

Dameon lightly placed me on a hard wooden surface. His face was tender as he did so. He brushed his thumb across my cheek as tears filled his eyes.

Dameon looked to Olgara, his face once again hard. "You better fucking save her or I swear to the gods I will end you myself."

Olgara chuckled, the sound sending shivers down my spine. "I thought you were smarter than to threaten a witch."

Dameon lunged at the woman, only for Selena to step in the way. "Stop, Dameon. She is Elora's only hope."

My skin bristled at that word. Hope had been my undoing too many times.

Selena turned to the crone, her eyes narrowing. "But I want you to know, witch, that I am on Dameon's side here. If you hurt her, if anything happens to Elora, you will *beg* for death before I am done with you."

"Nice to see you finally grew into your teeth, girl." Olgara laughed again, rattling me as I drifted to nothingness.

*   *   *

SOMETHING cold and slimy crawled across my abdomen. The sick feeling jolted me awake. I opened my eyes, finding myself in a cottage kitchen. Candles burned from the walls. Hundreds of jars of mysterious powders and ingredients lined dozens of rows of shelves along the walls. I sat up slightly and looked down, trying to see what slid across me like a snake. Black, limbless creatures anchored themselves to my skin with their mouths, covering me from waist to collarbones–leeches. Each horrid creature was as long as my forearm and as wide as my wrist. They were each such a deep black it seemed to absorb all light. I gagged and bile filled my mouth.

"Always so dramatic," Olgara muttered as her wrinkled hands dabbed a damp cloth on my temple. I wretched as she dropped another of the vile creatures onto me. I felt it latch, the sensation sending me over the edge.

Warm, rough hands enclosed over mine. "Take it easy, Princess." Dameon's voice soothed me as he squeezed my hand.

"Here, drink this," Selena said as she handed me a cup of water. I drank greedily until the cup was completely drained of the cool liquid. For the first time in days, my lips did not ache at the touch. Clearly the witch had healed those too.

"Can someone please tell me what is happening?" I breathed out.

"The witch is using magical leeches to suck out the poison," Dameon said. His tone was neutral, but with something else underlying it. He watched Olgara with narrow eyes, like he was still unsure how to feel about this whole situation himself.

"This witch has a name, boy. Or have you forgotten it on your journey?" Olgara snapped.

Dameon's eyes narrowed further as his face contorted in anger. "I'm sorry, let me rephrase. Olgara, you know the woman who essentially raised you is also the one who cursed you, clearly knew more than she let on the entire time, and sent you on a journey to find said witch to heal you, when she could have just fucking done it in Greyden," he yelled.

The old woman shrugged. "I did not have the proper supplies in Greyden."

"She almost fucking died, Olgara!"

Olgara's gaze at Dameon could only be described as dagger-like. "Don't you have horses to tend to?"

"Are you fucking kidding me, Olgara?" I bit out between clenched teeth. I did not know if it was the leeches doing their job or the sheer rage I felt, but the dragon was closer to the surface than it had been in days. I could feel my bones begging to shift but something still blocked them. As I looked at the witch, I thought it was probably a good thing the dragon was unreachable at this moment. Olgara narrowed her eyes as I sat up to be level with her. Several of the foul creatures attached to me slid off at the movement and thrashed aimlessly on the table. "Not only are you the one who cursed me to be a monster, but you sent me out to die instead of helping me days ago. We almost didn't make it! Was that your goal? If you wanted me dead so badly, why not slit my throat ages ago instead of stabbing me in the back like this?" I hissed.

Olgara seethed before turning to address Selena. "You were always the logical one, Selena. What do you think? Do you think the power I have given Elora is a curse?" Olgara smiled cruelly, "More importantly, do you think I even gave her this power to begin with?" Selena's face dropped and her skin paled.

"What are you saying? Of course you are the one who cursed me," I seethed.

Olgara slammed her hands on the table as her face contorted in anger. "How is complete power and autonomy a curse, Elora? Do you know how many people would beg for power like this? To be strong enough that they could do anything they wanted? That no one could ever hurt them."

"Then why not curse someone else?!" I screamed. We had drifted closer to each other, our faces mere inches away from one another. Our anger and frustration was mirrored, but for totally different reasons.

Olgara blinked, her face softened ever so slightly as she turned around and made herself busy with the jars behind her. "I did not curse you, dearie, nor did I give you your power. No being in this world is strong enough to do that. I merely delivered a prophecy. You were born with the power you held."

My face paled. There had been a secret hope this whole journey, one that I barely let myself think about. If the witch healed me, maybe she could remove the curse of evil she bestowed on me. Those hopes were instantly dashed, driven away like dust in the wind. I felt hollow as I took in a shaky breath.

"So I was always meant to be a monster?" I whispered. Tears stung the back of my eyes.

Dameon grabbed my face as he searched it for something. His eyes were frantic, confused. He turned to Olgara, his jaw set in anger. "What does she mean by this?" he commanded Olgara to answer. Tears flowed silently down my face as I waited to be gutted by the truth—for my friends to see me for what I truly was.

Olgara sat down in a worn wooden seat before waving her hand. A jar of clear liquid appeared and she poured herself a cup. From the smell alone I knew it was her special liquor that would knock a grown man on his ass. The wafted vapor burned my nose as Olgara took a gulp without a wince. "When the Queen Mother was in labor, I was sent for by one of the handmaids. She could sense something was not right. I masqueraded as the lead midwife. In my numerous years of life, I had assisted many people in birth, so I knew what I was doing, especially with difficult births."

"How old *are* you?" Selena whispered.

Olgara took another drink before a pained smile appeared on her lips. "I truthfully lost count years ago. All I know for certain is I have outlived all the empires that dotted the land when I was a child tenfold."

"How?" I asked.

"Magic," is all the old witch said before she continued her story. "When I got to the room, I sensed a great power immediately, along with an equally great evil. Twins," she said with a smile. "The gods, long forgotten, put a message in my head—a prophecy—a warning for the Queen."

"Say the prophecy," Dameon growled while looking at Olgara.

All my fears boiled down to this one moment. Before I could stop myself, I started to speak, reciting the words that Elrick tortured me with—the truth of my nature. "The true heir will be a champion to the kingdom. He will bring Albaria to a new age of prosperity never before seen. But the second, she will be a serpent sent to destroy Albaria. If the crown ever falls on the treacherous heir's head, Albaria will be destroyed." I paused as my voice cracked. I looked up at a stunned Dameon as the tears began to fall, "Guess which one I am," I said without humor.

Silence filled the room for several long moments. With each pump of my heart, I felt it breaking. Finally, Olgara broke the silence. "You misspoke, dearie."

"What?" I asked.

"I never said which child was which, nor did I say which was the boy or girl before they were born. I did not know that much," she said.

"But that doesn't matter," I said angrily. "Elrick was born first and that made him the true heir."

Olgara laughed, a sickening sound. "Elrick always was crafty." She took another gulp of her drink before setting her eyes on me. Her gaze was powerful and no matter how hard I tried, I could not look away. I studied her. The face was the same as the one I had always known, just younger. Gone were the sunspots and wrinkles that I grew accustomed to. The aura around her screamed absolute power. If there was such a thing as a god who walked among us, she was sitting before me. "You were born first, dearie. I should know, I caught you myself." She leaned forward as she covered my hand with her own. The intensity of her stare cut me open, freezing me in place. "You are the true heir."

Chapter Eighteen

THERE was not enough air in the room. Surely the witch had used her power to choke me without lifting a finger, I thought as I gasped for breath. Dameon's large, warm hand was on my back. His wide-eyed stare met my own. Selena seemed the least affected by this news. Olgara squinted before handing me the jar of clear liquid.

"This might help," she said as I took the jar in my hands. I took a long drag, the drink hit my mouth like liquid fire. I gagged, but swallowed down in one gulp. For a brief moment, the burn let me clear my mind of everything but the pain. The release was brief. Before I was ready, the weight of Olgara's words hit me like a wave taking down a ship.

"You're lying," I choked. Olgara sighed, her shoulders slumping as she reached for the jar in my hand. Her face did not contort as the infernal liquid met her lips. She sat the jar back down and turned her gaze to me again.

"Just because you do not want to hear it, dearie, does not make it a lie," she said.

I took a ragged breath, as anger rose up in me. "Why did you make me trek through the forest when you could have told me in Greydenn? Or even earlier," I growled. "How could you let me think I was a monster for all these years?"

Olgara turned her cool eyes on me as her face softened. Even though the face she wore now was not the one I grew up comforted by, the effect was still the same. She looked at me with the pity I had known only a handful of times from her.

"Dearie, I could not do that. It would have put you at risk."

"This means that Elrick is the evil heir. He is the monster." Dameon stepped out from behind me. His face was searching, hopeful even. He looked down at me and his face softened as a slight smile appeared on his full lips. "So he must be killed." Dameon's words did not match his face. He spoke of killing my brother as simply as one would speak of getting a new coat–joyful, but nothing of great importance.

"Go tend the horses, boy," Olgara said without looking at Dameon. Dameon looked at the witch, then at me. I gave him a small nod and he quickly exited the cabin, leaving Selena and me alone with the witch.

Olgara stood up and removed the leaches from the table. "Looks like the poison is gone," she said as she grabbed the last one. To my relief, my abdomen was no longer streaked with black. The stab wound was mostly healed, leaving only a wide pink scar. Olgara grabbed my hand and motioned for me to scoot off the table. "Easy on your feet, dearie," she said as I wavered. I sat down in an old wooden chair. Olgara motioned for Selena to do the same. The normalcy of it struck me.

"This feels more normal than I thought it would," I said. How many times had us three sat just like this, with me at the head and Olgara and Selena at either side of me?

"The only person we are missing is Katherine," Selena said as she eyed Olgara. Her voice was neutral, but she watched the witch with narrow eyes. Her shoulders were tight, like she was bracing for something or staring down a foe–waiting to see their next move.

Olgara heaved a sigh before locking her eyes on me. "There is another reason I never told you the truth, dearie." She paused and reached for my hand. I pulled mine back before she could touch me and placed my hands demurely in my lap under the table. Genuine pain flashed across Olgara's face so swiftly I almost did not notice it. "Very well," she said as she straightened herself and pulled her hand back.

"What was the reason?" I said in a voice more cool than I had ever dared use with her in the past.

Olgara took a deep breath. "Your mother commanded me not to."

Her words hit me in waves. My emotions moved through me swiftly, from anger to denial, to rage, and a deep sadness, all muddled together in the mess that was my mind. "You lie," I said through gritted teeth. "My mother thought I was evil, as everyone did. That is why she sent me away."

"She did it to protect you, dearie," Olgara said gently.

"You lie!"

"Why is it so hard for you to see yourself as an object of love, Elora?"

The chair screeched across the floor as I jumped to my feet. My finger was in Olgara's face as a rage filled me. "How dare you!" I screamed. "My parents sent me away after turning a blind eye to Elrick's abuse until I fought back. Now you say my mother loved me? That she knew all along? Then why did she not protect me? Why send me away?"

Olgara was calm as she looked up at me, almost serene. Like this was nothing more than a child's temper tantrum. "What was she supposed to do, Elora? Keep you at High Castle? That would be like sending a lamb to the slaughter. Now sit down and talk to me like an adult. Regardless of how you feel about me right now, I raised you."

I scoffed. "Oh, let me guess. You are going to say now that since you raised me you want something in turn. Tell me this, Witch. Is the only reason you were kind to me, the only reason you showed me any decency, is me being the true heir? Were you just hedging your bets waiting until you could get whatever you want from me? Not because you cared about me at all!"

Olgara stood up faster than I had ever seen. Despite the fact I still towered over her, the look on her face made me feel as if I was much smaller than her, like I was once again a little child about to be scolded for my behavior. The hard part was that I knew I deserved whatever scolding came to me. Even though I knew I was acting like a child, I could not stop it.

"Now you listen here, dearie, and you listen well." Olgara's eyes were like daggers in mine as she wagged her finger in my face. I squared my shoulders, even if the most powerful witch in all of Albaria, maybe the entire world, stood before me. "I did my best to be the mother you needed because the one you deserved was not able to. I loved you like my own and I still do, regardless of prophecy or title. I loved you not because you were the good twin, or for your power, but for all you are!" The truth of her words filled me with shame. "What was your mother to do? To tell the entire country, a country she was not a citizen of, that the princess who can shift is the rightful heir? Both of your heads would have ended up on a stake, Elora. Your mother was waiting until the right time when she could send you away to safety. If she hadn't, you would likely not be alive today. So sit down, listen, and do not let me hear you speak ill of Lillion *ever* again." I did as I was told, keeping my eyes on Olgara the whole time. The witch took another gulp from her glass, muttering after she did. "The queen was my best friend and she loved you more than anything–loved you enough to send you away though it broke her heart. There is so much you do not understand, Elora. So much I shielded you from. I now see that was the wrong decision."

"Like what?" I huffed. "Besides my entire identity being a lie."

"Oh, piss off! I never once told you that you were the evil twin. That was your own doing. I only ever agreed with you in order to protect you from that demon you shared a womb with!" Olgara took a deep breath to calm herself. Her mouth opened to speak when she was cut off by Selena.

"How do you expect Elora to listen to you when you have lied to her for her whole life?" Selena was exasperated as she spoke. She reached for my hand and I took hers in mine. The warmth steadied my racing heart.

Olgara smiled wickedly as she eyed Selena. "Oh, is that right, darling? Am I the only one that has lied to the princess?" Selena's eyes widened as Olgara turned to me. "Tell me, dearie, do you know of anyone else in the world that can change shape like you?"

Her words confused me. "No? What are you talking about? No one else has this power."

Olgara snickered as Selena's hand went limp in my own. "This is one of the things I kept hidden from you, dearie. But not me alone." She turned back to Selena. "Is there anything you would like to tell her?" Olgara smiled smugly as she spoke.

Selena took a deep breath before turning to me, her face unreadable. "Some people are born able to shift forms. Most are of common animals, though some, like you, can turn into great beasts. The ability–the magic–is passed down family lines. Long ago, your great-great-great-great grandfather feared the power the shifters held so he made it illegal. Anyone who is caught with the ability to do so is immediately put to death."

"There are others like me?" I whispered.

"Yes," Selena said with a smile. "So many like you." She squeezed my hand as a single tear fell down her ebony cheek. Her golden eyes shone in the low light of the cottage.

"Tell her the rest," Olgara said through gritted teeth.

Selena's smile faltered as she stammered.

"Now, pup."

"What?" I said, utterly confused. Selena stared deep into my eyes as tears flowed freely from her own. "Oh my god," I said as I pried my hands from her. "You can shift. The story, it was you!"

"Elora, I wanted to tell you! It just didn't feel like the right time! You just lost your powers," Selena stammered. I had never seen her so uneasy before. I stood up and backed away from her.

"How could you lie to me?!" I screamed.

"What was I supposed to do? Tell you and risk being killed?" Selena retorted. Her words broke something in me. I never felt more like a beast than at that moment.

"You think I would do that to you?" My voice cracked as tears dampened my cheeks. Rage mixed with an unending sadness filled me. The dragon in me was restless–begging to be released, but it was like there was a stone wall blocking her from emerging.

Selena softened. "No, Elora, of course not. I'm sor–" Before she could finish her words, I turned and ran from the cottage.

"Let her be," Olgara called to Selena as I ran through the door and into the blackness of night in the forest. I ran blindly until I hit something hard as hands wrapped around me. I moved to fight, but the smell of leather and peppermint soothed me. I buried my face in Dameon's chest and sobbed as he held me close.

*   *   *

"ELORA, are you okay?" Dameon whispered the words as he grabbed my face, pulling my eyes to his. His brows were furrowed, his face a mix of confusion and concern. I couldn't help but notice the way his full lips parted as he spoke my name, like the word alone was a sacred prayer. I averted my eyes before I pushed away as I wiped at my face.

"I am being foolish," I said as I looked down at my feet. There was very little light here. If I focused, I could make out the stones jutting out of the deep brown earth. I tried not to dwell on the fact that even though I could feel the dragon in me, I could not fully call on it.

Dameon walked forward, closing the distance between us as he placed a hand on my cheek. I leaned into it on instinct alone. The warmth from his hands comforted me, as they always had. His rough, calloused skin was gentle against my cheek. "Even good news can be hard to hear when it is the opposite of what you have been told your whole life, Princess." Dameon paused before placing his hands back at his side. "What happened?"

"My mother knew. This whole time, she knew and cast me aside. Olgara said it was for my protection." Dameon softened as he looked at me.

"Her doing it to protect you doesn't invalidate your pain. You are still allowed to feel abandoned, even if it was for a reason," he said.

"When did you get so wise," I said as I crossed my arms. Dameon's lips curled up in a soft smile.

"I've had a lot of time to think over the years." I smiled back at him, unable to stop myself if only for a second. "But that doesn't explain why you ran out of the cottage. I know you, Princess. It would take something much more than that to cause a dragon to flee."

"Selena can turn," I blurted out. As soon as the words left my lips the rest flowed like a flood, unstoppable. "I did not even know that other people could do this. They explained to me that it is illegal to discuss, but I have spent my whole life feeling entirely alone in this ability when I did not have to. That is painful enough, but to find out my best friend could do it too? And that she hid it from me? That she did not trust me to keep her safe?" I paused, hoping to stop the tears from falling that stung the backs of my eyes. "That made me feel like a beast."

"Selena can turn?" Dameon exclaimed with a shocked look. His eyes bulged from his head slightly as his head jutted out. The look of complete shock on his face caused me to laugh. "The wolf–she's the girl from the story," he muttered.

"Yep," I said as I kicked a stone at my feet. "Olgara sent her to look after me. It makes me question my friendship with her. I do not know how much was her actually caring about me or just her job."

Dameon scoffed. He looked incredulous, like what I just said was the most ridiculous thing in the world. "What?" I asked.

"You have got to be kidding me, Princess."

"Excuse me?"

"Elora," Dameon paused before continuing. "She was your maid that was ordered to attend to your every need from the time you were both children. The fact that it was the witch who said it versus anyone else in the castle does not change anything."

I scoffed. "It changes everything!"

"How?" he said with a humorless laugh. "She was still your employee, someone that was required to spend time with you and care about you regardless. It is evident that she and Katherine both became your friends over the years–your best friends. You three love each other and that is clear to everyone." He paused and his face softened. "Are you sure it isn't the betrayal of someone else having the ability to shift that is upsetting you?"

I opened my mouth to retort but quickly closed it. He was right, though I hated to admit it. The fact she could shift did not change much of anything except how I viewed my power. Suddenly, I wasn't so special. I wasn't chosen even if I initially thought of my power as a curse. I looked up at Dameon. He was a vision in the low light. His wavy black hair hung over his eyebrows as he looked down at me.

"Is there anything you are hiding from me, too?" I said as I narrowed my eyes at him.

The corner of his lip turned up as he took a step closer to me. The forest suddenly seemed to be devoid of air. We were so close, mere inches apart.

"There is only one thing I have ever tried to hide from you." He stared at me intently as he reached up and tucked a strand of hair behind my ear. "And I do not think I have ever been very good at hiding it."

My heart felt like it would beat out of my chest as I looked up at him. I knew he was right and it made me feel exposed. Dameon's face was unguarded, his eyes searching mine for recognition.

"Say it," I whispered.

Dameon took a shaky breath. "I love you, Elora."

His words crashed into me, though I expected them. I felt frozen to the spot. How many times had I dreamed of hearing those words from him?

"Dameon," I said. His face fell, and he turned to move away.

"I'm sorry, I shouldn't have said that," he stammered. "You've been through so much I shouldn't put that on you right now." His brown eyes shone in the moonlight as he moved away.

"Dameon." I reached for his hand, and pulled him to a stop. He looked down at me like he was hanging on my very word. His face was pained, a mix of regret and shame. But I saw something in his eyes that part of me resented, especially knowing it shone within me too–hope. And while hope was a dangerous thing, something that shatters people completely and breaks them, I knew Dameon would never break me–that I would die before I broke him.

"Kiss me," I said. As soon as the words were spoken, his lips were on mine. The kiss was soft but I could tell he was holding back. I pulled my head back, and our eyes met. I could see the hunger in his. "Like you mean it," I said. Dameon smiled.

"As you wish, Princess." Dameon kissed me with a ferocity that sent my head spinning. The kiss deepened as we tasted each other. Dameon wrapped his arms around me and I pressed my body to his. I needed to be closer, to feel his warmth and steadiness all around me. I nipped his bottom lip as his hands began to explore me. The warmth of them trailing over my body felt right as heat grew between my legs. I grabbed his neck, pulling him down to me so I could press myself fully against him. I wanted–no, *needed*–more of him, all of him. Without pausing, his hands were on my ass as he lifted me into the air. I wrapped my legs around his waist as we lost ourselves in each other. The fire in Dameon, the passion in our kiss, drove all thoughts from my head but *us*. Nothing else existed in that moment. I felt as though I was flying as I buried my hands in his hair.

We finally parted after several minutes, panting and with swollen lips. Dameon's chest rose and fell in swift succession, mirroring my own as he looked into my eyes. His eyes were wild as I brushed a curl behind his ear.

"We should probably go back inside now," I whispered.

Dameon pressed his forehead to mine as a soft smile painted across his lips. "Most definitely," he said as he started walking towards the cottage.

"Dameon?" I asked.

"Yes, Princess?" His face was serene, all the tension long gone.

"You should probably put me down first," I said while stifling a giggle. Dameon's cheeks heated as a sheepish smile spread across his face. I unwrapped my legs from his waist as he slid me down to my feet, the whole time our bodies pressed against each other. He looked down on me like I was the most precious thing in the world to him. Heat crept up my neck to be gazed on that way, though I knew I was looking at him with the same look in my eyes. What I felt with Percy was quick, merely a means to an end. But this–this felt different. Right.

Dameon kissed me softly one more time before we parted and walked towards the cabin. I hesitated at the door and adjusted my rustled clothing. I motioned for Dameon to do the same and he laughed–a deep musical sound that sent my stomach upside down.

The feeling of lightness did not last long, however. As soon as I opened the door and saw a teary-eyed Selena and a stone-faced Olgara, my stomach dropped.

"Sit down, girl. We are not done yet," Olgara said.

I moved to reclaim my seat as Dameon sat beside Selena. Olgara glared at me and my skin prickled.

"Are you done running from your problems like a child and ready to listen?" she seethed.

The serenity that Dameon's kiss had bestowed on me evaporated like water as I bristled at the insult, even though I knew she was right. "I am sorry I am not reacting the way you would like to the news that my whole life has been a lie," I said through gritted teeth.

"We do not have time for your self-pity, Elora," Olgara said.

"Well, what more is there to say? What other secrets are you two keeping from me?"

Olgara pondered for a second before responding. "Katherine is a young witchling, the best student I have ever had quite honestly."

For the first time tonight, the words from Olgara's wretched mouth did not shock me. It all made sense, the way Katherine was always near Olgara or doing errands for her. Even the poultices she had sent with me on the journey. "I figured that much," I said with a smirk.

"What a clever girl," Olgara bit out.

"I didn't even know that," Selena said with a quiet whisper. I looked her in the eyes and an anger filled my heart.

"Not so fun to be the odd one out, is it?" As soon as I said the words, the anger I felt revealed its true face–grief. I bit my lip, wishing I could take back my words as I watched them slice through Selena like a knife.

"Enough!" Olgara bellowed. "You are to be Queen, Elora. Put your petty feelings aside."

"Queen?" I asked. I looked around the room. Selena avoided eye contact with me and Dameon had a queer look upon his face as the color drained from his skin.

Olgara scoffed. "Elrick having the throne will spell the destruction of all of Albaria. We cannot let that happen."

"No, we can't," I said as my shoulders fell. It suddenly felt like the weight of the world was on my back. Shame filled me, because I was not sure I wanted the weight, let alone found myself worthy of the crown. "But I am not fit to rule," I exclaimed. If my actions tonight showed me anything, is that I was not fit to wear the crown either.

Dameon looked over to Olgara. "I have heard rumors of unrest in other townships. Greydenn is not the first to be hassled with a higher tax and new laws." Dameon chuckled dryly before continuing. "I think we were actually the last to have it. Probably didn't want to upset the dragon," he said as he nodded towards me.

"We could use that unrest to our advantage. That paired with the prophecy could be enough to propel the smallfolk around Elora." Selena looked at me as she continued. "You cannot take the crown without their support." Selena's face was neutral. I could see the wheels turning in her mind. She was always the best at formulating plans and seemed to be three steps ahead of everyone. I wondered why she still saw me as fit to rule, even after my outburst.

"That is very true," Olgara said. She smiled at Selena. "Clever girl," she said with a wink.

"I have no idea how to be Queen," I said. "Elrick may be a beast, but he has been groomed since we could walk to rule. He knows the laws and rules and everything. He knows histories and is seen by the people as the rightful heir. What will change that?" I looked out at the faces around me. They felt less like friends and more like a war council.

Olgara turned her attention back to me. "You know all he does, I made sure of that."

"No, I do not," I said.

"Do you think your father paid for you to have history lessons, language lessons, and everything else that has filled your days the last ten years?" My eyes widened as she continued. "Those lessons were not to prevent boredom or for a princess. I gave you everything I thought a good ruler would need." She paused as her face softened. "You also prepared yourself in a way that Elrick never experienced. You made friends with the small folk. I know you care about the people of Greydenn and they listen to you. Think about your seat on the small council. That was not just because you were a princess."

I moved to speak but the words would not appear. Selena and Dameon nodded their agreement to Olgara's words. My head was spinning at how easy they all accepted this—accepted me—as the rightful Queen. Bile rose in my throat at the thought. Before I could respond, Olgara threw her hand up.

"It is getting late. We all need rest before we journey back to Greydenn."

"How did you beat us here?" Selena asked. A sly smile spread across Olgara's face as she gestured towards me.

"This beast isn't the only one who can fly."

Chapter Nineteen

THE sun was shining through the windows of the cottage when I awoke from my dream of flying. I stretched my tired muscles and called to the dragon in me, hoping that a night of rest would allow her to answer. Hope once again proved to be a dangerous thing. Selena was asleep in a cot next to me soundly. Dameon had insisted on sleeping outside with the horses and had quickly left last night without a glance or word in my direction. His departure had left me feeling queer. He was just tired, I told myself. So much was revealed the night before that our feelings for each other were the least of his worries. That dam had been broken. There was no going back for us.

I crept from the corridor into the kitchen of the cottage. The fire was already crackling and the smell of freshly baked bread wafted through the air. Olgara was sitting at the well-worn table as the morning light shone through the open windows. A summer breeze carrying the song of birds wafted through the small kitchen.

"Good morning, dearie." Olgara did not look from her cup as she spoke to me. She motioned for me to take a seat across from her. As I sat, a tea set appeared before me out of thin air. I jumped back in my chair, startled. Olgara snickered–a joyful sound. Without a hand touching it, the kettle poured the perfect amount in my cup, followed by a dollop of honey.

"How?" I muttered in a state of bewilderment. Olgara winked. I took a sip of the tea, instantly comforted. It was my favorite blend that Olgara has been serving me since I was a child. The normalcy of it warmed me from the inside out.

"Magic," she said. "Breakfast should be ready in a few minutes." Olgara sighed. "We should talk, my dear." Her voice was softer than it was last night.

"Yes," I said with a sigh. "We should." I paused, taking another sip of my tea to collect my thoughts. "I am sorry for how I behaved. It was just too much to process at once, but that does not excuse my actions."

Olgara smiled half-heartedly. "Yes, it was a bit much. I was wrong to hide everything from you for all these years. There are things I could have told you and still kept you safe. I am sorry for keeping you in the dark for so long." Olgara took a sip from her own tea and I followed suit, allowing the silence to sit between us for a moment. Olgara was holding her cup in both hands and not looking me in the eyes. Judging by that, there was more she wanted to say.

"What else is there?" I asked. Olgara's face was shocked for a brief moment before it settled back into her usual coolness.

"I miss the days when it was easier to hide things from you," she said with a smile. I finished off the tea and before I could set the drained cup on the table, a strange force pulled it from my grasp entirely. My eyes followed the cup as it sailed straight for Olgara's outstretched hand. She studied the contents for a moment before her face contorted in a mix of horror and astonishment.

"The dragon is still inaccessible," she said with a gasp.

"How do you know?" I stuttered out. Fear filled me as I dissected her words. Did this mean I would never shift again? I did not know if it was possible for me to live without the other side of me. Once a heart knows the joy of flying or the feeling of warm sun on scales, there is no going back.

Olgara gestured to my cup. "The leaves, dearie. They tell me everything I need to know."

"That's how you knew Percy was going to shoot me from the sky," I said breathlessly. For the first time since our battle, the mention of his name did not break something in me.

Olgara nodded. "Aye, it was. The leaves do not tell me everything–some is left to assumption–but this is clear as they were that night." She held the cup up for me to see and gestured to the muddled dregs at the bottom. "You are separated from your other form."

"It's like there is a wall blocking me. I can feel the dragon. The second the poison was gone, the power was there." I slumped in my seat. "But now it's like there is a prison inside of me. I can't let the magic out." I looked up at Olgara as tears burned my eyes. "It is suffocating to be caged." The witch reached over and placed her hand on mine. It looked different than I remembered, less wrinkled and no age spots, but the calmness that swept through me at her touch was the same as it always was. "Magic," I said in a small whisper. Olgara smiled.

"Sometimes we all need a bit of a calming touch. The leaves aren't clear on this, but I think I know why your ability feels different."

"Please tell me," I said. I would do anything to be able to fly again. Once you know the taste of the sky, there is no going back.

"You haven't accepted your destiny, Elora. The ability to shift manifesting in you means something. You were sent here to lead Albaria and fight for those who are not able to. You must claim that in order to access your power. Your destiny and your power are woven together. You cannot have one without the other."

My jaw fell open. "There has to be another way. You saw how I was last night. I am not fit to rule."

Olgara smiled. "That is what all the greats say. No one who wants the power is fit to wear the crown. There is good in you, Elora. You have seen things others could only dream of. You've lived among the common people. You understand them and care for them deeply. That is what will make you a good ruler." She paused, seeming to weigh her words before continuing. "Perhaps you can see the weight of the crown as a driving force to be better. Humility is necessary for a just ruler."

"And what if I don't?" I paused as I looked at Olgara. "What if I do not accept my destiny?"

Olgara sighed. "Then Albaria will be led to ruin by your tyrant brother, who will never stop hunting you. Your powers will also never return." She paused for a moment and looked down at the dregs of her own cup. Her eyes glistened for a mere moment before she turned them back to me as she cleared her throat.

"So I have no choice," I scoffed, "because the leaves said so."

Olgara got up from her seat and kneeled at my feet, wrapping her hands around my own. "Oh dearie, there is always a choice." She reached into a drawer at the side of the table and pulled out a cloth bag with a note attached. "Here, your mother wanted you to have this."

"What were you to her?" I asked as I grabbed the bag. It was wrapped in a fine velvet of purple and was quite heavy. I recognized the script on the top as my mother's handwriting.

Olgara's eyes glistened with tears. "I was a friend when she needed it." She stood up and walked to the stove as she idly stirred the bubbling contents. I opened the bag and gasped. Inside, was a solid gold circlet with one large iridescent stone in the middle. The apex of the crown rose into a point. I had not seen it since the night I was sent away–the last time I saw its owner. "My mother's crown," I said with a gasp. My crown paled in comparison to hers but was designed to be a matching set. Where my crown was dainty and beautiful with intricate vine work, hers was powerful and regal in its solidity.

Olgara turned to me, her face damp with tears as she made her way back to the table. "A crown from the Queen, for the Queen." She paused and sniffled before taking a breath. "Lillion would be so proud of you. Read the letter when you are ready, and wear the crown when you accept your fate."

Fate seemed like such a foreign concept to me. I had lived my life to try and defy it, only to be told I had been playing into Fate's hand this entire time.

"Are the leaves always so loud? So clear?" I asked.

Olgara once again glanced at her own cup before looking back at me, her face softened. "Sometimes they are so loud it hurts."

*   *   *

OAK nibbled at my fingers as we packed up to go.

"No treats for you," I said softly as I stroked his head. He nipped at my fingers gently, making me laugh. Dameon had excused himself from breakfast early to tack up and check on the horses before our journey back to Greydenn. He still hadn't spoken to me, or even looked at me–since last night. A gnawing feeling was taking over my stomach, but I pushed it down. Something was off with him, but now was not the time to deal with it. I told myself that I was just reading too much into it. He told me how he felt last night, and I had never known Dameon to be a liar.

I watched as Olgara walked first to Dameon, and then Selena as she handed each of them a bag of supplies before hugging them. Something felt final about this goodbye in a way that made my skin crawl. I tried my best to shake the feeling. When it was my turn, the witch who raised me wrapped me in a tight hug.

"Be safe, dearie." Her voice crackled slightly as she spoke. Knowing better, I made sure to not point it out.

"We will see you in a few days," I said as I hugged her back.

Olgara gave me one last squeeze before she released me from her clutches. Her face was a mix of emotions as she looked up at me. She placed a hand on my cheek. "Yes, you will. In just a few days."

"Thank you," I said as I leaned into the warmth of her hand. "For raising me. You did not have to show me love, but you did. You were my mother when my mother could not be."

A single tear fell down Olgara's cheek. "It was the honor of my life."

"It's time," Dameon called back from atop Poppy. I tried not to dwell on the fact that he did not offer to help me on Oak. I was healed, he didn't need to anymore. I gave Olgara one last hug and goodbye before mounting Oak. With one last wave, we left the witch and her enchanted cottage behind. As soon as we all passed the stone, the cottage disappeared and we were once again surrounded by dense forest.

Hours passed by as we traversed the forest. Neither Selena nor Dameon moved to speak to me. We had not spoken much on the ride to the cottage, so it did not feel pronounced until we stopped for a break at a stream. Dameon was standing next to Poppy as she drank greedily from the cool and clear water. The summer sun danced on the water, making it glitter like gold.

I led Oak up to the stream and lowered the reins for him to drink his fill as I filled my own water skin. "How did you sleep?" I asked Dameon sheepishly.

"Like a baby," he said without looking up at me. His voice and face were completely neutral in a way I had never seen before.

"Is everything okay?" I asked. Dameon finally looked up at me. His brown eyes had no hint of joy as he looked at me like I was insignificant to him. Like he did not spend the night before tasting my skin and professing his love for me.

"Everything is fine. We should probably get going now." Without another word he mounted Poppy and trotted off. My blood began to boil as the rage burned through me. I mounted Oak and moved to gallop to Dameon and give him an earful. But as Poppy moved further and further ahead, and her cloaked rider did not glance back once, my rage burned away to reveal its true name—grief and shame.

Of course he could not love me. I am a monster, remember? Or maybe it is because I am no longer a monster, but someone who doesn't need saving. I mulled over and replayed our every interaction as the day went on until my shoulders were tense and my jaw hurt from gritting my teeth. I both longed for my other form to fly off the tension and was grateful she was distant to me. I feared what I would do if I was able to shift at that moment. A scorned woman is capable of so much, a scorned dragon though? Better the world did not find out that type of fury.

*   *   *

NOT a single word was spoken by any of us during the remainder of the day. We all made camp silently. Without a word, Dameon was off with his bow to hunt game, leaving Selena and I alone. Our camp for the night was a small clearing in the middle of a dense forest. A stream ran nearby and lush, summer grass padded the ground around us. Selena was making herself busy around camp and doing her best to not look at me. My body screamed for me to talk to her, to be acknowledged, but no matter what I tried, it did not work. Finally, I excused myself and made my way to the horses with an apple from my pack.

The horses were much more enthralled with my presence than my traveling companions were today as all three vied for my attention. I told myself it was because they loved me and had nothing to do with the apple I was cutting into small chunks and presenting to them. I gave the last chunk to Oak, who was quickly run off by Poppy. She licked my hand expectantly and I couldn't help but smile at the sensation. Selena's mount tried to edge Poppy away, but being the mare she was, Poppy quickly put the smaller horse in its place as she nipped at him.

"Don't bite," I said as I stroked her big black head.

"Some people can't help but bite." Selena's voice shocked me as I turned around. She was standing about ten paces behind. Her face was neutral as she looked at me, but her eyes were searching. They reminded me of mine–of the feelings coursing through my veins at that very moment. I suddenly realized it wasn't just that Selena was ignoring me today. In her eyes, I was ignoring her. Our pain was mirrored.

"No," I said. "Some people cannot." I knew why I bit, why I wanted to make her hurt. But knowing does nothing for the shame. If anything, it made it worse.

"We should talk," Selena said. I nodded and turned to face her fully. "I am sorry, Elora, for hiding my power from you. I should have told you when we began our journey."

"Why didn't you?" I asked.

Selena's face softened. "It didn't feel right. You had just lost the dragon and we were doing everything you could to survive. I didn't want to." She paused as if she was finding her bravery to finish. "I didn't want to make you feel as if I was rubbing it in."

"You think I'm so petty and jealous?" I bit out the question, my words ripping like teeth. Selena flinched and instead of feeling powerful, I felt shame. "I bared my secret to you and you swore there were no secrets between us."

Selena scoffed. "Gods, Elora. You still don't get it. You are the princess and you still only told me the truth when you were close to death! You were safe in your power all these years! Do you know what it was like looking up at the sky and seeing you fly away from your problems whenever you wished and I could not? Do you know what it feels like when you go months suppressing the need to shift? It is utter agony!"

Her words hit me like a slap. "How would I know if no one ever told me, Selena? I had no idea about other shifters, let alone the laws about them because no one ever spoke of it to me! Do you know how alone I have felt for years?"

"Do you know the ache I feel when I just want to run, and hunt, and do everything the wolf in me screams to do but I can't?" she exclaimed. Her eyes were wide and her teeth bared. If I looked closely, I could swear I saw her skin shift. Like I could fully see what she was below the surface for the first time. The woman before me was a stranger.

"So it has all been a lie?" My voice cracked, but I kept going, hoping she did not notice. "You have been jealous of me since the day we met? Our friendship, was everything a lie? Being with me was nothing more than duty?"

Selena scoffed. "Of course it was only duty at first. I hated the idea of caring for a spoiled princess! Realizing you were the dragon and the freedom you had made my blood boil."

"Then why stick around? Because of the promise you made to the witch? I believe you are absolved of that now. Leave if you can't stand the sight of me now!" My voice cracked as I lost the battle with the tears I was trying so desperately to repress.

Selena took a deep breath before looking back at me. "Elora, I know I could leave, but I do not want to. My anger for you faded each time you stood up for me. I stopped seeing you as a princess and as someone I was connected to only by duty alone." She walked forward and offered me her hand. After a moment of hesitation, I took it. "You piss me off sometimes, but you are more than a charge, or even a friend." Her elegant face softened. "You are my sister. I cannot imagine a life away from you because I do not want that."

I paused and mulled on her words. I wanted to respond to her in a way that let her know I understand her the best I could. Her pain was not lost on me. The words did not come, so I decided to show her in the next best way. I quickly wrapped my arms around her and hugged her deeply. After a moment, she returned the embrace.

"I am so sorry, sister," I whispered into her braids.

"As am I." Selena squeezed me tighter. "Sister."

After a moment, we released each other. Both of our faces were damp with tears when a thought danced through my brain.

"Wait, are you the wolf that has been killing livestock and everyone has been blaming me for?"

Selena blushed as a sheepish smile spread across her lips. "To be fair, it is usually you." I swatted her playfully with my hand. "More important than our late night eating habits," Selena mozied off to a fallen log next to us and took a seat. "Why don't you tell me why both you and Dameon returned to the cottage last night breathless with flushed skin and swollen lips?" She threw me a wicked smile as she patted the seat next to her. She kicked her feet excitedly.

Her words unlocked a rage in me that quickly turned into confusion and shame as tears began to fall freely. I sat down beside her and grabbed her outstretched hand. The joyful look on her face melted away instantly.

"What has happened, Elora?" Selena's face was contorted with worry.

"He told me he was in love with me and I reciprocated. We got a bit carried away," I said with a humorless laugh. The feeling of his hands trailing my body as he kissed me lingered in my mind. How had everything felt so perfect just last night and so wrong today? "Then we went inside and he has completely ignored me since."

"This isn't like Dameon," Selena whispered. "Something has to have happened."

"Like what? It seems he either lied about his feelings for me or after hearing the truth about me, decided he wanted nothing to do with me."

"That doesn't make sense, Elora. He has been pining for you for a decade now. Those feelings don't just go away in an instant."

"I feel so stupid." Selena suddenly shot to her feet and placed both her hands on my shoulders.

"You are not stupid, you are in love. And so is he. He is being a fool right now, and I do not know why, but you need to talk to him. I will not let you both ruin this for yourselves."

I scoffed. "And what am I supposed to do, Selena? Walk up to him and ask him why he doesn't love me?"

"Yes," she said neutrally. "But maybe worded a bit differently and less accusatory."

"I can't do that!" Selena placed a hand on her hip and looked at me with such intensity that I felt two feet tall.

"You can and you must. No matter what he says, at least you will have an answer."

"What if having an answer is worse than not knowing?"

Selena smiled. "We will just have to hope that isn't the case."

I rolled my eyes. Hope had become a four letter word to me.

*   *   *

I waited until Selena's breath had become shallow and even before I crept away from camp and towards the horses, knowing that is where I would find Dameon. As I walked towards the stream, my body screamed to drop it. But I knew I would not be able to live with myself if I let this go. It would be one thing if we went back to normal, but Dameon completely brushing me off is something I had never known from him. This couldn't be how we ended, I wouldn't allow it.

I walked down the hill carefully. The moonlight was barely visible through the dense tree cover. I longed for my dragonsight as I walked blindly toward the stream. I didn't even try to call on the dragon–I could feel she was too distant to answer.

I was relieved when I finally saw the outline of the horses in the lowlight. I let out a sigh of relief as Oak walked up to me and nuzzled me. I could hear the rhythmic sweeping of a brush. Looking over, Dameon's tall frame was visible over Poppy as he groomed her. I approached quietly, hoping not to startle him. I waited until I was right beside Poppy to speak. I knew Dameon knew I was there because his sweeps of the brush had become more erratic, like he was hoping he could brush me away as well.

"Couldn't sleep either?" I asked as I stroked Poppy's shoulder. It was too dark to make out Dameon's face on the other side of her aside from the hard set of his jaw.

"You should go back to camp, Elora. We have a long day ahead of us tomorrow." His voice was cool and hit me like a slap. I was grateful for the darkness at that moment–it hid the shock on my face. Poppy stomped her large hoof on the ground, earning a grunt from Dameon.

I took a breath, trying to cool the rage and bitter sadness that was building in me. When I finally thought I had won the battle with my tongue, I began to speak, but the words I carefully planned were not the ones that were uttered from my lips.

"What the fuck is your problem, Dameon?" I shuddered at my own voice. I had lost the baĖle.

"What do you mean?" he said coolly as he continued to groom Poppy.

Before I could stop myself, I walked around Poppy and grabbed Dameon's arm, pulling him to face me.

"Dameon I have known you for ten years but I have never known you to be senselessly cruel." My voice cracked, but I willed myself to push through. "And I have never known you to go back on your word. You said all those things to me last night." I paused, knowing I needed to say the words. "You said you loved me and now you have treated me like utter shit all day. Why?" Dameon gently covered my hand with his own before shoving it off his arm entirely.

"You are to be Queen, and I will do everything in my power to help you attain what is rightfully yours." He paused for a moment before letting out a breath. "But I cannot be what you need, Elora. I care about you, but I think my proclamation last night was just the feeling of watching my friend almost die. I do not love you."

Without saying a word, I turned away from him and began to walk back to camp.

"Elora," he called out.

"We have a long journey ahead of us tomorrow, Captain Grey. We should both rest while we can."

I held my breath until there were dark spots in my vision, hoping it would stop the sob building in my chest from escaping. I wanted to roar, to release the pain in a storm of fire, but I refused to give him the satisfaction of hurting me. I lay down on my bed roll without disturbing Selena and silently wept, all the while promising myself that I would never be this weak again. I cried until my sadness became rage and then fell into a dreamless sleep.

Chapter Twenty

OUR second day of riding mirrored the first. Dameon did not so much as look at me–his final act of kindness. The rage and embarrassment I felt was only surpassed by the pain of losing my best friend. He had always seen me in a way others had not. Or, at least I thought he did. Dameon was obviously eager to be rid of me–our pace never fell below a trot the whole day. We arrived at the lake well before sunset. The sight of the glistening waters soothed my broken soul.

I walked Oak to the edge of the water and dismounted as he took a long drink.

"I bet I know what you want," I murmured to the horse as he pawed at the water. I made quick work of the saddle and packs attached to the horse. As soon as he was free, Oak shook himself and ran into the water. His gleeful noises made me laugh as he swam to the deeper water. I had never seen a horse enjoy swimming as much as Oak.

Dameon and Selena had started to set up camp on the shore. I lugged the saddle there and did not ask for help–I could not bear it.

"We will stay here until late tomorrow," Dameon said to no one in particular. "We can't return to Greydenn until nightfall." Dameon quickly departed to take care of the horses, leaving Selena and me alone.

"Have you decided yet if you will take down Elrick?" Selena's face was neutral as she asked the heavy question.

I struggled with a response. How could I know if I was worth starting a war for? Countless people would die because of a prophecy, more blood on my already stained hands. A knot grew in my stomach at the thought.

"Olgara made it seem like I do not have much of a choice." I took a breath and tried to calm my mind. "Either I take the throne or Albaria is ruined. But I am not sure I want the throne. I do not think I am made for it."

"Ruling will take time to learn, just like any other skill, Elora. No one would expect you to excel at it immediately."

I scoffed. "You speak like running a coup is an easy task. I would not even know where to begin."

Selena smiled. "Advisors. You would begin with advisors who you trust. It will be a long battle, but I know that the people will rally behind you if they know the truth."

I took a breath and let Selena's words sink in. Before I could respond, Dameon walked into the middle of us and threw our longswords at our feet.

"Pick them up. I am not letting either of you go back to Greydenn until I can be sure you know how to use these."

"Do you really think that is necessary?" I bit out. Dameon's face contorted with disgust.

"Yes, Elora, I do. You do not know how to use a sword properly and need I remind you, you might be leading an army soon to claim your rightful throne. So pick up the sword!"

I threw him an icy glare and did as he asked. The weight felt good in my hands as Selena and I both squared up.

"You aren't fighting each other," Dameon growled. "That would do no good." He struck like a snake as his blade sliced out at me. I barely had time to move out of the way.

"What the fuck!" I yelled.

"You could have killed her!" Selena exclaimed.

"War isn't pretty, Princess." He lunged again. This time, I used my blade to block, earning me a wicked smile from my opponent. Dameon prowled around me, seeming to see my every flaw. I had never seen him look so animalistic before.

"You are horrible with a sword," he said.

"I killed a knight, so obviously not that bad."

Dameon growled as he lunged again. His sword nicked my ear, just enough to sting.

"That useless piece of shit couldn't teach you to fight properly. Plus you were a dragon then. Now you're just a woman who doesn't know how to defend herself." He chuckled. "Do you expect people to follow you like this?"

His words broke something in me. I could not shift, he was right about that, but there was still a beast in me. I could feel the claws of the dragon ripping across the barrier between us as I roared and charged. Dameon deflected, but not before my blade sliced his cheek. He touched his cheek and smiled when his fingers came back tinged red with blood.

"There you are, you little killer," he purred.

We fought until my arms burned, the whole time Dameon insulting everything about me. The sword was slipping from my hands from sweat as Dameon lunged at me again. I blocked his advance and threw my sword to the ground.

"Enough," I exclaimed.

"We are not done," he growled and he prowled towards me. "Do you think your fucking beast of a brother will allow you to walk away from a fight with him? Didn't seem to work in the past."

"How fucking dare you!" Selena seethed. My eyes widened in shock. I had never heard Selena curse in all our years together.

Dameon looked fully unhinged. "There is going to be a war, Elora. A fucking war. You must learn to fight hand to hand, even if you are able to shift again, you will still need this skill. Percy didn't teach you to fight, he taught you how to dance with a sword. Do you think the men you meet on the battlefield fight like that? What about your fucking beast of a brother? Will he parlay and wait for your attack or will he try to find your every weakness and kill you in the most painful way possible? I can't let that happen! So pick the fucking sword up." The fury on Dameon's face melted away. "Please," he begged.

"Why can't you see your life would be easier–everyone's life would be easier if I was gone? We are going to war because of me! ME!" I paused and took a deep breath. "You made it exceptionally clear last night that you do not care what happens to me."

Dameon walked forward until there were mere inches between us. He towered over me as I stared up at him defiantly. If he thought I was walking away from this, he never knew me.

"Pick up the sword, Elora." My skin crawled at the way he enunciated every single word.

"No."

"Why are you being so difficult?"

"Why are you such an ass?"

Dameon threw his hands up in exasperation. "That's it, I'm done. You want to make this harder than it needs to be, so be it." Dameon turned away and sulked towards the tree line. Within moments, his form was enveloped by the forest.

I refused to let him get away with this. Rage drove me forward as I ran to the forest, to Dameon. I grabbed his arm and forced him to look at me, to see the pain he has caused. "No, what's ridiculous is you! How dare you tell me you love me and then just decide the next day to take it back with no explanation. If that is how you feel, that is one thing, but the Dameon I knew would never do something like that."

"Do you know how hard it was for me to do that?" he yelled.

The color drained from my face. "You are the one who professed feelings. You kissed me!"

"Yes, and I shouldn't have."

I blinked away the tears stinging my eyes. "Do you think I'm such a beast that you no longer care for me at all?"

"No," Dameon yelled. "I'm the beast! You are going to be Queen. You are the rightful Queen of Albaria. In what world does a Queen end up with some stable boy bastard, Elora?"

I paused. "So you do have feelings for me."

Dameon's face contorted in pain as he stepped forward before stopping, like an invisible rope held him back. "I have loved you since the moment I met you," he ground out. "But you need better than me—a marriage for power, or alliance. Someone who can help you more than I can."

"You haven't been a stable boy in years," I called out.

Dameon threw his arms up. "That is not the point, Lor! You need better than me if you are going to take down Elrick."

"Oh, so you want to take my agency out of it completely. What about what I want?" I exclaimed.

"And what is it you want, Princess? Because I guarantee-" before he could continue, I kissed him. His words made me so angry that it was the only way I knew how to shut him up. I held my breath until he began to kiss me back. As quickly as it started, he pulled back.

"You deserve better than me," he whispered.

I looked into his deep brown eyes and wiped the tears falling down his tan skin. "There is no one better for me."

Our lips met in an instant again as we moved with each other.

"Finally," I heard Selena yell, her words startling us apart. "I wanted to make sure you weren't going to kill each other, but I see that is no longer the issue," she said awkwardly as she began to back out of the forest. "I am going back to camp, where I will be staying, all night," she called out.

We both chuckled at her departure.

"Are you sure?" he asked. His voice was soft–scared. He looked at me like I might disappear at any moment.

I squeezed his hand and then touched his cheek. "I have never been more sure of anything in my life." The truth of it scared me. I did love Percy, but not in the way I love Dameon. Percy had been a desperation, the culmination of my caring for him and my desire to not be his demise. Dameon though, I felt my love for him woven in every fiber of my being.

"No more fighting now," I said.

Dameon smiled. "Well that seems presumptuous, Princess." Dameon grabbed my hand and led me deeper into the forest.

I followed him into the woods, like I knew I would follow him anywhere. As soon as we were alone, Dameon fell on me like water once again. His lips moved against mine slowly, like he wanted to explore every inch of me–to remember this moment.

Dameon pulled back. "I am so sorry, Elora. I thought pushing you away would be for the best."

I smiled. "You are a fool, Dameon." I kissed him gently. "But good thing I already knew that." Dameon's wicked grin sent chills down my spine as he feigned pain.

"You wound me, Princess."

"You'll live," I whispered into his lips. He kissed me again as his rough hands grasped my face. I was on fire with happiness and desire.

"Promise me something, Dameon."

Dameon stared into my eyes as he stroked his thumb across my cheek. "Anything."

"Do not ever try to push me away again. Let me make my own decisions."

He smiled. "I should have known better. You are too stubborn. I assure you, Princess, you are never getting rid of me." Dameon paused as tears welled in his eyes. "I love you, Elora. Always have and always will."

His proclamation left me stuttering. I was so sure of my feelings for him, but a small part of me was still afraid to admit them. I pushed those thoughts to the side as I stared into his eyes and pressed my lips against his wrist.

"I love you too, Dameon. Always have and always will." His eyes shone in the waning light of the forest as I proclaimed my feelings.

If anyone in the world had the power to hurt me, it was him. There was no assurance that he wouldn't but as we lost ourselves to each other, as we gave all we were and all we ever would be, I found myself hoping for a lifetime of him by my side.

Suddenly, in the distance I heard a wolf howl–one I recognized. Dameon chuckled.

"It appears Selena has opted to give us privacy," he said as he pulled me close to him again.

I batted my eyelashes. "Whatever for?" I asked in the most innocent voice I could muster. I lightly grazed a finger over his breeches, and Dameon's eyes bulged at the touch. He grabbed the offending hand lightly and pulled it to his lips.

"What's wrong?" I asked. "Do you not want to…" my voice trailed off.

Dameon's eyes widened. "Oh gods, nothing is wrong, Elora. Of course I want to," he stammered as he pulled me close. "I have thought about this for years." He kissed me deeply as he held me close. "I just need this moment to last."

"You've thought of this for years?" I teased.

"Longed for it," he whispered as he kissed me deeply. My fingers moved adeptly over my corset as we kissed, undoing the laces. He kissed me fervently as his hands covered mine, taking over the job of undoing my corset. He pulled it gently over my head and hung it on a nearby limb. Heat gathered at the apex of my thighs as I walked forward and undid the buckle of his leather armor, placing it on a limb as well. His eyes were ravenous as I removed his shirt. I ran my fingers down his tanned chest. His muscles rippled under my touch. I moved my hands down, tracing the muscled v of his abdomen, utterly transfixed.

Dameon grabbed the hem of my tunic gently and pulled it over my head. The cool summer breeze nipped at my exposed breasts. Dameon looked at me hungrily as his hands came to my hips. His eyes pleaded with me, a silent question on his lips. I nodded my head and his hands moved up slowly, gently cupping my breasts as he kissed me. He trailed one hand down my side and pulled me closer until our bodies were pressed against each other.

"Gods, you are perfect," he whispered with one hand grasping my ass, pulling me closer to him. My hands traced the lines of him until they hovered over the waist of his breeches. I needed him, needed to show him how much I loved him. I began to fall to my knees, only for Dameon to halt me with his arms. I looked up at him quizzically.

"A Queen gets on her knees for no one," he growled as he righted me. Suddenly, he fell to his knees, his eyes never leaving mine as he took my hard nipple in his mouth on the way down. He suckled before dragging his teeth gently across the sensitive peak and then releasing me.

"What are you doing?" I asked breathlessly as he moved to the other breast. Dameon smiled wickedly.

"I am showing my appreciation to the crown." He slid down my breeches slowly before pulling me close to him. In one fell movement, he fell to his back, pulling me on top of him. I straddled his face as his tongue parted me. A deep moan fell from my lips and I threw my head back as my hips rocked rhythmically back and forth. I cupped my breasts in my hands as Dameon devoured me.

"Dameon," I moaned as he slid a finger inside of me. His tongue was working the bud between my legs in rhythmic circles. Each round brought me closer and closer to the edge of my undoing. The curving of his fingers in time with that devilish tongue was too good–I felt too good. Heat built between my thighs as my body prepared for my climax. With his free hand, he pulled my hips down to his face more, allowing me no escape as I came hard, his name falling from my lips like a curse.

Dameon's finger slid from me as I arched my back. He grabbed my hips as he sat up quickly, picking me up like I weighed nothing. I yelped as I landed on his lap. He grinned wildly at me and his mouth glistened from me. I could feel his hard cock pressed against the heat of me.

I needed him like I needed air. I pulled at his waistband, exposing his hard cock. He wrapped his arms around me as he kissed me hungrily, desperately.

"I need you," I said into his full lips. He moved down and kissed my neck, taking the delicate skin between his teeth. My hips bucked against his shaft. He moaned into my neck as a dull ache built in me.

"Then take me," he breathed as he lay back onto the ground. He wrapped his hands around his cock and placed it at my entrance, waiting for me. I kissed him deeply as I lowered myself on him. I dug my hands into his chest as the size of him stretched me, filling me up. "Elora," he moaned when I was fully seated. I started to roll my hips slowly, getting used to him. I rocked up and down slowly, but it was too good. My eyes rolled back and I began to ride him wildly, losing all control. Dameon dug his fingers into my hips, pulling me closer to him. "You feel so fucking good," he ground out.

"Dameon," I whimpered as heat built in me. My movements became erratic, instinctual as I rode him until we reached oblivion together.

Chapter Twenty-One

THE late morning sun was shining through the trees as we untangled ourselves from each other. I sat up and stretched as Dameon sat behind me and kissed my bare neck.

"We need to go pack up and check on Selena," Dameon whispered into my skin. I turned around and pressed my lips to his. He groaned as I nipped his bottom lip between my teeth.

"Time to go back to the real world," I said.

Dameon placed a hand on my cheek as he gazed into my eyes. "This is our real world. I am not running from this any longer."

"Neither am I." I was tired of running from the inevitable. I may not have believed in my own destiny as it was spoken, but I believed in this.

By the time we arrived back at camp, Selena had already packed most of the belongings away. She looked at us both like she knew our every secret as a sly smile spread across her lips.

"Sleep well, you two?" Her smirk only deepened my blush. I couldn't help but laugh at Dameon's embarrassed face.

"Like a baby," I said in the sweetest voice I could muster.

"I am surprised you two are back already," Selena said. "We have hours until we need to leave." She paused as a wicked smile spread across her lips.

I stared longingly at my lake. Everything would change once we arrived back, no matter what I decided. This lake was the place in the world I felt most free. "Can we swim?" I asked my companions. "Until we need to leave?" Until I needed to accept my destiny. Dameon and Selena nodded in fervent agreement. We spent several hours that day playing in the water together and lounging in the sun. Everything felt good and right in my life. In the water, I could pretend the weight of the world did not rest on my shoulders. We played like children to pass the time and for the rest of the day I spent our trek dreaming about the next time I would find myself enveloped in the lake's cool embrace, accompanied by the love of my life and my best friend.

Night had fully fallen by the time the mountain Mirador became visible. We agreed to separate at the base under the cave. Dameon would take the horses back to the stables and meet us in Mirador while Selena and I would return to the castle the same way we left.

The path up to my cave seemed taller at night. There was very little light on this side of the mountain without any torches burning in the cave. I found it odd that Katherine had not lit any in her duties, but brushed the thought aside as I began my ascent ahead of Selena.

"How are we going to get to the ladder?" Selena asked. I eyed our surroundings in the low light. We couldn't risk going up the path to the mountain–this was our only way in. I eyed the trees, seeking out our savior.

"I have an idea," I said as the perfect limb came into view. "But you will not like it."

The limbs were thick and perfectly spaced for our purpose. I scaled the tree until I was at the height of the ladder. I took a deep steadying breath before walking out on the limb, grasping a limb above for leverage. I wrapped my arms around the limb, preparing myself for the next step.

"Be careful, Elora," Selena called. The bark dug into my skin as I reached a foot out. The wooden rung of the ladder swayed with the contact. With one hand and one foot on the tree still, I reached out a hand slowly. My fingers wrapped around the wrung and I lunged, leaving the safety of the tree entirely. I let out a shaky breath as the ladder swayed. Once the ladder stilled, I took a breath and began my ascent.

The climb up was grueling and took twice as long as the descent. By the time the entrance to the cave was visible, my hands were raw. The edge of the rock was one rung away. I took a deep breath and prepared myself for the worst part. I threw my leg over the edge as I pulled myself onto the ledge. My breath was ragged as I lay in the dust and collected myself.

I pulled myself together and walked to the wall of the cave, blindly running my hands along the wall until I found what I needed. The flint in my pocket made lighting the torch much easier than expected as I walked to the edge and signaled to Selena that it was her turn.

By the time Selena made it to the top, I had caught my breath and was more than ready to lend a hand as she crawled over the edge.

"I am never doing that again," she said between rapid breaths. I laughed and she tried to smack me, but missed.

"Take a moment to breathe. I am going to pull up the rope." This job proved more difficult than I thought as I was panting while pulling the massive weight in mere minutes. Selena came to my aid and by the time the ladder was brought back up, we were both panting messes.

"Gods, I am ready for a bath," I said. Selena nodded in agreement as we made our way to the back of the cave. The white stone surrounding us glowed in the torchlight. "You should stay in one of the spare rooms tonight–we can figure everything out in the morning."

"That would be excellent," she said as we began our ascent up the winding staircases in the hidden passage. We walked the rest of the path in silence. I opened up the door concealed by the painting to an eerily quiet castle.

"Katherine must be sleeping somewhere," Selena whispered.

"Go clean yourself up," I said to her. "I am going to do the same and then wait for Dameon's arrival." Selena nodded before heading out of the chambers and down the corridor to one of the vacant rooms.

My chambers were just the same as I had always known it, but something felt different. I took my pack from my shoulders and removed the items. The parcel with my mother's crown was last to be unpacked as I placed it on my bedside table. I moved to open the card, feeling finally ready to read her words, when something out of the corner of my eye caught my attention.

Atop my dressing mirror was a large box, wrapped carefully in red paper with a bow on top. I walked towards it and removed the top. The smell of metal hit me first as my brother's clean and clipped handwriting took my focus. A note lay atop folded cloth. My heart was beating relentlessly as I moved the note to the side and held my breath as I looked under the paper.

A sob built in my throat as I saw her there, just as I had left her. She must have flown back to Mirador soon after we departed. Olgara's hair was an unbound, silver halo framing her serene face. Her decapitated head lay atop a white silk pillow, as if she was sleeping. The blood was obscenely red–fresh. I took a step back and opened the note in my hands, its words sending a chill down my spine.

> *You have killed the one person I loved, so the only person who was foolish enough to love you paid the price.*
>
> *As for your servant, she will be punished until you turn yourself over to me.*
>
> *Do hurry. Or don't–I plan to have all kinds of fun with this one. I have been practicing just for you.*

The anguish rocking through me was something I had never known before. I was breaking into pieces, I was sure of it. Olgara couldn't be dead–no one could kill a god. Elrick did not have that much power. A shrill scream built in my throat, but it came out a roar as fire filled my chambers. The smell of burnt fabric filled my nose as the tapestries lining my walls turned to dust. I did not care–I wanted it to burn, I wanted it all to burn. I ran to the window, throwing it open and myself out as the dragon leapt from my skin.

He would burn for this.

Acknowledgements

This book would not have been possible without the support of so many others. To start, thank you to the team at Line by Lion Publications, specifically Amanda. Words cannot begin to describe how grateful I am for all the work y'all do. Meeting you at the Renaissance Festival after just finishing this novel is one of the most important things that has ever happened in my life. Thank you to Adam Prack for the amazing cover art. You have brought my words to life in such a beautiful and meaningful way. Thank you to my beta readers Jessica, Matthias, Sydnee, Mackenzie, and Caitlin. Your feedback was so helpful and encouraging in my moments where I doubted myself. And to all the people in my beta reading group–sorry I got a deal before you could actually beta read. The outpouring of support from so many people, especially those I grew up with and haven't seen in a decade, was astounding to me and powered me through the editing process. A big thank you to the amazing musician Jenna Soderling for assisting with the lyrics to Olgara's lullaby. You rock (literally). Thank you to my loving husband for supporting me through this process and holding me when things were tough or I doubted myself. Thank you for showing me a love I could only dream of before you. And last but not least– my students, past, present, and future. My goblin creatures bring so much joy to my life and I would have not completed this project without you all. If you are reading this, please put down this book, it is not for you.

www.ingramcontent.com/pod-product-compliance
Lightning Source LLC
Chambersburg PA
CBHW060650190726
48289CB00002B/349